THE LONG WAY

THE WAY HOME
BOOK 2

MAY ARCHER

ACKNOWLEDGMENTS

A sincere thank you to everyone who made this book possible: Leslie Copeland, who did a great beta on a fast turnaround, coordinated my ARCs, and saved my sanity (such as it is) more than once; Ann Attwood, who did a thorough proofread at super speed; Shanoff Designs who totally understood my guys and created a gorgeous cover; Kara Kelley, for her encouragement and virtual hugs; Jane Henry, for her constant support and virtual whip-cracking; all the Slackers who sprinted with me and inspired me; and most of all my family, who were remarkably understanding when Damon and Cain tagged along on our beach vacation.

Last but never least, thank you to every single reader who's taken the time to read and/or review my books! You all rock, and thanks for choosing to spend your free time with my guys!

CHAPTER ONE

"...Although the senator remains coy about the possibility of a presidential run, it's clear to all observers that his star is on the rise.

Since appearing on the political scene several years ago, Emmett Shaw has been the darling of the ultra-conservative Family Ethics Group. Becoming a standard-bearer for the Group's push to 'restore traditional values in America,' Shaw has championed bills seeking to overturn marriage equality, cut funding for family planning clinics that provide abortions, and to protect public and private employees from charges of discrimination provided they are acting on a sincerely held religious belief.

Critics have called these measures unquestionably unjust and un-American, but the choice to support these bills, Shaw says, was an easy one.

"I'm a parent of two fine children myself," the senator tells me, leaning back in his office chair and producing a family picture. "When I'm presented with legislation that really comes down to a question of morals, I ask myself what kind of future I'd like for my son and daughter, what kind of legacy I want to leave them. And then the path forward becomes clear. There's nothing on earth more important than my family."

His pride in his children is clear, and Shaw seems to have every reason to be proud. His daughter, Arcadia, a runner-up for Miss Tennessee last year, has been an active part of her father's staff since his first campaign, and his son, Cain, a second-year law student, has taken a semester off to help his father raise money for other Family Ethics Group candidates around the country. Certainly, the younger Mr. Shaw, with his classic good looks, has become a campaign favorite, inspiring many young voters to explore the Group's platform and to become more politically involved.

"My boy is loyal to his family, and committed to doing the right thing," Shaw beams. "My children are a joy, both of them."

Though the senator speaks easily of joy, he's also a man who's all-too-familiar with tragedy. It was just over a year ago that his best friend, Levi Seaver, along with Seaver's wife Charlotte and their future daughter-in-law Amy McMann, were killed when their private plane crashed into a Tennessee mountain on the way to visit the Shaw family.

Levi Seaver was best known as the genius behind Seaver Technologies, the company that he and Emmett Shaw, along with mutual friend Jonathan McMann, founded more than two decades ago.

The cause of the crash was found to be pilot negligence, but because the pilot, Damon Fitzpatrick, was killed along with his passengers, he never formally faced charges.

Shaw says the shock of the loss made his family closer than ever..."

CAIN'S STOMACH churned as he read the words. The lights of the crowded function room suddenly seemed far too bright, the air starved of oxygen. He clicked his phone off without finishing the article, and glanced at his sister as he slid it back into his pocket.

"Jesus. This article is…" He shook his head as he struggled to complete the sentence. *Disgusting? Ridiculous? Outright lies?*

"Brilliant! I *know*!" Cady squealed, staring at her reflection in the mirror over the bar and smoothing down a non-existent flyaway from her long, blonde hair. She swiveled on her stool to face Cain, excitement on her face. "That's why I wanted you to read it. Such a major coup for Daddy to have Gary North writing about him in the first place, and for him to have garnered this level of attention without even officially declaring his candidacy."

She made an excited noise so high-pitched the dolphins in the Harbor outside could hear it, and Cain motioned to the bartender to refill his water glass, wishing it was something stronger. That sham of an article - hell, of the whole spectacle tonight, could really only be swallowed with alcohol.

Cady took a tube of lip-stuff from her tiny purse and dabbed it on her already-pink lips, then hopped down from the stool. "You ready to get your game face back on? The photographers are going to want a couple of pics with just the two of us for Daddy's donors' Christmas cards, and then a couple more with Ed Burke."

Cain's blank face must have given him away, because Cady sighed. "Ed Burke? The conservative candidate for senator here in Massachusetts? The one the Family Ethics Group endorsed? The one we're here to raise money for?"

Jesus. Right.

Cain pulled his lips into a grotesque smile and widened his eyes, approximating the look of utter rapture that Senator Emmett Shaw's campaign donors no doubt wanted to see on their holiday cards. His reflection above the bar showed he looked like Jack Nicholson from *The Shining*.

Perfect.

Cady caught his expression and rolled her eyes, before

casting a surreptitious glance around them, likely making sure no one had captured his comical expression on a cell camera, but she knew better than to say a word. After two months of being forced to attend back-to-back fundraisers, two months of living under his parents' iron-fisted control, it was probably obvious to anyone who knew Cain even a little that he was *this* close to a breakdown.

Of course, nobody close enough to recognize the symptoms actually gave a shit about his mental state.

He put a hand on Cady's waist and guided her toward the crowded area near the front of the room where his father was holding court.

"I'm sure it's great that this Gary North person has written the article, but am I supposed to have any idea who he is?" Cain asked, mostly to distract himself from the growing horror of stepping closer to the laughing, fawning flock of conservative voters who hung on Senator Shaw's every word.

It could always be worse, he reminded himself. *You could be trapped under a rockslide or dangling off a balcony. Oh! Or actually stuck talking to the donors, rather than smiling and shaking hands.*

Cady turned to him in surprise. "Duh! You don't know who Gary North is? I mean, I know you were pre-law, not journalism like me, but the guy is a big deal. I mean, a flaming *liberal* of course, in case you couldn't tell by the fact that he writes for *The Herald*. But he just won an award for some undercover reporting he did."

Cain nodded mechanically, already tuning out her words as they drew closer to the senator and took their appointed places at his side. As always, the photographers' flashbulbs turned in Cain's direction.

He sucked in a deep breath and slowly let it out.

Another day, another photo op.

It could always be worse. Pits of lava. Hungry sharks. This is a cake-walk, he reminded himself. But he couldn't quite make himself believe it.

Cain could recall a time when pretending hadn't been this difficult. He was a Shaw, for God's sake. Pretending was probably in his *blood*, or if not, it was definitely something he'd learned from the cradle. When his kindergarten teacher, Mrs. Lafferty, had asked what he wanted to dress up as for Halloween, he'd known better than to say "princess," no matter how amazingly sparkly the costumes had been. Later, when all the other guys talked incessantly about sports, he'd been careful to memorize all the crucial stats for all the Boston teams, so no one would guess he was more interested in the hot players than the games.

And when his father had run for office years before, Cain had stood on the platform behind him and faked agreement with every homophobic thing the man had said, all the while trying not to pop a boner because the celebrity donor standing next to him was so fucking hot. (Rule number one: Getting wood for Adam Baldwin was not acceptable when you were the son of a man with serious political ambitions who was trying to woo the ultra-conservative Family Ethics Group, no matter how amazing Adam had been on *Firefly*.)

He'd accepted all the pretense - *hated* it, but accepted it - because as annoying and controlling as his father was, as much as they'd disagreed on all things political, as much as he'd blamed the man for all the shit that had gone down with Jesse back in high school, he'd *loved* his father. He'd known without a doubt that his father was a *good* man.

Jesus *God*, Cain had been so criminally naive about everything concerning Senator Shaw, he wanted to go back in time and slap himself.

"For God's sake, Cain, look *happy*," Lucy Shaw hissed in

his ear, her own brilliant smile not dimming one iota. "Remember who you are. Remember why you're here!"

Oh, he remembered why he was here alright; he was unlikely to ever fucking forget. But he couldn't imagine how his mother felt that it was any reason to smile.

The photographer gave Cain a thumbs-up and moved on to taking fake-candid shots of the senator with his donors. Cain scanned the room, looking for a familiar face or preferably an empty corner he could escape to. He didn't expect any of his old Boston friends to be here tonight - he hadn't exactly been a popular kid in high school, and he'd hardly kept in touch with them, especially after what happened to Jesse. His college acquaintances were all near his parents' new house in Tennessee. And his other childhood friends - Sebastian and Camden Seaver, and Drew McMann - weren't likely to attend any event hosted by Senator Emmett Shaw.

They knew the truth about him, too.

Cain's eyes passed over a hundred curious faces, all watching his family with some combination of awe and respect, but his gaze snagged on one man who stared at him way more intently than the average Shaw supporter, and smiled like he could guess Cain's secrets.

Cain's pulse kicked up.

The guy was completely nondescript - average height, build, and face, light brown hair, skin, and eyes - the kind of man who'd be impossible to pick out of a lineup, if it weren't for the determined, knowing way he met Cain's gaze.

Cain didn't allow his eyes to linger, but he moved to stand behind his sister. Arcadia Shaw prided herself on knowing everyone worth knowing, and she'd sure as hell know everyone on tonight's guest list.

"Who's that guy at your two-o'clock?" he asked. "Pink shirt, brown hair."

Cady turned her head just past two o'clock to nod benevolently at a tall woman in red, then turned back to Cain excitedly. "That's Gary North!"

"He's here?"

"Were you even *listening* when I explained this to you earlier?" she demanded. "He's doing a whole series of articles on Daddy. It's going to be excellent publicity."

Cain did another casual room-sweep with his eyes. Gary still watched him, and Cain didn't like it. Gary looked like the kind of guy who'd happily exploit his secrets. Cain forced himself not to dwell on the thousands of worst-case scenarios running through his head.

"Senator Shaw, I cannot tell you how thrilled I am to see you up here campaigning for Ed Burke!" Cain refocused his attention on the pink, balding man who was apparently trying to wrench the senator's arm from its socket with the force of his handshake. "Next best thing to luring you back to Boston yourself. What we need here in Massachusetts is a strong, conservative voice. We've been without one for too long!"

Emmett Shaw's immaculately-groomed sandy-blond hair gleamed in the light from the chandelier, and his avid blue eyes, two shades lighter than Cain's own, locked on the pink man with what Cain knew would be the force of a laser.

God help the man who defied those eyes. Lord knew, Cain rarely managed it.

"I couldn't agree more, Mister?" his father said, with an upward inflection at the end of the sentence that invited the man to give his name… along with his credit card number and ATM pin.

The pink man, thrilled to have caught the attention of

the Senator Emmett Shaw and not realizing that he'd just walked himself into a trap, provided it eagerly. "Bill, er, *William*. William Fassbender. Of Fassbender and Sons Auto. The largest importer of luxury vehicles in the Northeast. You might have heard of us?"

Oh, Bill. Bill, Bill, Bill. You poor sap, with your pride and your luxury vehicles. You just sold your soul.

Cain held his breath and watched the ensuing carnage with something like sympathy. Bill, who had likely never been called William except by his mother, but had decided his full name made him sound more distinguished, was quick to agree that liberal immorality was the cause of so much suffering in the world today, and that every American had a duty to put a stop to it. Would William be willing to stand up and do what so many men were too weak to do?

Why, of course he would! Gladly! Did Senator Shaw need money? A house? A *kidney*? Coming right up! Anything for *the* Senator Shaw, with his perfect hair, charming manners, spotless record, and incredibly, *unbelievably* wholesome family!

Emmett wrapped an arm around Bill's shoulders and turned him toward his assistant, Darla, who would be happy to take down details and welcome him into the cabal.

Cain looked away. At a certain point, he couldn't stand to watch the bloodbath anymore. Beneath the sleeve of his tailored charcoal suit and blue dress shirt, Cain could swear he felt his tattoo - the forbidden, secret ink he'd gotten in a Fireball-induced rebellion months ago and had hidden zealously ever since - pulse hotly against his skin like a caged creature trying to break free.

Not long ago - a mere three months, though it seemed like it had been in another lifetime - it wouldn't have been Darla standing at the senator's side, but Jack Peabody.

Jack, Senator Shaw's most trusted right-hand-man.

Jack, the man who'd committed murder at the senator's behest, tampering with the engine of Levi Seaver's private plane and setting up Damon Fitzpatrick to take the fall for the crash.

Jack, Cain's former lover.

Now there was a pair of secrets Gary North would give his left nut to reveal, he thought, glancing back at the reporter who was still eyeing him.

It was a sad irony that Cain suspected which of those sins would be most damning in the eyes of the Family Ethics people, and it wasn't the murder.

Senator Shaw had killed his own best friend - a betrayal so heinous Cain could still hardly believe it, despite having accidentally overheard Jack's confession with his own ears, along with Cam Seaver and the pilot Jack had framed for his crime, the very-gorgeous and very-much-alive Damon Fitzpatrick.

And still, the moral code of Emmett Shaw and his Family Ethics cronies was crystal clear. Three amazing people dead, a dozen or more lives destroyed, but by God, no dicks touching. *The* Senator Shaw would have been lucky to get a job washing William's luxury imports if that truth had come out.

Fortunately for his father's political career, the truth had been buried six feet under... and so had Jack, killed in prison before he could testify.

Cain's fingers clenched into a fist, and he was positive that he'd come out of his own skin if he had to stand in that spot a minute longer. He checked his smile to make sure it was firmly in place, and bent to whisper in his mother's ear. "I'll be back."

Lucy, who'd been watching the shakedown of William Fassbender excitedly, turned to look at him. "Where are you going?" she demanded.

"Bar. Again." He shrugged helplessly. "It's dry in here."

She pursed her lips. "You know what we discussed. No alcohol. This is *not* the time for you to indulge in any of your questionable behavior."

Cain felt rage gnawing a hole in his gut. He was twenty four years old. It had been months since he'd touched a drop, and that had been *his* decision, completely unrelated to his father's campaign. Still, he didn't allow his smile to slip. "Only water," he said brittlely.

"Fine. Five minutes," she warned, like he needed her fucking permission.

Then again, who could blame her for thinking that way when he'd fallen in line with every other ridiculous dictate and demand his parents had laid down recently? He hadn't balked when he'd been told he'd be taking a semester off law school - perhaps not surprising, since he'd only chosen law as the path of least resistance in the first place, and didn't give two shits about missing a semester. But then he'd been told he'd be coming on this months-long campaign tour, raising the senator's national profile in preparation for his possible presidential run. Surely his mother had to have been suspicious when he agreed to *that*, since he made no bones about the fact that he considered small-talk to be *Saw*-style psychological torture.

He wondered if his father had ever explained to his mother exactly how he'd ensured Cain's compliance, or if it was just another of Senator Shaw's many secrets.

Maybe his mother thought it was his weak nature that had him agreeing to all this *bullshit.*

Cain was pretty sure that's what Cam and Sebastian Seaver had thought when he'd told them he wouldn't be going to the authorities about the crimes Jack had confessed to.

"Cain," a voice said as he approached the bar, and he

turned to find Drew McMann, wearing an immaculately cut suit and his trademark wry grin. Cain smiled, and Drew embraced him like a brother. He and Drew had never been close when they were growing up, despite traveling in the same circles and having parents who were close friends. Funny how adversity and kept secrets had a way of binding people together even more tightly than shared history.

"Hey," Cain returned, before asking the bartender for another water and adding a hefty tip to the glass on the counter. "Didn't expect to see you here tonight."

Drew lifted his chin in acknowledgment.

"*Not* my idea. My mother's." Drew shrugged as though this were explanation enough, and Cain nodded because Mary-Alice McMann and Lucy Shaw had been cut from the same cloth.

"How's everyone? Seen Bas and Cam?" Cain asked. He winced internally. *Yeah, bring up Cam Seaver, who dumped Drew just a few months before getting a new boyfriend. Smooth, Shaw.*

But Drew smiled warmly as he took a sip of brown liquid from his glass. "Yeah, they're good. And I can't seem to get away from them - I see them at work every day."

Cain nodded. Right. *Duh.* Drew worked at Seaver Tech, the company Cam and Sebastian had inherited from their father. In fact, as the senator liked to remind Cain, Drew was head of the legal team already, despite only being thirty, *because that's what ambition looked like.*

"Cam's got Cort working at Seaver, too," Drew continued, referring to Cam's new boyfriend who, through some coincidence Cain didn't totally understand, was Damon Fitzpatrick's brother. Drew rolled his eyes, but there was no bitterness in them. "His asshole-good-humor's growing on me. *Like a fungus.* But he makes Cam happy, so." He shrugged.

"And Bas?" According to the senator, Bas Seaver, head

of Seaver Tech, had been pretty much steamrolled by grief and depression after the crash, and had only recently emerged from his self-imposed exile. *"Poor boy will never be the same,"* the senator had told Cain's mother sadly, and Cain remembered thinking that his jerk of a father couldn't be all bad if he could feel so much compassion for his friends' son.

Lying asshole.

"He's fine, I—. Hey, you okay?" Drew asked. His dark eyes looked concerned and a frown marred the handsome face below his trademark-perfect brown hair.

"Yeah." Cain swiped his water off the bar and nodded to the bartender before turning back around so that he and Drew could watch the party together. "Just, you know. I can't stop thinking about shit." He shook his head in frustration at all the things he couldn't say.

How was he supposed to live with his father, knowing what the man had done?

How could he toe the line they'd laid out for him, when he hated himself more every day?

How could he do anything else after his father had threatened Jesse, whose only crime had been dating Cain, once-upon-a-time?

Christ, he hated being forced into this position. And while it shouldn't matter what Drew or the Seavers thought of his decision not to come forward, it did.

"Nobody blames you for not going to the authorities about your father, you know." Cain turned his head to Drew and found steady, knowing brown eyes watching him. "If it were my mother, or even my father, I don't know if I'd be able to turn them in."

Cain grimaced. *Yeah. Right.*

It was bitterly ironic that Drew thought filial love was what kept him from doing the right thing, but it wouldn't change anything for Cain to tell them his real motivation -

that the senator had the power to destroy the life of an innocent man, one Cain felt responsible for.

And anyway, why *shouldn't* everyone be pissed at him? Cain was pissed at himself.

Sure, Cam and Damon had overheard Jack's confession, too, and knew what the senator had done. But Damon was widely believed to be dead, like everyone else aboard the Seavers' plane, and he couldn't come forward without potentially facing charges. Cam, the grief-stricken son, accusing the senator on his own, with no proof, would be futile at best and downright dangerous at worst. They'd needed Cain to come forward, to get justice for Cam and Bas's parents and Drew's sister, to get Damon his life back.

And he simply couldn't.

He knew for a fact that Cam and Bas were pissed, but Damon... Damon was the one Cain *really* didn't like to think about, for more than one reason.

Damon was all tall, broad-shouldered, confident grace, complete with flashing hazel eyes and distinctively long, prematurely-gray hair that gleamed like silver silk. Gorgeous and proud, even with the scars and the limp he'd received as souvenirs from the Seavers' plane crash. He was hot as hell, but there was more than that. Something about the man had called to Cain from their very first meeting. Maybe because Damon had been dealt a shitty hand too. Unlike Cain, though, he'd never backed down. He was still working to clear his name, still proud and determined to see the senator brought to justice.

Damon must hate his guts.

And still, he couldn't stop himself from asking Drew, "And, um, Damon? What's he up to?"

Drew shook his head and glanced away, his eyes roaming over the crowd. "I'm not sure. He fell off the fucking map again a couple days ago. He won't answer

Cort's calls." His voice hardened. "I don't understand that guy. Bas wanted to give him money - kind of compensation for the fact that Bas had stirred shit up with the media after the crash and blackened Damon's name, you know? Not that we accept any responsibility for defaming his character." Drew's lawyer-voice was smooth and polished.

"Uh huh."

"Asshole wouldn't take it," Drew continued. "Not for himself anyway, though he did let Bas send a check to that sister of his - remember, the one he'd never known he had until the tabloids dug her up after the crash? He let Cam and Cort harass him into taking a job as an airplane mechanic at Seaver Tech, since he had no other way to get a job. And he moved into his brother's old apartment, since Cam and Cort are joined at the hip now, and Cort spends most of his time at Cam's place. Guy seemed happy enough the last few weeks from what Cam's said. Then, three days ago, *poof*. He and Cort had barely been able to reconnect, and now he's fallen off the radar again."

Cain said nothing, but he was pretty sure he understood exactly where Damon was coming from.

Cam and Sebastian were stand-up guys, but who would want to live on someone else's sufferance? Who'd want to spend every day walking on eggshells, hoping their bene-factor wouldn't decide that today was the day to take it all away? Who'd want to live under someone else's thumb?

Cain looked over at his parents, who were still chatting eagerly with Billy Fassbender. They'd been joined by two women, the younger of whom was so pink and shiny, she could only be Bill's progeny. From this distance, Emmett Shaw looked like a sweet, portly, middle-aged man, whose guiltiest secrets were dying his gray hair blond and eating a few too many Cheetos on football Sundays. Millions of voters had gone to the polls and said *Yes. Trustworthy.* And every one of them had been wrong.

So, yeah, Cain could understand why Damon would find it hard to trust Sebastian, who'd fucked up his life so well in the first place.

Drew shook his head and clapped Cain on the back. "Gotta get back to my mother. You have my number if you need me for anything?"

Anything, like being ready to confess to all he'd heard? Not gonna happen. But he nodded and smiled his goodbye, then turned back to the bar for another refill. "Double water this time. With ice."

The reporter, Gary North, was standing just a few feet away, watching him again, and Cain's heart beat faster. He mentally reviewed his conversation with Drew, trying to imagine what Gary might have overheard, or read on his lips. Nothing like an ill-timed comment to blow the entire charade of your life wide-fucking-open.

To his surprise, Gary stepped forward and offered Cain his hand.

"Mr. Shaw?"

Cain reluctantly extended his hand. Damn his ingrained manners.

The man smiled affably. "Gary North. Reporter for *The Herald*?"

Well, he didn't lie. Cain would give him that much.

"I know who you are. I have no comment," Cain said firmly, turning away.

To his shock, North laid a hand on his arm, stopping him. "I haven't asked you for one yet." He sounded reasonable, and also amused.

"But you will. So let me tell you upfront, I have no comment on *anything.*"

"So suspicious. Maybe I just want to buy you a drink,"

Gary said, and holy cats, the man's smile was *flirtatious*. He wasn't Cain's type - he preferred men who were taller and broader, but he still felt heat flood his face, even as he took a step back. *Danger, danger.* Was Gary the type to flirt with every man? Somehow Cain didn't think so.

"I'm only drinking water. Thanks, but no thanks."

"Ah. I wondered if it might be vodka."

Cain looked down at his glass, startled. "Oh?"

Gary shrugged. "Occupational hazard," he said apologetically. "I've spent the last two years undercover chasing Russian criminals all over the country, and even to Moscow. I see vodka everywhere," he said in a mock-whisper.

"Russian criminals? Jesus." Cain took a literal step back from the man.

"A group named SILA, founded right here in Boston," Gary agreed. At Cain's blank look, he explained. "It's Russian for *power.*"

"Oh-kay. So you write about Russian gangsters and now you're chatting with me?" Cain forced himself to laugh. "I can't tell if I'm supposed to be impressed or horrified."

"I'd prefer you went with impressed," Gary joked, though his hand hadn't moved from Cain's arm.

Cain forced himself to laugh it off, just like any straight guy would in that situation - *wouldn't they?* - and take another step away. "I'm sure that's true, Mr. North. Excuse me. I need to get back." He nodded to where his father was holding court.

Gary's eyes swung toward Senator Shaw, and then turned back to Cain, his gaze coy. "Your father seems to be having a great night. The rumors are swirling about a possible White House run."

"I told you," Cain repeated. "No—"

"Comment," Gary recited, along with him. "Yes, I know. And I promise, I won't ask about that. I'm confident that if and *when*, he makes a decision, we'll all be well aware." He flashed a hard smile. "No, I'm looking to write about things your father *won't* be mentioning in a press conference. A piece on the *real* Emmett Shaw. The one the public never sees."

Wow. There were so many things that could come under that heading. And Cain would not be talking about any of them. "I can't-"

"Your father gave me permission to ask you for an interview."

Cain's eyes swung toward Gary's, startled.

"Just a couple of hours ago," Gary continued with a firm nod. "You can check with him."

"He wants me to do an interview with you?" Cain sipped his water again, praying that any visible terror was blanketed by a heavy dose of skepticism.

What was worse than making small talk? A fucking *interview* with a man who saw too much.

"Hey, I'm a talented reporter." The man's smile widened and he winked.

"You're a liberal mouthpiece," Cain corrected, and Gary's smile dimmed.

"We tend to draw in a lot of the younger voters. Just like having someone young, handsome, and *relatable,* like yourself, helps your father increase his visibility with that demographic."

Shit. That was probably true. Still.

"I can't imagine what I'd have to say that would interest anyone," Cain said. He shrugged, as though amused. *Drop it. Drop it, Gary.*

"Oh, you let me worry about that," Gary said. "I think you're plenty interesting."

"I assure you, I'm not. Just an average guy who likes to keep to himself, low-key and --"

"Lonely," Gary interrupted.

Cain blinked. Not one person in a thousand would look at him, at Senator Shaw's son, with his money, his pedigree, and his picture-perfect family, and see that he was lonely.

But Gary North somehow had.

And it was absolutely true, Cain realized. How long had it been since he'd had physical contact with anyone beyond a simple handshake or a pat on the shoulder? How long since he'd had a conversation with someone who had nothing to do with his family? How long since anyone had seen the *real* Cain?

God, even Cain himself hardly knew who the real Cain was anymore.

The fact that this reporter had recognized that loneliness made the idea of doing an interview immeasurably more dangerous. Gary North wanted a reaction, a sound-bite, and Cain would be damned if he'd let someone else use him that way. Not when there was so much at stake.

Still, what the senator wanted, the senator fucking got.

"Contact my father's office then," Cain agreed finally. "Have them set something up."

"Or you could give me your number."

Now Cain didn't have to feign amusement. He laughed out loud as he met the man's eyes. "That's not ever going to happen. My father's office will want to approve the questions."

"And you always do what your father tells you to do?"

Cain's skin prickled, but outwardly he ignored the taunt. Or maybe it wasn't a taunt at all. Maybe Gary could see what everyone else saw in Cain.

"Here's my card," Gary said, sliding the thin white

paper into Cain's breast pocket. "In case you change your mind."

"Set up the damn appointment," Cain said, meeting Gary's eyes, then he walked away before the man could reply.

God, an interview. Awful. So many things to keep from saying and, more difficult still, *implying*. So many things to dodge and lie about. Too bad Cain's concerns meant jack shit to his father, if his mind was really set on this thing.

Cain needed to get out of town, and not in the sense of going back to his parents' house in Tennessee, or moving on to the next stop of the Senator Shaw Baby-kissing Tour, but going someplace where none of his family could reach him.

Maybe when he got there, he could forget how to be Senator Shaw's kid, and remember how to be Cain.

As he bypassed the center of the room, where his father was standing, and attempted to make a getaway to the restroom, he saw a flash of red hair in his peripheral vision as his mother moved to intercept him.

He stifled a sigh. "Just water, Mother." He handed her his glass, and she accepted it, taking a brief sniff of the liquid to confirm. *So much trust.*

"Excuse me, I need the men's room," he told her tightly, nodding towards the door.

"Just a minute. I saw you chatting over there," she said, voice chilly with disapproval. "With that man, that *Gary North*. He's a *reporter*, Cain. For that revolting rag, *The Herald*."

Cain raised his eyebrows. "I know. Cady told me, and the man confirmed it, himself just now. What's wrong with *The Herald*?" He'd heard this tirade a million times, but he enjoyed watching the struggle play on her face, her need to remain relentlessly cheerful and photo-ready winning out over her absolute hatred of the media outlet that had blasted his father's political platform from the very beginning.

She gave him a sharp look. "You know very well what's wrong with them. Dirt-slingers. That's all they are."

Cain's eyebrows flew up. This was tough talk for Lucy Shaw.

"Funny, because Dad already gave him an interview, and now Gary tells me that I'm supposed do an interview with him, too."

Lucy's lips pinched together and she exhaled through her nose. "Your father mentioned it. He wants to appeal to a younger demographic. It's a ridiculous idea."

Cain's chest loosened. "I agree. He's calling the senator's office to set it up, so have Darla give the guy the brush-off."

His mother shook her head once, and a tiny line of frustration appeared in the middle of her forehead. "He's not going to back down. You're just going to have to handle things."

Right. Totally. Easy enough. He just had to remember not to mention anything important that had happened to him during the last six months.

"Mom..."

But Lucy merely nodded decisively, as though there was nothing more to be discussed. "You'll talk about school," she told him firmly. "Your studies. The girls you've dated." Her face brightened. "Oh, and Sebastian Seaver. Talk about him."

"Bas? What for?" Cain and *Cam* had dated briefly in high school, not that his mother knew that. But Cain and *Bas* had never been close, even before Bas had every reason to hate him.

"Because he's sympathetic. He lost his fiancée *and* both parents in that horrible plane crash. People will instantly sympathize with you, too."

"Cam Seaver lost his parents as well," Cain pointed out. "And I'm far better friends with him."

She raised an eyebrow. "Yes, I'm well aware that you and Camden were good friends, but that's not the image we're trying to cultivate for you, sweetheart."

Cain squinted down at her. Though he was no mighty giant himself, he was still far taller than his petite mother.

"What image? What's wrong with Cam?"

"Nothing's *wrong*, we just want to make sure you spend plenty of time with *all* your friends, " she hedged.

Oh. My. God.

"Is this because he's *gay*?" Cain demanded. His voice rose, and several people nearby turned to look at him, but he would not lower it. "He's your godson!"

The hypocrisy was nauseating.

"Don't be so melodramatic." Her whisper was cold and furious, as were her eyes as she glanced around to make sure no one could hear them. "Nobody is suggesting that you don't talk to him. We occasionally travel in the same small circles, and it's only right to be polite. Just... don't seek out reasons to talk to him. Or to Andrew McMann, either." She scowled at the place where Cain had stood talking to Drew.

"To what end?" Cain drew a hand through his hair, heedless of the mess he knew he would cause, and his eyes pled with his mother. "Everyone knows we've been friendly with the Seavers and the McManns for years. Cutting them off now achieves nothing."

Her mouth twitched. "Who we've been *friendly with* doesn't matter, Cain. It's all about who can help us *succeed* in life, and who is setting us up for failure." She wrapped a hand around his neck and leaned in close. "You can be just as happy with friends who help you cultivate the image you want."

The image *he* wanted. A successful, conservative, *straight* asshole, just like dear old dad.

Right. His stomach clenched, the lies eating away at his insides like corrosive acid. He looked back at the senator, imagined the blood that stained the man's successful, conservative hands.

Gary North was right - Cain was so fucking lonely. In this entire function room crowded with sycophants and yes-men, there was not one person who really saw him.

"I'm going to the restroom," he told his mother stiffly. Bile clogged his throat.

She nodded and stroked a comforting hand down the lapel of his jacket as though he were a skittish animal who might bolt. "Alright, darling. Alright. And when you get back, I'll tell you all about Mr. Fassbender. He's planning a little ski vacation next week for his daughter Penny and some of her friends. I was sure you'd want to go, so I gave him your number."

Skiing? He hadn't been skiing in years, but apparently he needed to cultivate the image of a man who skied. And never mind that Thanksgiving, the general time of family togetherness, was next week.

"Sure," he said hollowly. "You can tell me all about it."

Honestly, it might be better than sitting at his parents' DC house, or wherever they planned to spend Thanksgiving. If he had to listen to more conversations like this while trying to cough down dry turkey, he might actually shoot himself.

The worst part was, he suspected that his mother honestly believed what she was telling him was true - that he'd have a happier life if he cut out any friends who could cause a potential scandal. It was almost amusing, because as far as he knew, *he* was the greatest potential for scandal in his mother's life, and rather than cutting him out, she was determined to rein him in.

He reached out, squeezed her forearms, then stepped away. "Be right back," he told her, and she nodded.

Even though he knew she was watching again, he practically sprinted from the room.

TONIGHT'S EVENT was held in a large and spacious function hall, one he knew for a fact looked like a thousand other function halls in other cities around the country. A large crystal chandelier that had to weigh a ton dominated the foyer outside, but the furniture was Spartan, probably to discourage parties from spilling out into the lobby. There were a few leather benches off to one side, not far from the hallway to the restrooms... and not far from the main exit.

One of the two black-suited security guards he'd been introduced to earlier nodded at him from the doorway, watching as he sank down onto the leather bench and shifted forward, cradling his head in his hands.

God, escape was tempting. What would it be like to walk out the door and just keep on walking?

But then, of course, there was Jesse.

Blond-haired, blue eyed, with a cocky smile that had peeked out whenever he'd caught Cain saying something stupid or outrageous, which was pretty regularly, Jesse Porter had been his childhood sweetheart. For one spring, Jesse had been a living, breathing dream - someone who'd only wanted to love Cain, and let Cain love him in return. Someone who'd understood the life Cain led and the restrictions therein.

Come kiss me, Jesse.

But... dude, someone's gonna see.

Shut up. Everyone's busy swimming. No one's gonna notice if we head behind the pool house.

But, Cain, your parents…

Are too busy schmoozing with your parents and everyone else to even notice.

You're such a child, Cain Edward Shaw.

See if you can kiss some responsibility into me, then. It'll be fun.

And it had been, until Cain's father had caught them and brought his considerable power to bear, forcing Jesse to choose: Cain, or his scholarship and any hope of a happy future.

It had broken his heart at the time, but Cain didn't fault Jesse for walking away from him. Hell, the only guilty parties in this mess were Cain himself, for thinking he'd ever deserve someone like Jesse, and his father, who *to this day* had kept tabs on every aspect of Jesse's life and had threatened to take it all away if Cain didn't toe the line.

So here sat Cain Shaw, the rich, white, educated son of one of the most powerful men in the country, unable to visit the restroom without permission from his mother.

Fucking pathetic.

Shouts at the door caught his attention, and he looked up, expecting to see gatecrashers or (his personal favorite) protesters. At this point, *any* drama would be a welcome respite from his own.

Instead, he saw the duo of security guards wrestling a tall man in a black hoodie to the floor - *hard.*

"I said I want to see Shaw!" the guy shouted, as one of the guards practically knelt on his back. "He owes me!"

No shit. Get in line, buddy, Cain thought. But then it struck him that something about the guy seemed weirdly familiar. The voice - gravelly and rough, like he was perpetually angry - made prickles of sensation dance through Cain's chest, and he got to his feet in a second, heading toward the man.

"Parker, call for backup," the guard holding the man down said to the one still standing. "This guy's drunk and belligerent."

Cain's heart beat faster and time seemed to slow down. The broad shoulders and sturdy frame - so proud and powerful - were familiar, but it was the steel-gray hair pulled into a queue at the nape of the man's neck that was a dead giveaway. It was the very last person he'd expected to see here, despite the fact that the man had been on his mind, directly and indirectly, all night. For one stunned second, Cain wondered if he'd somehow conjured him.

"I am *not* drunk," Damon yelled, although the slur in his voice belied his words. "I have a right to be here. To speak to the senator."

Oh, Damon.

The security guard called Parker saw Cain approach and took a step forward. "You're gonna wanna stand back, Mr. Shaw," he said, forearm thrust out to block Cain's way.

Fuck that.

Cain couldn't say precisely why he felt compelled to intervene on Damon's behalf - the guy was drunk off his ass, and had every reason to hate Cain's guts, so maybe he *was* a threat. Maybe the guards were right to want to contain him.

But Cain was so damn *tired* of being powerless. He'd be damned if he'd let Damon self-destruct this way, getting himself arrested or *worse.*

Not if he could help it.

He drew himself up straight, managing to look down his nose at the guard though the man was a full six inches taller than Cain.

"I think *you* are going to want to stand aside," he said haughtily. "I know this man."

"But Mr. Shaw," Parker said, looking dubiously from Cain to the man on the floor. "He's not on the invitation list, and he doesn't have any identification on him. Says he wants to see Senator Shaw, and he's three sheets to the wind."

"He's a friend of mine, and his pain medication makes him disoriented."

Parker seemed unconvinced, looking to the guard on the floor for advice. Damon struggled to break free, and the guard on the floor shook his head. *No way are we letting him go.*

"And what is your name?" Cain demanded of the second guard.

"Rodney."

"Rodney," Cain said, repeating the name like he was committing it to memory, which he was. "Do you know who I am?"

The guard was fighting Damon, so he grunted as he replied. "You're Shaw's kid."

"I'm Cain Edward Shaw, yes. Senator Shaw's *son*. And I am telling you right now, you need to let my friend go."

On the floor, Damon immediately fell silent and stopped struggling, though he didn't look up. The guard hesitated, so Cain continued.

"Is violence generally your way of handling things, Rodney?"

"Violence?" Rodney looked at the other security guard helplessly.

"We haven't been violent, Mr. Shaw," Parker interjected.

"Really? What do you call it when you've taken an injured man, who I can state for the record was causing no physical harm to anyone until you jumped him, and forced him down on his already *injured leg*? Do you understand how liability works in Massachusetts?"

The guards exchanged looks.

"We have orders to detain anyone who…" Parker began, but Cain interrupted, dialing his attitude up to stratospheric levels.

"Parker. That's your name, isn't it?"

"Er. Yes?"

Cain sighed gustily, just as his father would. "Are you asking me or telling me, Parker?" he demanded. The man was perhaps a foot taller than Cain, and twice as broad, but his eyebrows twitched with discomfort at Cain's tone.

"Uh. Telling you?"

"Right. Okay, here's what we're going to do, Parker. You're going to find us a room, a private room where my friend and I can chat until he feels a little better, and then I'm going to make sure he gets home."

Parker nodded, still throwing a cautious glance at Damon, who hadn't moved nor even raised his head.

"*Now*, Parker," Cain said, making a shooing motion with his hands and shaking his head in disbelief.

"Yes, sir," Parker finally acquiesced.

Cain took a quick glance around and saw that the foyer was blessedly free of any witnesses. But he knew it wouldn't stay that way for long.

"And you, Rodney. Help me get him up," Cain told the other guard, who removed his knee from Damon's back and stood.

The minute he moved his knee, Damon pushed himself to his feet. His hair had gotten mussed in the struggle, and he shoved the long iron strands back from the rough perfection of his face.

"I'm capable of standing on my own."

Those eyes. *God*. Green-gold like a cat's and every bit as wild, they seared into him, focused and clearly sober. Damon was *pissed*, but despite the slurred words and the acrid smell of alcohol that radiated from him, not nearly as drunk as he seemed.

Cain swallowed and nodded, robbed of words. Being a condescending asshole to the huge-as-fuck armed guards was one thing. Standing firm in the face of this gorgeous, compelling man was definitely another. He was excited and terrified in equal measure, like he wanted to run away and push his luck at the same time.

"Manager found you a room with a sofa. This way," Parker informed him proudly, like a child who'd just completed a task and wanted a cookie. "It's the place where brides get ready when they have weddings here."

Cain nodded.

When Parker turned to show them the way, Cain took a deep breath and slung his arm around Damon's waist, encouraging the man to lean on him under Rodney's watchful eyes as they made their way across the lobby to a back hallway.

"Capable of walking on my own too, kid," Damon muttered. His voice was pitched low enough that only Cain could hear, and the harsh, breathy rumble once again made Cain shiver with something that wasn't quite excitement and wasn't quite fear, but a strange amalgam of the two.

Cain was annoyed at himself for letting something so trivial affect him so badly. He was also annoyed at Damon, who wasn't going along with Cain's rescue.

"Okay, first off," Cain retorted in an angry whisper that would have done his mother proud. "Given the fact that you were thirty seconds away from being arrested, how about you wait until later to tell me how capable you are?" He could feel Damon's muscles stiffen beneath his arm, and he gripped Damon's waist more tightly, forcing him to lean on Cain even though it clearly wasn't necessary - the man was carrying his own weight, despite his evident limp. Still, Cain was committed to the story he'd spun for the guards. "Second, you went to a lot of trouble to get drunk - or make yourself seem that way, at least - so for God's sake just go with it."

"Jesus, kid." Three syllables laced with disgust and frustration.

At the end of the hall, Parker and a neatly-dressed woman with a name tag stood by an open door.

"And last but not least, my name is *Cain,* not *kid,* because I'm not *a* kid, and I'm definitely not *your* kid. Got it?"

Cain smiled at Parker as he shuffled Damon through the doorway and into the room. Against the back wall stood a purple tufted sofa, and he hobbled toward it, then dropped Damon down with an utter lack of care.

"Thanks, Parker," he said, walking back toward the door and ushering the guard and the woman - *Amy Patel, Guest Service Specialist,* according to her nametag - back into the hall. "I'll make sure the senator hears about how helpful you've both been in taking care of this sensitive situation."

Amy beamed, and Parker nodded solemnly. "You need any more help with him, you let me know," he said. And then he looked at Damon again, a bit awkwardly. "Uh, sorry about before. You, uh… feel better, bro."

Cain cleared his throat and shut the door in the man's face. One problem down, one giant problem to go.

CHAPTER TWO

Damon let his head fall back against the ridiculous purple sofa and watched with slitted eyes as Cain turned to face him, his arms crossed over his chest.

Well, well, well. Seemed the Shaw kid had a pair of balls after all, despite all appearances to the contrary.

My name is Cain, not kid, because I'm not a kid, and I'm definitely not your kid. Got it?

Damon got it, alright. Though this was hardly the first time he'd met Cain Shaw - they'd both been present for Jack Peabody's bombshell confession a few months back, and they'd seen each other a couple of times after that - tonight he couldn't help but see him with new eyes.

Right now, Cain definitely wasn't looking like a kid. His cheeks were flushed, and his blue eyes were dark and stormy with anger.

It was the kind of look that, in another lifetime, would have set Damon on fire. Even now, he felt a brief, unwanted pull of attraction, before his own anger rose up to quench it. He'd had a perfectly good plan working back there, and the kid had cocked it up completely.

He brought his aching right leg up onto the sofa and flexed his toes back and forth as much as he could, given the boots on his feet. He wanted to reach down and knead the pain away through his jeans, but he'd be damned if he'd do that while the Shaw kid watched. His life was fucked up enough without showing weakness and, honest to God, if this kid looked at him with pity, that would be the last straw.

"What the hell are you doing here?" Cain demanded, shattering the silence like the words were being pulled from him. He started pacing the floor, hands thrown up in some overdone caricature of frustration.

Damon opened his eyes fully. The *kid* was angry at *him*. Oh, for fuck's sake.

"And I know you're not drunk, Damon, so don't bother pretending!"

Interesting.

"And how the hell would you know that?" Damon demanded. God, he hated the sound of his own voice - the grating noise of a poorly-oiled engine, croaky and out-of-tune from disuse.

Cain opened his mouth like he was about to speak, then snapped it shut like he'd thought better of it. He shook his head instead. "Irrelevant," he said, though his cheeks burned even redder. "At least the guards bought it, and I was there in time to save you before they caught on."

Damon frowned up at him in blatant disbelief. "Save me?"

"Uh, yeah. They were two seconds away from calling the police on you." Cain stopped his pacing a step away from the couch, and folded his arms again to glare down at Damon like he'd been personally offended by Damon's actions. "Seriously, man, what were you thinking?"

Damon imagined if he'd ever had a real mother, rather

than the lackluster collection of foster parents he'd had forced on him during his tenure in the system, she would have scolded him with the same expression Cain was wearing now - utter disappointment in both his life choices and his lack of gratitude.

But seeing that expression on the face of a man at least a dozen years younger, several inches shorter, and fifty pounds lighter than Damon, was so entirely incomprehensible that, despite the slow-simmering anger that had been dogging him for weeks and his outrage at the way his plans for tonight had been ruined, he threw his head back and laughed out loud.

It was such a weird and unexpected sound, more like a deep bark than anything else - *God, how long has it been since I laughed, if I don't even recognize the sound?* - that Cain's face lost its frustrated expression. He uncrossed his arms and looked down at Damon in concern.

"Are you okay?"

Which set Damon off again. *God, what a fucked-up night. What a fucked-up* life.

He felt the strange pull toward Cain Shaw flare again - found himself looking at Cain's mouth, the anxious frown that pursed his lips, and wondering what he tasted like. Of all the people in the world, why should this kid - this kid who'd fucked him over and refused to do the right thing - be the one to summon up emotions Damon hadn't let himself feel in fucking forever? It was ridiculous.

"Yeah," he said finally, sitting up and wiping at the tears leaking from his eyes. His stomach felt hollow, like he'd overdone a workout, and he wondered if it was possible to be out-of-shape from lack of laughter. He sucked in a deep breath that was more like a sniff. "Yeah," he repeated. "I'm good. I'm fine. You caught me off-guard."

"Are you sure? Should I call someone? Cort, or…"

Damon's laughter fled as quickly as it had appeared. He scrubbed a hand over his eyes.

'*Cort, or…*' There wasn't any *or*. Damon had no one else to call. God knew, even his own long-lost sister wanted him to stay away from her. Hell, the one and only time he'd tried to call her - the dictionary definition of an awkward call, right from the, "Uh, hi, I'm Damon. I'm your… brother? The media found your name and camped on your doorstep when they thought I was dead?" - she'd hung up on him. She'd refused to open the door when he'd tried to visit, and hadn't even acknowledged the money he'd had Sebastian Seaver send to her and her little girl, a niece Damon would never know.

So, *no*, Damon had no one but Cort. And now Cort had Cam, so Damon needed to extract himself from the equation. He was tired of relying on his little brother, and he wouldn't drag Cort down with him.

"Nah. I'm good," he said belatedly. He adjusted himself more comfortably on the couch, and couldn't help wincing at the ache in his leg. "Believe it or not, it was going to be even better before you interfered."

"How the hell do you figure that?"

Cain grabbed a chair from in front of the long, mirrored vanity and dragged it over to the sofa. He frowned as he sat down and propped his feet on the edge of the sofa near Damon's waist with his knees bent and his arms crossed over his chest. His position was half-armadillo, half-bodyguard, like he wasn't sure whether Damon was going to hit him, or try to escape back to the lobby, but he wasn't going to let either thing happen. It was infuriating and *intriguing*, and left Damon wondering whether he'd underestimated the Shaw kid.

He sighed and ran a hand through his hair.

The kid - *Cain. His name was Cain* - seemed like a decent

enough human, for all that he was completely lacking the balls, or conscience, or whatever one needed to bring their father to justice. Hell, in a way, Damon could almost understand it. In his quest to get his life back after the crash, Damon had asked his own brother to do some pretty underhanded, not-exactly-legal things in order to keep Damon's name off everyone's radar. And Cort had done them, not because he was a shitty person, but because love and family loyalty sometimes trumped everything else. But understanding why Cain had made his choice didn't mean that Damon wasn't angry about it - not when it was Damon's fucking life that hung in the balance. And understanding didn't mean that he and Cain were friends. Not by a long shot.

"That's none of your business, kid." Damon tried to swing his legs around, but Cain's feet were in the way. "Move," he said.

Cain swallowed hard, but shook his head and planted his feet more firmly on the cushions. "No. Not until you tell me what you'd planned."

Was he fucking kidding? "Not happening. I said, *move,*" Damon yelled. He pushed at Cain's feet, but from this angle Cain had all the leverage.

"And I said *no.*" Though his eyes betrayed some hesitation, Cain cocked his head with pure determination. "Gee, I hope Parker and Rodney aren't standing outside the door listening, just in case I need their help with the drunk, belligerent dude they apprehended. All that angry yelling would be *way* tricky to explain, wouldn't it, since I said you were my friend and all?"

Damon blinked, stunned. *Oh, that fucking brat.* The kid had maneuvered him perfectly. He sucked a breath in through his nose and let his eyes go hot. It was gratifying to see Cain squirm, even though he kept his feet braced right where they were.

Damn it.

"Now, as I was so *politely* asking," Cain said, no hint of a quaver in his voice. "Why were you here? I'm gonna assume you had some kind of plan, however misguided."

Damon huffed out a laugh. This was what his life had come to - answering to a punk like Cain Shaw. *Jesus.*

"I came to see your father," Damon drawled, and since he couldn't get off the sofa - well, not without hurting himself and/or Cain - he flopped back down and propped his hands behind his head, resting and watchful. He'd see what the kid had to say about that.

"Yeah, duh." Damon lifted an eyebrow and Cain shrugged. "Well, I figured you weren't here for the hors d'oeuvres." He gave Damon a small smile, and his eyes flashed with mischief. "Or to make a campaign donation."

Once again, Damon found himself laughing. "Maybe for the free drinks?"

Cain rolled his eyes. "Maybe for the scintillating conversation. And there are any number of eligible women in the crowd." He flexed his hand against his bent knee and his smile dimmed. "Just ask my mother."

"No eligible guys?" Damon teased.

Cain's shocked eyes flew to his.

"What's that look for? You remember I was there when Jack confessed everything, right? You know I know that you and he had an affair, just like you know that Jack and I hooked up a couple of times, too." God, *Jack.* A name he didn't even like to think about, let alone say, and judging from Cain's expression, he didn't like hearing it any better. He hurried on. "I'm aware that you're gay, Cain. Just like you're aware that I am."

Cain swallowed and gave a shaky laugh. His eyes

darted around the room like he was looking for cameras. "Jesus, just hearing you say it out loud gives me chills. Like, if anyone else heard it… Damn."

Damon levered up on one elbow and leaned until his chin was directly above Cain's knee. "*Voldemort*," he whispered.

God, the kid's smile was electric- the even white teeth glowing against his perfect skin sent a pang of frustrated arousal directly to Damon's groin… And *holy shit*, there was a feeling he hadn't had in a really long time. At least as long as it had been since he'd laughed. Possibly longer.

Why this kid? Why was he suddenly so charming?

Maybe the double shot of whiskey he'd downed to sell his drunk act had hit him harder than he'd thought.

"What?" Cain chuckled. "What are you even talking about?"

What *was* he talking about? Not his dick. Oh, right. "*Voldemort*. You know, from Harry Potter?"

"Yeah, I know Harry Potter. I'm just surprised *you* know Harry Potter."

"I can *read*, kid. God."

Cain flushed. "I just meant I didn't know you'd, you know, read *those* books."

"Hasn't almost every human on the planet read those books? Or at least watched the movies?"

Cain cleared his throat, his embarrassment somewhat endearing. "Well, I guess I figured it was mostly, you know…" His hand fluttered in the direction of Damon's head, as though this should somehow explain something.

It didn't.

Cain sighed. "I thought it was mostly a thing younger people would reference," he blurted out. His cheeks were so red, Damon could feel the heat of them from a foot away, and he felt his own lips twitch.

"Exactly how old do you think I am, sonny? I'm forty, not a hundred and forty. And this hair has been gray since I was younger than you."

Cain pressed his lips together like he was fighting a laugh. "Right. No, I knew that. You're right. Sorry."

Was the kid humoring him? "Now I'm annoyed. I could kick your ass, you know."

"I know," Cain nodded seriously. But then his head tilted to the side. "Like, assuming you didn't get winded while you were chasing me."

Damon squinted and lifted himself up higher, so he was propped on one wrist. "Say again?"

Christ, this was the craziest conversation Damon had ever had. Why did it feel so good?

Cain laughed, high and light, but he didn't move away. "Nothing. I said nothing."

"Hmm," Damon agreed, laying back down again. "That's what I thought."

"But what the heck does anything have to do with Harry Potter?" Cain demanded.

"Oh, right. Voldemort. Remember, none of the good guys in the books would say his name because they were so scared of him. Even when he wasn't around and had no power, they'd *give* him power by refusing to name him out of fear." He shrugged his shoulders as best he could with his hands behind his head. "When you own the words, you keep the power."

A whole parade of emotions chased one another across Cain's face - surprise, fear, wonder, anger, and finally, a sad sort of acceptance. "It's a really nice analogy," he allowed. "But I don't think it's entirely the same thing."

Damon thought it was probably more apt than Cain was willing to admit, but it was none of his business. He shrugged again. "If you say so."

"You haven't distracted me, either," Cain warned. He crossed his arms again, and he looked so fucking adorable, all self-righteous and innocent, with that hint of hesitation peeking out beneath his bravado, that Damon rolled his eyes. "I still want to know what your big plan was for tonight. Or did you even have one? Was being arrested *part* of the plan, or just a fun little afterthought?"

Did he have one? Little brat. "Oh, I had one. The plan was to cause a scene, *Cain*," Damon sighed. "Such a loud and disruptive scene that people would come running out of the fundraiser, phones held aloft like Lady Liberty's torch, ready to stream it all over social media."

"What?" Cain sputtered. "That's the stupidest plan I've ever…"

"And then, when it was plastered on Facebook and trending on Twitter," Damon continued. "Your father wouldn't be able to ignore it anymore. He wouldn't be able to just *go on* like nothing had ever happened, like he hadn't ruined lives and killed people. Maybe the authorities would look into it. Maybe they wouldn't even have to. Maybe just getting him involved in a scandal would be enough." He glanced over and saw dawning comprehension in Cain's eyes. "Reporters would dig deeper. Voters would remember."

"Oh my God," Cain whispered.

Damon nodded. "It would've been beautiful." He sighed again and said grudgingly, "But I get that you didn't know. That you thought you were doing the right thing."

Cain shook his head rapidly. "Oh my *God*," he repeated. "Not oh-my-God, what an amazing plan, you fucking idiot. I mean *oh-my-God, that's the stupidest thing I've ever heard.*"

"The fuck it was." Damon scowled, sitting up. "It would have worked. People would have flooded out in another minute."

"Yeah, maybe." But Cain waved this away with a flip of his hand and he leaned forward, getting in Damon's face. He smelled clean and woodsy, like some subtle, no doubt outrageously expensive cologne. Damon was momentarily distracted by the desire to bring him even closer, but then his words brought him back. "But who gives a shit? You're missing something vitally important here."

"Oh, really. What's that?"

"My father would not have sat by and allowed that to happen, Damon! God. First of all, there have been a million negative stories written about him over the years."

Damon raised a skeptical eyebrow. He'd found nothing negative about the senator in all his searching, and while he didn't believe for a second that the Seavers' deaths were the only skeletons in the man's closet, he assumed Emmett Shaw had been too crafty or too lucky to get caught.

Cain grimaced and looked away. "My father was a businessman for years before he ran for office. You know that, right? Hell, he was one of the original founders of Seaver Tech, along with Cam's father and Drew's. You don't think there were dozens of disgruntled former employees who'd have been only too happy to dish about him? Colleagues who remembered he made some shitty hate-speech comment, or people he'd passed over for promotions they deserved?" His face grew bleak as he added softly, "Or maybe something even worse that I don't know about yet."

"The point is," he continued, "every one of those stories got buried, Damon. My father's record is spotless, which is why he's such a political darling. No one has said a damn thing against him."

"Impossible," Damon said. "You can't bury *every* story, Cain. Not every disgruntled employee can be bought off, not when tabloids are happy to pony up just as much cash to get dirt."

"You'd think," Cain agreed, and he seemed to shrink in on himself as he spoke the words. "I never really thought about it, about how convenient it was that he made everything go away. I mean, sure there are plenty of people who write articles disagreeing with my father politically, but… those are almost like advertisements for him, you know? What seems like a bullshit human-rights-violation to one party sounds like the path to American greatness for the other. The stuff about my father personally, though, all goes away. And I know there have been things." When he lifted his eyes to Damon's again, they were wide and hurting. "I've heard my father talking with… with Jack."

Damon inhaled sharply and rubbed the back of his neck. Once again, speaking the man's name was like launching a verbal grenade. Knowing he'd been idiotic enough to fall for that asshole was bad, but knowing Cain had also been taken in made it even worse somehow.

Damon took advantage of Cain's distraction and knocked his feet off the sofa. He swung his own legs around, despite the screaming pain in his leg as he did so.

Fuck, fuck, fuck. That altercation out in the lobby had really messed him up again. He dug in his jeans pocket and produced a single tiny tablet of pain medication, which he dry-swallowed.

"So what you're saying is that your dad's been offing people for years? Every cop who wrote him a parking ticket, every secretary whose ass he grabbed?"

Cain's face paled. He bit his lip, but didn't reply.

Fine, yes, he was being a complete asshole, but between the throbbing in his leg and the hot rage that made his gut cramp, Damon didn't care. He pushed himself to his feet, desperate to move, but at the last second, his leg nearly gave out and he had to catch himself against the arm of the sofa. *Jesus Christ*, he hated being this weak, especially in front of Cain. It made him irrationally angrier.

"How the hell would that even be possible, Cain, huh? How could a person hide that much for so long?"

"I didn't say he *offed* them," Cain said hotly, staring at his knees. "He doesn't have a crew of hit men hanging around the house." Then he huffed out a dejected little laugh. "Besides Jack."

Unwelcome sympathy coiled in Damon's chest. Cain was a kid. Just a kid. It was the senator who deserved Damon's ire, and Christ knew, Damon would never want anyone judging *him* by *his* absolute dickwad of a father.

Besides which, the kid surprised him. He was a contradiction, for sure, with the way he seemed to be totally cowed by his father, but had no problem standing up to Damon.

"What I'm trying to say," Cain continued in a stronger voice, "is that I have no idea what he did in the past. But after what Jack did, and then what happened to Jack in jail? If I hadn't happened to be in the lobby tonight, Damon, what would have happened?"

Damon limped forward, bracing his fists on the vanity. From the mirror, he could see that Cain hadn't turned, and was still facing the empty sofa, his shoulders hunched over in a way that signified simultaneous tension and defeat - like an animal that knew it had been bested, and was just trying to protect itself.

"I'll tell you," Cain said a second later, his voice hollow. "People would have heard you making a racket, yeah. And the video of you, all drunk and disorderly, suddenly back from the dead, would have gone viral. You'd have been arrested for being threatening tonight, and maybe they would've tacked on something about you being the cause of the plane crash. Any chance you ever had of getting your life back would have disappeared in a puff of smoke. And then? Before any reporter had a chance to dig up anything, before any investigator had a chance to ask you a single question?" He spun to his feet and pierced Damon with a glare. "You would have disappeared."

Damon returned his look steadily. "Well, maybe it would have been worth it. Maybe my disappearance would seem pretty fucking suspicious to an investigator."

Cain's eyes widened and his mouth went slack. "Your disa... *what*? You understand what I mean, right? You wouldn't be disappearing to witness protection? To a farm in Topeka or *whereverthefuck*? They would kill you, Damon. If Jack was killed before he could talk, they would definitely kill you."

Leaning a hip against the vanity to take the weight off his leg, Damon folded his arms across his chest and looked back at Cain. "I gave it sixty-forty odds. That was before I knew he'd done this shit before, though." He stopped to ponder. "Now, I'd say maybe eighty-twenty."

"Jesus," Cain breathed. "You know, Drew said Cam and Cort are worried about you. That you've just fallen off the radar entirely. But I don't think any of them realize you're actually suicidal." If Cain saw Damon flinch, he didn't show it. He took a step forward, getting in Damon's space. "They care about you. Cort is your brother. Did you stop for even a *second* to think what it would do to him to lose you now? *Again?*"

Damon's pulse kicked up, throbbing in time with the ache in his leg, and he blinked against the fog that crept around the edges of his vision as the pain pill, amplified by the double-slug of Jack, hit his nearly-empty stomach. Rich kid. Privileged and entitled. He had no clue what Cort was to Damon - that he'd give anything for his brother, that this *was* for his brother, in a way, because who the hell would want a brother like Damon? Messed up leg, messed up head, no future, no fucking *name*, for God's sake.

He hadn't realized he'd spoken some portion of that aloud until Cain shook his head. "So what you're saying is, you're feeling sorry for yourself."

"No. Fuck." Damon rubbed his forehead with the heel of his hand. "No. I just want this *over*. I want Cam and Cort to ride off into the sunset and not worry that someone's gonna find out what they know."

"And you think showing up like this, getting your name on my father's radar, will keep them safe? It can only make things *worse*."

The room wavered when Damon's head shot up, then wavered again as he shook his head. *God*, the pills weren't usually that strong. Then again, he'd never attempted to take them with nothing but liquor in his gut, either.

"I need something to happen. I need to *make* something happen." His explanation came out more like a plea. "Everyone else seems fine *waiting*, but what the hell are we waiting for? Is your father going to wake up one morning and just confess? Call a press conference and start groveling? Evidence isn't going to fall into our laps, and I can't… I can't sit in this holding pattern forever." He shook his head. "Maybe that's me feeling sorry for myself, kid. But I want this over. One way or another."

He leaned back more heavily on the vanity, bracing his palms on the slick surface. He was tired. So damn tired. But he met Cain's deep blue eyes defiantly.

The kid's gaze held none of the pity Damon was sure he'd find. Instead, Cain was staring at him like he was a complicated math problem, his brow furrowed and eyes squinted as he ran a risk-benefit analysis on Damon's life.

He hoped Cain got a better result than he'd found when he'd tried to do the same thing.

He tilted his head back against the mirror and closed his eyes. The lights in the ceiling made pink and white sparkles dance across his eyelids, and for just a second, he could imagine he was leaning on the little dock by the pond back in Johnsville, soaking up summer sun while Cort played in the water. He'd hated his life back then, stuck in that shitty foster home. He'd spent hours planning a way to get them both out of there, never letting himself think about the possibility of failure. *Hard and easy don't matter when there's no plan B,* he used to say. He wondered if he would have pushed himself so hard if he'd known how things would end up.

"Sometimes," he told Cain, surprised at how slurred his voice was. "Sometimes you get to a point where shit *can't* get any worse and doing *anything* is better than doing nothing."

He opened his eyes to find Cain standing right in front of him. *When had he gotten so close?* Damon's vision was wonky and he couldn't seem to clear it. Cain wrapped his arm around Damon's waist and hauled him to his feet, like they were going to dance, and Damon went without protest.

He tried to search for his earlier anger, to conjure up some defense against this new, incredibly attractive Cain Shaw, but the medication seemed to dull all of those negative emotions, and the way Cain watched him made Damon's mouth go dry.

"God, the look in your eyes, Cain."

Cain seemed startled. "What look?"

"That look, like you think I'm a better person than I think I am," Damon whispered.

Deep blue eyes stared into his, and Damon was lost. He leaned forward and brushed his mouth against Cain's, and his senses exploded. With his eyes closed, the press of

Cain's lips - tentative at first, then firmer, the shocked inhale of his breath, the sexy smell of his cologne, were all magnified until Damon was drowning in sensation, lost in Cain. He wrapped his hand around the back of Cain's neck, his fingertips rubbing the short, soft hairs at his nape, and took the kiss deeper, his tongue licking into Cain's mouth. Cain opened for him with a low moan that came from deep inside his chest, and as their tongues tangled, Damon felt honest-to-God electric currents zinging down his arms to his fingertips. He was a dying man shocked back to life by the fire of Cain's touch.

He broke the kiss with a small gasp and stood staring at Cain, stunned into speechlessness. He'd kissed many people before. Nothing had ever felt like this.

"Sorry. Sorry." He brought his hands down, caught himself against the counter again. He couldn't trust himself to stand, and he couldn't trust himself to lean on Cain. "It was the pain medication," he said, more to convince himself than anything. "I'm... a little fucked up."

Cain pushed the back of his hand to his mouth. "Join the club," he muttered.

"What?"

"Nothing." He shook his head and sighed. "Come on, up you go." He grabbed for Damon's waist again.

Damon shook his head, and the world tilted slightly. "Maybe..."

"Don't worry. Your virtue is safe with me," Cain told him with a huff as he levered Damon off the counter. "You're not even going to remember this tomorrow, are you?"

"Remember what?" Damon was confused.

Cain just rolled his eyes. "I'll call for a car. Let's just see if we can get you to the curb, okay?"

"Kay. Where are we going?" he managed to get out as

he and Cain shuffle-stepped to the door and then out into the hall.

"Anything's better than nothing, you said. So right now we're doing *anything*," Cain said grimly. "I've got an idea, but I'll wait to tell you about it until you've come back down from whatever cloud you're floating on."

Damon nodded, or thought he did. Somehow this made perfect sense.

"I'm not walking so well." He frowned, but Cain snorted.

"I noticed. But don't worry, I've got you."

Damon staggered slightly, pushing Cain into the wall. For a minute, they stood there, bodies aligned, faces so close they were breathing each other's air. "Yeah? You think you can handle me, kid?"

The moment held, and Damon's entire world narrowed to Cain's blue eyes. So dark. He could dive in there and drown before he ever reached bottom.

"I can handle you," Cain whispered.

Huh. So much conviction. Damon smiled, or at least he tried to. His last thought before everything turned gray was *I'd like to see you try.*

CHAPTER THREE

Cain sat, half-asleep, curled up on the huge outdoor sofa at his parents' cabin. The cool morning air brushed his face, the hard arm of the couch dug into his cheek, and he could smell coffee somewhere in the distance, but he was so incredibly comfortable, he couldn't bring himself to fully open his eyes.

He'd been having the most amazing dream - hot hands coasting along his stomach, callused fingers leaving trails of goosebumps that scorched a path straight to his dick, while a warm weight settled firmly against his back, and a ragged voice breathed in his ear. *"You want this, don't you?"* the voice had said. And miracle of miracles, Cain *had* wanted it, wanted *everything* without reservation - the exploring hands, the heat, the desire that swamped him.

It had been a delicious, disorienting sensation to want something so much, and to feel no shame in the wanting. It had been as natural as the mountains that rose up behind the cabin - something unquestionably real and beautiful, something that had existed for ages before anyone had thought to put a name to it or try to bend it to a purpose.

He couldn't remember how he'd gotten to his parents' mountain house, but right at the moment he didn't care. He wrapped the memory of the dream around himself, knowing as soon as he opened his eyes, it would all fade away like mist.

"Your nose is twitching."

It was the voice from the dream, but… not. Cain's eyes flew open.

Well. Okay, then. Fuck.

So, he was *not* on his parent's porch - which would explain why he didn't remember traveling from Boston to Tennessee. That was probably good. But for a second, he couldn't remember exactly *where* he was, or how he'd gotten there.

He was in a living room, curled up on a leather sofa that had seen better days, and covered by a quilt that smelled like lavender. The enormous black hole of a flat-screen TV and a small window with a view of the milky gray sky took up nearly the entire far wall, and a large, wooden coffee table sat on a brightly patterned rug directly in front of him. In the leather chair closest to his head, sat none other than Damon Fitzpatrick - fully dressed in jeans and a *Wolves in the Throne Room* t-shirt that didn't hide the light pink scars curling up his forearms. With his silver hair damp and combed as though he'd already showered, Damon watched Cain with steady hazel eyes.

Cain sat up quickly, pushing back the quilt and swinging his feet to the floor, but that was as far as his momentum got him. He rubbed his eyes with the heels of his hands. "What… uh. How?"

Damon made a sound that could have been annoyance or humor, or maybe some combination of the two, had Cain been awake enough to distinguish. "And here I thought *I* was the one who'd gotten myself so fucked up I blacked out last night."

Cain's brain came fully online and memories from the night before came flooding back. After calling for a Lyft to Cort's apartment, where Damon was living, Damon - with all the belligerence of the truly fucked up - had insisted on stripping naked before Cain could tuck him into bed. Cain had decided to sleep on the couch instead of going back to his hotel in case Damon needed him. And beyond all, he remembered that kiss.

So hot, so consuming, so stupid. He'd known even in the moment that it was the product of Damon's pain medication lowering his inhibitions. Hell, he wasn't sure if Damon even *liked* him, and certainly not in that way. But for a brief second, when he'd stood with his arm bracing Damon's waist, and Damon had opened those hazel eyes to meet Cain's, Cain had seen something all too familiar in his gaze, an echo of Cain's own loneliness and his desperate need for connection.

It had seemed so right at the time, but now it felt distinctly uncomfortable, as if maybe he'd taken advantage of the man while he was drugged up.

Fuck. Did Damon even remember it this morning? Cain shot him a glance, and like he could read Cain's mind, Damon said, "There are some blank spots in my memory."

"Blank spots," Cain repeated, heart sinking.

Damon sighed. "Places where I can't remember what happened." He cleared his throat and tapped his hand on his knee. "Or things we might have done."

Cain blinked. "Do you remember the fundraiser?"

"Yes, of course I remember that part. I meant..." He turned his gaze on Cain, scorching and direct. "Look, I woke up naked in my bed. I don't think anything happened, but — "

"Oh! Oh, no, no, no." Cain's face was on fire, and he waved a hand through the air as though he could somehow dispel his own embarrassment. "Everything was fine."

"Fine?" Damon looked panicked. "*What* was fine?"

God. "Nothing happened last night. Between us." Damon looked relieved, and Cain couldn't tell if he should feel insulted or not, so his tone was sharper than he intended when he admitted, "Except that we kissed."

"Oh."

That one little word gave nothing away, and Damon's face was blank. Was it a regretful *oh*, a shocked *oh*, or an appalled *oh?* Or perhaps an *oh* that meant he remembered that unimportant little moment, but not anything after it? One syllable was really not enough to go on. And why the hell did he care? Why did it make his stomach twist to think Damon didn't remember what had clearly been a mistake? Cain rubbed his eyes. He needed to get back to the hotel.

"Are you okay? *Were* you drinking last night?" Damon demanded. "You didn't seem drunk, from what I remember."

"What? No. I wasn't drunk." *Horny. Not drunk.* "I don't drink at all anymore," Cain said, looking up. He pushed the blanket off himself, then frowned at it. "Hey. This wasn't here when I went to sleep." *That* he remembered clearly. In fact, he hadn't been able to find a blanket at all, so he'd ended up removing his dress shirt and tie, and huddling under his suit jacket.

Damon ignored the question in Cain's voice. "Do you always wake up like you're coming back from an out of body experience?" he asked instead. "How long until it wears off?" His voice was still the same deep, broken rasp from last night, and it did crazy things to Cain's insides.

"I, uh. I don't sleep much at all," Cain found himself saying. He could feel a hot blush climbing his cheeks, and rubbed the back of his neck, hoping Damon couldn't read his thoughts. "So, like, I guess when I finally do sleep, I sleep hard."

Like a statue, Cady sometimes said. *If statues snored and drooled.*

"Yeah, I noticed," Damon said dryly, almost like he was replying to Cain's thoughts, and Cain's eyes widened. *What* had he noticed? Oh, mother of God, if Cain had spoken during his dream, or…*worse*. His cock was still semi-hard in his pants right now, for Heaven's sake. What had he been doing or saying while Damon watched?

The heat in his face doubled, counteracting the cold, damp air of the apartment, and he stood up, grabbing the blanket in his arms and turning away to fold it.

At least you were clothed. At least you didn't wake up with your cock in your hand. At least…

He cleared his throat. "I was dreaming."

"Figured that, too. You kept saying something."

Oh, God. He *had* been talking! Was spontaneous combustion real? Could you induce it? He was attempting it right now, if the heat of his cheeks was anything to go by.

"Did I?" Cain's voice was meant to be casual but came out strangled.

"You kept saying, 'I *do* want it. I *do*.' Do you remember what you were dreaming about?"

"Donuts?" Cain blurted the first thing that came to mind. He averted his face and squeezed his eyes shut. "Probably, you know, donuts… Or something like that."

"Donuts." A statement not a question, like he knew Cain was lying.

"Oh, yeah. Mm-hmm. Love donuts. They're just… the best." *Kill. Me. Now.*

"Donuts?" Damon asked again.

"That's what I said!" Cain fixed him with a glare. "Who *doesn't* want donuts?"

"Right," Damon allowed. "Anyway, I covered you in the night when I got up. I wanted the windows open and you seemed chilly. You didn't move at all, even when I took your jacket." He nodded to the vacant chair near Cain's feet, where Cain's discarded jacket, dress shirt, and tie had been laid out.

Okay. Alright. That wasn't too bad. They'd just confirmed that Cain had donut fantasies and slept like a corpse, and the kiss last night had been so totally forgettable that Damon had likely blocked it out, but this morning definitely could have gone worse.

At least he'd remembered to text his mother the night before and make an excuse for why he hadn't returned to the party. Darn his sensitive stomach for acting up *just* as he was having the time of his life at the fundraiser, but what could he do but go back to the hotel so he didn't spoil everyone else's fun? His mother's terse reply had suggested she could think of a few preferable alternatives. *We will be discussing this in the morning, Cain.*

In comparison, this mortifying conversation with Damon was a walk in the park.

He looked out the window as he smoothed the blanket. "Wow. It's pretty gross out there today," he said, taking a deep breath to calm his nerves. There was no visible sunlight, just a bleak, gray soup that hugged the glass tightly and seemed to seep in through the opening.

Damon shrugged. "I like the fresh air, even when it's murky. I don't like being cooped up." He pursed his lips together like he hadn't meant to say that much, and Cain found his mind going back to last night.

Everyone else seems fine waiting, *but what the hell are we waiting for?*

Damon had been locked in a kind of static prison for nearly a year and a half now, and Cain could only imagine he had to fight tooth and claw to regain whatever control he could over his circumstances. For the millionth time, Cain wondered how Damon had survived the plane crash that had killed the Seavers and Amy McMann, and where he'd been for the year before he'd reappeared.

Not that it was any of Cain's business. Not that he and Damon were friends. Not that they were *anything.*

"Is that coffee?" Cain asked, inhaling deeply as he deliberately changed the subject.

It wasn't a total ruse. The scent was strong in the air - so strong he'd smelled it in his dream - and right now he needed a cup more than his next breath. His brain was full of sticky cobwebs that kept latching onto random thoughts, making him sympathize with Damon more than he could afford to since he still couldn't come forward about his father, and making him want things from Damon that would only spell heartbreak.

Last night he'd had a pretty good idea about how he *could* maybe help Damon fix things, though. And maybe, *maybe*, he'd still tell Damon about it. He was fairly sure he would take some convincing, and Cain required appropriate caffeination for that.

"Yeah. What passes for coffee here, anyway." Damon gave that annoyed, humored grunt again, and Cain realized that even wide-awake, he couldn't tell which emotion it conveyed. "Had a cup a little while ago."

"Is it instant?" Cain asked. He'd drink it even if it were - he wasn't *too* much of a coffee snob, and these were desperate times - but still.

"No, not that bad." Damon's eyes met his, and this time the amusement was plain. "But you've got to heat the water in a kettle and pour it."

Cain nodded. "That's cool. My college roommate had a setup like that. Very hipster."

"*Hipster,*" Damon said, testing the word in his mouth. "Yeah, no. Cort's just a Luddite. Hates all forms of technology.'

"He does?" Cain made his way into the neat, sparsely furnished kitchen, and found the makings for coffee still sitting on the counter. "But Drew said he's working at Seaver Tech now." He turned on the flame beneath the kettle.

"Yep." Damon pushed himself to his feet, and Cain pretended not to notice the grimace on his face as his injured leg took his weight. "Ironic, huh?"

"Maybe," Cain agreed as Damon shuffled towards the kitchen. He busied himself preparing the coffee grounds to keep himself from watching, and babbled on. "Though, you know, maybe that's part of why they're good for each other. Yin and yang. Light and dark. Tech-junkie and old-school. They balance each other."

Damon stopped as he reached the counter that separated the kitchen from the living room, and leaned on his elbows. "Christ, you're young," he said.

Cain lifted an eyebrow. The way Damon said the word made it sound like an insult, and it hit harder than Cain would have imagined. The number of years he'd spent on the planet had fuck-all to do with how old he felt. "I'm almost twenty-five," he said, a bit more defensively than necessary.

"*Almost!* God."

"Hey. Twenty-five is not *that* young." Cain shut the water off as it started to hiss and gestured threateningly at Damon with his coffee spoon. "You'd better not call me kid again."

A snort. "Not even if that's what you are? I'm old enough to be your father."

"Only if you got started really, *really* young!"

Damon snorted again and Cain sighed. It was hard to explain how in some ways, he felt like the most bumbling, inexperienced child on the planet, while in others he felt like he'd been eroded by glaciers.

"Fine, have it your way *Big Daddy.*"

"Oh, Jesus," Damon said in disgust. "You will *not* call me that, ever."

Giving Damon an exaggerated shrug, Cain poured the water in a slow stream over his coffee grounds. "No? Keep calling me kid and see what happens," he challenged, and he counted it as a victory when Damon raised one eyebrow but didn't reply.

He turned his attention to the coffee, watching it drip, giving himself a second to gather his courage. Then he grabbed the mug and leaned against the back counter, facing Damon.

The coffee smelled amazing. He took a deep sip, feeling the liquid burn a path down his throat.

Ugh. Bitter and dark, exactly the way he *didn't* like it. Given that he usually took it extra light and sweet, this was the equivalent of running a lawn mower on jet fuel. But he'd be damned if he'd ask for cream and sugar. No doubt, in Damon's mind, grown-ups drank their coffee black and poisonously strong.

He set the mug on the counter took a deep breath, just as Damon came into the kitchen. "Listen. I had an idea -"

"Yeah, speaking of brilliant ideas…" Damon went to the refrigerator and took out a cardboard container of cream, setting it on the counter. "I owe you a *thank you.* And probably an apology." He opened the cabinet above the stove and got down a little dish filled with packets of sweetener.

"Cort probably has real sugar around here somewhere," he said. "But fuck if I know where." Cain blinked in shock and Damon rolled his eyes. "I've eaten squirrel with greater enthusiasm than you're showing that coffee."

Cain opened his mouth - to thank him or demand why the fuck he'd eaten a squirrel, he wasn't sure which, but Damon had already moved back to his spot at the far counter, leaning his weight on his arms again. Cain wisely closed his mouth again and doctored his coffee exactly the way he liked it. *Perfect.*

"I screwed up last night and went off half-cocked," Damon continued. "Wasn't thinking." He shook his head like he was annoyed at his own foolishness, and Cain frowned. He brought his coffee over to the counter Damon had claimed, and leaned his forearms against it too.

"Yeah, you weren't making much sense." He looked into Damon's eyes, which were so close he could pick out the threads of brown and gold among the green. They looked like shattered sea glass, the green cracked open so the amber-yellow could shine through. He could watch them forever. He remembered the way Damon's eyes had looked just before he'd leaned in and laid his lips on Cain's…

No. That was not real. He quickly turned away.

"So does this mean you're gonna think of a different way to get info on… *him?*" Cain couldn't bring himself to say *my dad.* Frankly, he couldn't remember the last time he'd really thought of the man that way, even before finding out about his ties to the Seavers' deaths.

Damon eyed him speculatively and didn't answer. "Want some eggs? Or toast?"

"Uh. No?" Cain cocked his head to one side. "Does this mean you *are* still going with your stupid plan? Because, honestly Damon…"

Damon leaned forward and grabbed Cain's coffee mug

off the counter, holding Cain's eyes as he took a sip. He shuddered as he swallowed. "That's more like melted coffee ice cream than actual coffee."

Cain would not be sidetracked by this insult to his coffee. "It's still massively stupid. Think of Cort. Think of…"

Damon held up a silencing hand. "Cain," he said, uncharacteristic hesitation in his deep growl. "I think what we lost sight of last night was that you and I are on very different sides when it comes to this topic. Maybe you feel responsibility to your family, to your dad, and you don't want to come forward about what Jack told us. So let's skip the discussion about what my plans might be. That way, you won't feel like you have to warn him."

Shock hit Cain like a blow to the solar plexus. "You think… you think I would tell him?"

Eyes on the counter, Damon licked his lips. "I think you'd probably feel like you should."

Cain shook his head as laughter bubbled out of the hole Damon had punched in him. "You really don't know shit about me, do you?"

"I know enough." Damon's voice was soft, and Cain got the impression that the man was trying to be *gentle*, and just going about it completely wrong.

Fuck him. Fuck him and his stupid *misguided gentleness.* He'd already made up his mind about Cain, and he didn't care to hear the truth. The crushing loneliness Cain had felt the night before came flooding back.

"You know, *what*, Damon? My last name? The fact that I won't bring hearsay about my dad to the authorities?"

"That you're lying to cover shit up." Damon ran both hands through his long hair. "Look. Don't take it personally, because it's *not* personal. It's just that you and I have different agendas. You're a good kid. I can't *really* be mad at you when I know you're being loyal to your family."

His voice said that he'd tried to be mad and couldn't sustain it, which maybe Cain should have taken as a compliment, but he couldn't, because... *Kid.* Jesus.

"My agenda is keeping my father from hurting anyone else! Do you know why he hasn't come for you, Damon?" Cain asked softly. "Why the authorities aren't banging down your door?"

He dared a look into those hazel eyes, and found Damon watching him steadily. "It's because I haven't told him you're alive. I kept that secret."

"You want a medal?"

"I want some respect. I'm not your enemy."

"You're not on my side, either, kid."

"Jesus *Fucking* Christ. I'm *not a kid!*" Cain grabbed the spoon off the counter and flung it into the sink with a loud *clang,* then immediately looked up at Damon, horrified. "Sorry," he whispered, his gut clenching. *You fuck-up. Way to show you're not a child.* He felt hot tears stinging the back of his eyes. "I'm sorry. I lost my temper. That was a very inappropriate display. I… You know what? I should go."

He turned to hurry out of the kitchen before he got a lecture, but Damon grabbed him by the wrist and propelled him back in.

"Inappropriate?" Damon seemed rattled, and he blinked at Cain in shock.

Cain's heart beat in triple-time. He didn't really believe Damon would hurt him, though even with Damon's injury, Cain was no match for his size and breadth. He simply couldn't handle Damon's anger right now, even if he had a right to it.

"You lost your temper," Damon said, his hand still firm on Cain's wrist.

"Yes, I know," Cain couldn't meet Damon's eyes. "I acted without thinking. I don't think I damaged anything, but if I did, I'll pay for it."

Damon goggled at him. "Who gives a shit, kid?" He grabbed the spoon from the sink and held it out to Cain. "Throw it again."

What? "No. No, I'm good." Was Damon trying to humiliate him?

"It was a freakin' satisfying sound. Throw it," Damon encouraged, but Cain shook his head wildly and Damon shrugged. "Suit yourself."

He threw the spoon into the sink with a resounding clatter loud enough to make Cain wince.

"You good? That terrifying display injure you in any way?" Damon asked, heavy irony lacing his words. His thumb stroked the inside of Cain's wrist where he held it, and Cain wondered if he could feel his frantically scrambling pulse.

"N-no."

"No. Right. Me neither." He picked up the spoon again - an ordinary metal spoon, but just the sight of it now made Cain nauseous. "Throw it, kiddo."

"W-what *for*?" Cain demanded, looking down at the floor. *God, just end this. Kill me now.*

"Because it was nothing but a noise. It's not the end of the fucking world." Damon's hand left Cain's wrist and wrapped around his waist instead, like Cain was a toddler and Damon was helping him pitch.

Fucking embarrassing. And even so, there was a pleasant warmth where Damon held him. A connection. An acceptance. An instinctive feeling of safety, where there shouldn't be any.

"I'm aware that it's a noise. And I made it because I lost

my temper," Cain said impatiently. "Which I won't do again, alright? Now please, let me go."

"Why?"

"Because I asked you to, and I should probably get home. I need to find my phone. I texted my mom that I was sick last night, and she probably..."

"No." Damon squeezed Cain's hip. "Why won't you do it again?"

"Lose my temper?" Cain nearly shouted, well aware of the irony he had going on there. "Because it doesn't fucking feel good!"

"Yeah it does!" Damon's face was nearly in Cain's now, looming over him. "Especially when you're not hurting anyone else. Just let it go."

"No."

"Do it."

"No!"

"*Kid.*"

"Fine! Fucking *fine.*" Cain grabbed the spoon from Damon's hand and hurled it at the sink. "Are you happy now?" He grabbed it and hurled it again, and again, and again, until he was breathing hard and shaking.

"I'm sorry," Damon said. He rubbed his thumbs under Cain's eyes, and Cain was mortified to realize there was wetness there. He'd been crying and hadn't even realized.

Super mature and adult behavior. No wonder he doesn't trust you.

"Sorry for what?" Cain whispered, closing his eyes.

"Because I was being selfish. This isn't only about me, and I... I keep forgetting that."

Cain's eyes flew open. Damon was so close, *so* close. "I wanted to help you," he admitted. "I had this idea. Stupid idea, probably. But I wanted to help you. I'm not... *not* on your side, Damon. There are things I just can't do."

God, what was it about this guy that had him spilling his guts all over the floor? Why did he give a shit what Damon Fitzpatrick thought of him? Guilt was part of it, but... He looked into Damon's eyes and knew for a fact it wasn't the only, or even the largest, part.

"Yeah. Alright." The gruff words were spoken into his hair as Damon gathered him into a hug. "Can't very well call you a kid and then be pissed off because you made an adult decision I don't happen to agree with." He sighed and rubbed his hand along Cain's arm, tracing the tattoos there with his fingertips.

Cain didn't protest, even when the gentle touch tickled. He was exhausted, as though he hadn't slept at all. One half-cup of coffee and a trip on the emotional roller coaster that was Damon Fitzpatrick, and he was completely wrung out.

"I was looking at these while you slept," Damon said. "I didn't realize you had tattoos. I didn't know you were the type."

"I didn't realize there were rules I was supposed to stick to." He sighed. "Okay, no, that's a lie. I definitely know there are rules I have to stick to. My father is great for rules. But I went through a rebellious phase a few months back."

"That so?" Damon was too close, his breath hot on Cain's neck in a way that made his pulse beat frantically. It made Cain think about other rebellious, ill-advised things he could be doing, and he wondered if the shift of Damon's body, the hitch of his breathing, meant his thoughts were running in the same direction. "I kinda like the idea of you breaking the rules."

Cain's cheek buzzed with the vibrations from Damon's chest - pleasant little chills that soothed and excited at the same time, just like in his dream. His mind helpfully conjured up the kiss from last night, the bone-melting heat and all-encompassing security of Damon's lips on his. He wanted more, even though hooking up with Damon would only complicate the Gordian-knot complexity of Cain's life.

Should he kiss Damon? Did Damon want him to?

Damon's gentle fingers continued their motions, but otherwise he didn't make a move, so Cain kept talking just so he could put off the inevitable moment when he'd have to step away.

"I was drinking a lot. I mean, not like I was an alcoholic, except... maybe I was? Am? I don't know how it works, exactly. I started out drinking on the weekends, just to unwind from school. And then Thursday and Friday became the weekend, too. And I wasn't having enough to unwind, I was having enough to... you know, forget where I was and who I'd been with and what I'd been doing."

Damon's chest froze and his arms squeezed Cain at the waist and arm. "Did something bad happen?"

Cain shook his head slightly. "Not like I was attacked or anything like that. It could have happened," he admitted. "I was lucky. But I did some really stupid shit. Hooking up with people who didn't know enough to keep their mouths shut. Getting caught on a cell-phone camera with a bunch of people skinny-dipping."

"Other than the hookups, that sounds pretty typical."

"Yeah, not when you're the only son of a senator. He made it all go away, because..."

"Because that's his M.O., and he needs to keep up appearances," Damon concluded.

"Yeah. Pretty much. One night, he was discussing my future - telling me how I needed to step up, get some ambition, grow some balls." Cain sighed. "I was pissed, so I went and got this done." He held up his arm, the scroll of the words and the outlined flames dancing over his skin. "My roommate has a friend who's a tattoo artist. I described to him exactly what I wanted, and he did it for me."

"It's gorgeous, but it looks half-done." Damon's fingers danced over his skin again, and Cain felt like the flames inked on his skin had become real.

"Yeah. Yeah, I got it all outlined that night. Took fucking forever. And I had originally been even more ambitious, but fortunately Quinn - the tattoo guy - knew how much I could probably handle. He told me to come back later for the color."

"Why didn't you?"

"Good question." Cain shrugged. "Jace – he was my roommate. He teased me relentlessly for being scared of the pain, but that wasn't it."

"You didn't wanna get caught," Damon said, his voice carefully neutral.

Cain appreciated the diplomacy, but it wasn't necessary. He recognized his own weakness better than anyone.

"Yeah. By the time I got this, my parents had already threatened things I... couldn't afford to lose," he said simply. *Like Jesse's future. Like his own.* "So I backed off. Story of my life, right?" A sudden thought occurred to him. "I do the right thing, but only to a point. Always straddling a line."

Never losing, never really winning. Probably explained why he was shit at making connections with other people.

He gave a huff of laughter and took a step away from Damon. He felt the loss of heat immediately.

"Anyway," he said, rubbing his suddenly-damp hands on his pants. "Thanks for the, um, coffee. And letting me crash." He stepped around Damon into the living room and headed for his shirt.

"You're leaving?" Damon raised an eyebrow.

"Probably. Yeah. I..." He put his hands into the sleeves

and started buttoning the shirt in record time. "I mean, you've got stuff to do, and I…"

"I thought you had a plan." Damn that raspy, wrecked voice. It made Cain's fucking knees go weak, and his fingers tremble on the buttons. "I'd like to hear it."

Damon stalked closer, leaning heavily on one leg, and Cain lifted his eyes helplessly. "I don't want to… I don't want *you* to…" He groaned in frustration as his words seemed to pile on top of one another, clogging his brain. "You don't owe me anything."

Damon stepped closer again, crowding Cain against the wall much the way he had the night before, except this time those hazel green eyes were completely lucid and focused on him. "You're right. I don't. And you don't owe me anything either. Okay?"

The words were important, freeing.

"Yeah, okay."

Damon's gaze drifted down, focused on Cain's mouth, and Cain wet his lips nervously. He felt like he was standing on a precipice, unable to decide whether to risk the jump. Did Damon want him to kiss him? Their mouths were just inches apart, and Cain wanted very badly to find out what Damon tasted like in the light of day. Once again, the moment was ripe with possibility.

Then Damon pushed himself upright, clearing his throat. Cain shut his eyes tightly as the chance he hadn't taken spun off into the land of might-have-been.

Once again, he'd played it safe and lost.

"So, let's hear this plan," Damon said, taking a seat on the sofa again. "I'm all ears."

CHAPTER FOUR

"That's a terrible idea."

"It isn't," Cain insisted. "I've been thinking about this for a while. It's a perfectly good idea. My father is too much of a control freak to have let Jack off the leash completely. He's organized. He's meticulous. He's got records of every appliance he's ever purchased, every oil change he's ever gotten. He has something to cover himself in case Jack ever wanted to confess, I can almost guarantee it."

Damon leaned back on the sofa, with his bad leg propped on the coffee table, and watched the man pacing back and forth in front of him. Cain Shaw, baby-faced and model-perfect, dressed in wrinkled suit pants and a half-buttoned dress shirt, dark hair sticking up like he'd stuck his finger in an electrical socket, and blue eyes flashing as he unveiled his plan.

It actually wasn't half-bad, as plans went. Probably, he admitted to himself, better than the half-baked scheme he'd come up with the night before. But that didn't mean it was good or advisable. Damon risking his own life was one thing, but Cain's idea would stick his neck out there too.

Sure, the senator was Cain's father, but Damon wouldn't put it past that asshole to get vengeance against his son, one way or another.

And then there was the nagging question of just how much Damon could trust this kid.

Kid. Cain hated the nickname, so Damon was trying not to use it, but in his mind he clung to it like a drowning man to a lifeboat, because if he didn't put that distance between them, it would be far too easy to think of all the things that made him want to pull Cain close. The man was a metric-ton of gorgeous packed into a one-hundred-fifty-pound frame. That huge tattoo on his arm was intricate and intriguing, a thing Cain had done solely for himself. And their one misguided kiss the previous night had brought something to life in Damon that had been dormant for nearly forever.

Hell, yes, he remembered that kiss. It was probably a dick move to let Cain think he'd forgotten but again, it was safer that way than letting either of them think it could happen again.

Cain didn't just do it for him in a physical way - those eyes, that quirky mouth, the slight frame that just begged to be held down and fucked hard (and *yeah*, he'd thought a lot about that while he watched the man sleep this morning). It was something about the guy's mind, too. The way he always said the unexpected. The way his demons called to Damon.

That was a very inappropriate display.

He'd thrown a spoon into the sink, for Christ's sake. He hadn't killed anyone, hadn't crashed a plane into a mountain, hadn't hurt a soul, but the stark terror on his face, like he was expecting Damon to hit him or curse him out over a fucking piece of silverware, made Damon's heart clench hard with the need to protect him.

Ironic, since these days Damon couldn't even manage to protect himself.

"And you're convinced this magical unicorn of evidence, this file that names all the names and dates and bank account numbers, is a physical thing? Not something he has on a cloud somewhere that Bas Seaver could hack?"

The ache in his leg distracted him. He'd been getting better, slowly but surely, thanks to the physical therapy provided to him as an employee of Seaver Tech - *Yet another thing he didn't want to have to be grateful to the Seavers for* - but he'd managed to set himself back in a big way thanks to those security goons. He fought the urge to rub it. It wouldn't do much good, and he'd be damned if he'd call attention to it. For a second, he even contemplated the little bottle of pain medication calling to him from the kitchen counter, but he dismissed the idea just as quickly. He hadn't had to take a pill in nearly a week before last night, and clearly his tolerance was all fucked up. He'd rather take the pain than the loss of control.

Cain shook his head and sat down on the coffee table. "Nah. No way. What did you say about Cort? That he was a Luddite?" He leaned forward, resting his hand on Damon's leg in his excitement. "My father is the same. Not about everything. I mean, my parents at least have a coffee maker." He rolled his eyes. "But he's not a computer guy. Even when he and Cam's dad founded Seaver Tech, he was one hundred percent behind the scenes, managing the contracts and negotiating deals. He never helped with development. When it comes to keeping records, it's got to be in a physical location. And I can get you to those locations."

"Ki...Cain," he corrected himself just in time, although Cain's narrowed eyes showed that he'd noted the slip. "Let's say we can find this file, neatly labeled *Evidence Against Me.* Okay?"

Cain rolled his eyes again and nodded shortly.

"Okay, then what? You've said you don't want to come forward about what happened on the plane, but if we can find the stuff you think we will, we're going to have to present it to the authorities. And the media too. It's going to come out, and your father will probably be arrested."

Gentle fingers began to knead the muscles of Damon's leg through his jeans, and *holy shit* it felt good. Cain instinctively applied the perfect level of pressure to loosen Damon's knotted muscles without causing further pain. The man was staring into middle distance, his brow furrowed, like his mind was more occupied with his plan than the massage. Unfortunately, the same could not be said of Damon's cock, which had woken up like a bear coming out of hibernation and scenting food for the first time in months. In the absence of pain, he couldn't fail to appreciate Cain's nearness, and the feeling of those long fingers pressing against him.

Jesus.

Not now. Not this guy. Inconvenient didn't begin to describe the attraction he had going on. Impossible was closer to the truth. Even whole and uninjured, he wouldn't have been anyone's choice of partner, certainly not someone with as much beauty, charm, and potential as Cain Shaw. Not to mention, there was an entire lifetime of age between Damon's forty and Cain's *almost-twenty-five* - a long and fucked up lifetime.

"The thing is," Cain was saying, drawing Damon's thoughts back to reality. "It's not that I don't want to see my father punished, Damon." His cheeks were flushed, but the gaze he shot Damon was firm. "But I can't be the one to do it. I can't risk him knowing it was me. Because if it didn't work? If he managed to get out of it like he's gotten out of everything so far?" He shook his head and looked away again. "I know it makes me a coward, but there are some things I can't risk."

Damon took a deep breath and tried to concentrate.

"That's exactly what you'd be doing if I went along with your plan," Damon reminded him. "If you sneak me into his office to look through his stuff, you think no one is going to know it was you?"

"I think it's *very* possible they won't know it was me, yeah," Cain said staunchly. "I'm not going to call my parents and announce my intentions, and they won't be back in Nashville for weeks. I still live in their house, and there's nothing so unusual about me entering my own home. Besides..." He gave a self-deprecating smile. "The upside of having your father think you're mostly spineless is that you're never going to be the first suspect."

Damon shook his head. "I still don't like it." Cain looked like he was going to argue, but Damon grabbed his hand and squeezed, silencing him. "I appreciate you wanting to help. I do. But I can't ask you to do this." *And I don't know if I can trust you to go against your father. And I don't know if I can handle having you near me for that long without kissing you again, and how the fuck would that end?*

"You're not — "

Whatever argument Cain would have made was cut off when Damon's phone rang shrilly from the kitchen counter where he'd plugged it in that morning. He went to stand up, but Cain stood first. "Rest your leg. I'll get it." He stepped over Damon's leg to get the phone and returned to his spot a minute later, holding the phone out.

"Who's Chelsea?" he asked.

Damon stared at the screen for a second, too stunned to

speak. He'd never expected to hear from her again, after the way they'd left things the other day.

"My sister," he whispered finally, and Cain's face broke into a smile.

"Oh, right. I remember now."

Damon reached for the phone, hope and panic churning together in his mind. "I don't know what she wants." And please, God, don't let it be about the money Bas had sent her, or her reaming him out again for being a criminal asshole.

"You know, I sometimes find the best way to figure out what a caller wants is to actually *answer* the phone," Cain teased.

Right, yeah. Answer.

He slid his finger across the screen and cleared his throat. "Chelsea?"

"What did you *do*?" Her voice shook with outrage.

He groaned. "Listen if this is about the check…"

"Not the check!" she cried. "Although I already told you I didn't want your blood money, and you were asshole enough to send it anyway."

"Yeah, I was," he agreed. His voice had gone raspy again, so he cleared his throat before he continued. "I am. I know it doesn't make up for missing all those years with you, or for what the media did to you after I disappeared, but I wanted you to have it anyway. To keep it for Molly. For college or… whatever."

"College? Oh, my God, Damon!" Chelsea was nearly hysterical. "We'll be lucky if she makes it to kindergarten thanks to you!" She broke down into sobs. "You're going to get us killed."

"Killed!" His eyes flashed to Cain, whose face wore the same expression of shocked worry he imagined he was wearing. "What are you talking about? Chelsea, is Molly okay?"

"Don't pretend like you care about her, for God's sake," his sister wailed. "You came into our lives and brought nothing but trouble. I grew up without you, and from the second I learned you existed, you've done nothing but make my life harder."

Damon's heart sank to his stomach, dragging the breath from his lungs.

"I'm sorry," he whispered. "If I had known, Chelsea. If I'd known about you, if I'd ever had even a tiny clue that you were alive, I would have come for you. I would have protected you."

"Fuck that! All I wanted from you was for you to leave us *alone*. But you couldn't even give me that, and now my baby is… my baby is…"

"What?" Damon leaned forward, hardly even aware that Cain was still in the room. "What happened to Molly, Chels?"

His sister's crying was overlaid with the high-pitched warble of a three-year old, asking "Whas' wrong, Mama?"

"It's okay, baby," Chelsea told the little girl, who had to have been Molly. Damon heard her take a deep breath, like she was trying to compose herself.

"Chelsea, tell me what the hell is going on," he demanded. "Is Molly alright?"

"She's alright," Chelsea said, her voice cold and hard despite her sniffles. "Thank God. But Damon, this is the last phone call. Do you understand? I don't know what you're involved in, but I don't want any part of it. No more calls, no more checks. I don't know how your friends found us, but…"

"Wait. Chelsea! Don't hang up!" Damon said, pushing

to his feet, not giving a shit about the pain in his leg until it almost collapsed beneath him.

Without thinking, he grabbed at Cain's shoulder for support, and Cain stood, wrapping an arm around Damon's waist.

"Chels, I don't know what you're talking about," he said, as calmly as he could. "Tell me what's happening."

"Like you don't know!"

"I swear to you, I swear to *God*, I have *no* idea what you're talking about!"

"I worked a double last night," she told him, and he nodded even though she couldn't see him. He knew she waitressed at some all-night diner not thirty minutes from the house where his last and longest foster family had lived, the home where he'd met Cort --the only family he'd ever claimed. The knowledge that a sister he'd never known had been so fucking *close* all those years, dealing with their shit-head father on her own, struggling to raise a daughter when she was barely out of her teens, herself… it absolutely flayed him. If she was too disgusted to allow him into her life, to be there for her personally, he'd thought he could at least help her financially, that maybe she'd take that much from him.

But somehow apparently even that had gone to hell.

"I got off work at eight this morning and got Molly from the sitter - she stays with this retired lady, Mrs. Danport, downstairs when I'm working. We came upstairs and… and-" She broke off into a round of fresh sobs.

"And what? Chelsea, *and what?*"

"And the door had been broken open!" she cried. "Our stuff was thrown around. Every dish in the cabinet was broken. M-my sofa, Damon. My new sofa. Someone took a knife to all the c-cushions and the st-stuffing was ripped out. I thought, it had to be a robbery. I went to grab some stuff for Molly so we could go back down to Mrs. Danport's apartment and c-call the police, but when I went in Molly's room…"

Damon's stomach flipped. "Chelsea, honey." He kept his voice low and calm. "What happened?"

"There was a note stuck to her pillow," she whispered. "Stuck to my baby's pillow, Damon. They rammed a knife right into the place where my daughter's head would have been. And it said, '*Tell your brother to disappear, or your daughter will.*'"

Beside him, Cain froze in place, and Damon realized he'd been close enough to hear the entire conversation.

"It's my father. He's doing this, isn't he?" Cain whispered. His face was paler than Damon had ever seen it. "Fuck!" He stepped away and grabbed at his hair with both hands. "Fuck him!" He turned toward the window, his body curled in on itself.

Christ.

Damon sucked in a deep breath as things began to click in his mind. He hadn't been careful enough. Either Cain had let it slip to his father that Damon was alive - but, *no*. Looking at his anguished expression, Damon didn't believe that. He simply couldn't. Okay, then. It had to have been last night at the fundraiser. He'd thought he'd gotten away, but there were probably security cameras all over the place. Someone had seen his face and figured things out.

The element of surprise was no longer a factor.

"Chelsea, I know you're pissed right now." She made a noise that was a cross between grief and outrage, and he winced. "But you've got to let me help you."

"Help me *how*, Damon? They know who I am. They know where I *live*."

"Stop panicking and *think*, Chelsea. Is there anyone you could be safe with? Any place out of town you can go?"

"You want me to take my baby and, what? Just leave? How will I work? How will we live?"

"Don't worry about the money," he told her. "Do you have a place? Nowhere in Boston. Out of state would be better. Any friends who could help you?"

"No! God. My friends are all local, and I wouldn't bring this shit to their doorsteps either! That's your deal, not mi-"

"Okay," he interrupted. "Okay. I have an idea. I'll come get you. Pack what you need - not too much - and I'll take you somewhere you'll be safe. One hour, okay?"

"Damon." There was a world of warning in those two syllables. Then Chelsea sighed, totally defeated, and Damon's heart squeezed again. "Yeah. Fine." She hung up without another word.

He held the phone in his hand for a second, staring as the screen went black, then lifted his gaze to Cain, who still stood in front of the window, staring blankly at the rain-slicked parking lot below.

"You heard?"

Cain startled, like he'd forgotten Damon was there. "Yeah. Yeah, I heard."

"I'm gonna take her someplace safe," Damon said, and Cain nodded, but didn't turn.

"Tell me if you need anything. Money, or… anything."

Damon closed his eyes. The parallels were not lost on him. Cain felt guilty for what had happened to Chelsea, the same way Damon did. And just like Damon, he was offering money because he was pretty sure anything else he had to offer would be rejected. The difference was, in this particular case Cain had nothing to feel guilty about.

"Actually, I need something more than that," Damon said. This time, maybe sensing the change in his tone, Cain turned to look at him. "You might have noticed I'm a little dinged up." He gestured towards his leg. "I can drive, but I haven't driven for any length of time since I've been back. The place where I want to take Chelsea… it's far. Two days' drive, at least. Maybe more, with a kid, especially since we'll need to take the long way. And I don't want to fly. We can't use anything that can be traced."

Cain's eyes were huge. "So, you want me to come with you?"

"Can you?"

"Yeah. Yes." His face clouded. "I'll figure out something to tell my parents."

"You sure? We have no idea what we're getting into here," Damon warned.

Part of him wanted Cain to back out, both to keep him safe and because the man was a complication Damon didn't need. But another part of him wanted Cain to be with him. Improbably, the guy kept him sane.

"I'm positive," Cain said. "I won't let you down."

God.

Without conscious thought, Damon lifted a hand to Cain's face, his thumb tracing Cain's cheekbone for an instant before he pulled it back and turned away.

"I'll go pack a bag," he said roughly as he dragged his broken body into his room.

The way Cain looked at him - just as he had the previous night - made Damon's chest tight with nerves and hot with an emotion he couldn't quite name. With all his scars, all of his failures, Damon was nobody's hero, and he could only hope Cain figured that out before one or both of them got hurt.

CHAPTER FIVE

"Well, well, well," Sebastian Seaver said twenty minutes later, opening the door to Drew McMann's sprawling Colonial like he owned the place. "This is an unexpected Saturday morning treat."

Cain could say the same. Bas had one arm propped against the edge of the door in a way that displayed his impressive height, the lean muscles in his arms, and the hard, hairy line of his abs that peeked out from beneath his ratty *Harvard Crew* t-shirt. His brown hair was neatly trimmed and swept back from his forehead, and his blue eyes were clear. It was a far cry from the thin, ravaged man he'd been three months before, consumed by guilt and grief.

"Not my idea," Damon said by way of greeting, folding his arms over his chest and nodding his head in Cain's direction.

Cain rolled his eyes. It *was* his idea to contact Drew and ask for a favor, but Damon had agreed it was necessary. If they were going to drive Chelsea somewhere safe and keep her under the radar, they couldn't very well take *her* car. Damon's beat-up old pickup, which Cort had kept in storage for him, wasn't going to work for transporting four people - Cain had felt cramped with just the two of them on the short ride to Drew's house. And Cain's car was down in Tennessee, parked in his parents' garage. They couldn't take a chance on renting a car with the paper trail that might leave, so there was only one decent option. After stopping at Cain's hotel to grab a bag of clothes, he'd called Drew.

Bas gave Cain an appraising glance, his mistrust clear, and Cain did his best to hide the squirming discomfort in his gut.

Why the hell couldn't Drew have answered the door?

Finally, Bas raised an eyebrow and stepped back.

"Drew, *darling*, your company's here!" he drawled. He shut the door, and his bare feet made a soft sound as he led them down the long hallway through the center of the house, ushering them into a large, surprisingly cheerful kitchen. Pale green cabinets and cream-colored walls set off the dark wood of the island, and sunlight gleamed off the wide plank floors.

Off to the left, Drew rose from the battered oak farm table where he'd been typing at a laptop. The impressive pecs beneath his tight blue t-shirt flexed as he took off a pair of black-rimmed glasses, and ran a hand through his hair - though somehow, miraculously, every strand fell back into its proper place - and crossed the room to greet them.

"Wow," Cain said, glancing around the room. "This is cool."

Drew followed Cain's glance, and smiled with unexpected shyness. "Yeah, thanks. I just redid it a few months ago. Took forever to get right."

"You designed it?" Cain asked, looking around again in light of this new information. He wasn't sure why he'd imagined Drew picking something less homey and more...

marble and stainless-steel perfection. Maybe he'd misjudged.

"I did." Drew shrugged. "Architecture and design are a hobby of mine."

"A man of many secrets, our Drew," Sebastian said, flopping an arm over Drew's shoulders and shaking him. Though both men were tall and solidly-built, Drew was the more heavily muscled of the two, and Bas was slightly taller. "Aren't you, buddy?"

Drew flushed and pushed Bas away, but didn't respond, and Cain got the distinct impression there was a subtext he wasn't understanding.

Damon cleared his throat, and Cain shook himself out of his thoughts.

"Listen, we need your help," he began.

"So you said when you called." Drew ushered them over to the table. "You want anything to drink?"

"Not a social call," Damon growled, and Drew shot him a glare.

"Right," Drew snapped as he resumed his seat. "Okay, then. What do you need?"

"A car." Cain slid into the seat to Drew's left.

From across the table, Bas blinked, then smirked. "Time for an upgrade, Shaw?"

"Leave him alone," Damon said, grabbing the seat next to Cain and pulling it out fully so he could stretch out his leg as he sat. His position brought his entire injured leg to rest along the length of Cain's, and Cain had to stifle a gasp at even that casual contact. *Jesus.*

Bas narrowed his eyes at Damon, who ignored him. "My sister called this morning," he explained instead.

"Chelsea?"

"Yeah," Damon told Bas. "Someone broke into her apartment last night."

"Shit." For the first time, Drew looked at Damon with something other than dislike. "Is she okay?"

"Yeah. She and her daughter are fine. For now." He glanced at Cain and repeated, "For now. But we need to get her out of town, fast. And we need a car to do it."

In a few words, Cain explained the threat that Chelsea had received. "Someone knows Damon is alive," he concluded. "They're harassing his sister in their attempts to keep him quiet. We have limited options."

"Fuck." Drew sighed. "I wondered how long we'd be able to keep that under wraps."

"What do you mean?" Cain demanded.

"Damon is a human being living his life." Drew shrugged. "He didn't move to Alaska to hide out, so it makes sense that he'd be seen at some point."

Damon nodded, like he'd expected that. Apparently, Cain was the only one who hadn't realized Damon would eventually be discovered.

"It was never going to be a long-term solution," Bas said, giving Cain a significant glance. "Which is why we need a way to make Damon safe permanently."

Cain rubbed a hand over his scalp in frustration.

"Not now, Seaver," Damon said, making a slicing motion with his hand. "That's an issue we can figure out later, and Cain and I have some ideas."

"You and Cain?" Bas scoffed. "You and young Shaw here are, what? A team now?"

Cain swallowed hard and focused intently on the wood grain of the table, waiting to hear what Damon would say.

"How about for once you stop being a dick," Drew told Bas in a low voice.

"Me?" Bas crowed, leaning into Drew's space. "That's rich, coming from a man who generally only relates to people by being a dick or kissing ass."

"You use peoples' feelings as ammunition against them!" Drew fumed. *"Christ."*

He pushed his chair back from the table with a loud screech and stood up, stalking toward the kitchen. He stood by the island for a second, taking a deep breath like he was composing himself, then turned and opened a cabinet door, taking down a ring of keys.

"Here," he said, handing Cain a key chain with a tag shaped like a Crayola-blue sand dollar. "You can take my Acura. Leave your truck in my garage."

"Camp Burgess?" Cain said, reading the clumsy black letters inscribed on the tag.

Bas frowned. "Let me see that." He leaned across the table to grab the keys from Cain's hand.

Drew crossed his arms over his chest and rolled his eyes. *"Yes,* it's from that summer camp we went to when we were thirteen."

"I made this," Bas accused, staring at Drew. "I painted it in that stupid arts and crafts class."

"If you say so," Drew said dismissively, like he didn't remember one way or the other, but even Cain could tell he was lying.

"You kept this for… twenty years?" Bas demanded.

"Apparently," Drew challenged.

Silence fell as Bas and Drew stared at one another, and tension thickened the air around them.

"We need to go," Damon whispered in Cain's ear, and Cain stood. He was more than ready to leave anyway.

Sebastian took one last long look at the keychain, then placed it in Cain's palm. "Uh. Be careful," he said without meeting Cain's eyes.

"Yeah." Cain agreed. He walked to Drew and put a hand on his shoulder, feeling the coiled tension in the other man's frame. "Thanks."

Drew nodded. "No worries." He seemed to collect himself and frowned at Damon. "I want a text from one of you every day, letting us know you're okay."

"You gonna call out the cavalry if we fall off the map?" Damon joked, but Bas nodded seriously.

"Yeah. You're not alone anymore. Cort is my family now, thanks to my stubborn brother, and that means you're family too."

"I don't want Cort involved in any of this," Damon said. "That's why I didn't go to him for help. He's too close to me. Last thing I need is somebody fucking with him the way they fucked with Chelsea."

Drew rolled his eyes. "You do recall that Cort is an FBI-trained security expert, right? He can probably take care of himself better than you."

"He's also my kid brother," Damon reminded him, and Drew nodded reluctantly.

"Fair enough. But he's going to want to know where you are," he warned. "If you're gone for longer than a day or two."

"I'm not going to lie to him," Damon agreed. "I did enough of that. You feel free to tell him what you know, if he asks. Just don't volunteer anything."

Drew nodded, a small smile curling the edges of his mouth. "I can do that." He reached out and clasped Damon's hand. "Take care."

"Will do." Damon lifted his chin in acknowledgment. Drew ushered them out a side door from the kitchen to a three-bay garage, where a silver Acura SUV was parked alongside a cherry-red Dodge Charger and a half-restored classic car that sported a patchwork-quilt of various colors.

Damon and Drew stepped through the door, but Sebastian held Cain back.

"He's been through enough," Bas warned, tilting his

head toward Damon. His voice was low and his blue eyes anything but friendly. "Whatever you're thinking, whatever idea you and your dad are planning? Think again. I will ruin you both."

Cain pulled his arm out of Bas's grasp, sudden fury suffusing him. He was tired of this bullshit. Sebastian Seaver had *no* grounds to judge him. *Fuck that.*

"Suddenly you think you're Damon's defender?" he hissed.

"He's family," Bas said again. *And you're not* was left unsaid, but couldn't have been clearer.

"Let's get one thing straight. Damon *has* been through enough, partly because you couldn't keep your fucking mouth shut after the crash. *Who* worked up the media? *Who* wanted his pound of flesh even from a man he thought was dead?" He watched in satisfaction as Bas's face flushed. "Yeah, that's right. And I am *well* aware that my father is an asshole, but don't you *dare* lecture me about the choices we make for the sake of our families before you take a long look in the mirror, Sebastian Seaver."

Bas's eyebrow twitched. "So you're not totally incapable of finding your balls when you need to stand up for something? That's comforting, Shaw."

Cain shook his head. He couldn't believe he'd tortured himself over Bas's opinion of him when the guy was fucking clueless. "Once again, *Seaver*, look in the mirror. I have no clue what's going on with you and Drew, but how about you man up and stop dicking him around?"

Bas's chin went back and his jaw set.

"Cain? You coming, kid?" Damon called from the garage.

Cain's gaze swung in his direction. *Kid.* Really? Again? Cain was in a temper, and Damon had been warned.

"Yeah, *Big Daddy*," he said sweetly. "I'll drive."

CHAPTER SIX

"What did Bas want?"

Cain glanced over at Damon. The man looked deceptively calm sprawled in the passenger seat of Drew's Acura, with his long legs stretched out and his leather seat tilted back, unless you noticed his hands. His right was coiled into a fist and digging into his injured leg, while the left beat a relentless rhythm against the center console.

The dashboard GPS Damon had programmed showed they were about twenty minutes into the forty-minute drive to Chelsea's house, and Damon had been silent the entire way. But Cain felt the man's tension building, much the way he'd watched thunderstorms brewing in the heavy clouds on the far side of the mountain back at his parents' cabin - he wondered when it would break, and whether he would be in the path of destruction when it did.

Cain considered his response for a second as he shifted into the left lane and poured on the speed. Damon had told Chelsea an hour, and they were running late.

He really didn't want to tell Damon all the shit Bas has spouted. Cain was pretty sure Damon had doubts about him already - all those pointed remarks about Cain's *loyalty* this morning had made that abundantly clear - and he didn't want to fuel the fire. But he also recognized he couldn't show he was trustworthy by lying.

"He warned me that I'd better not be planning to mess things up for you," Cain said simply.

In his peripheral vision, he saw Damon's head tilt back. "What?"

"Don't sound so shocked. You heard him earlier. You're *family* now."

Damon shook his head. "I do *not* understand that guy."

"It's not real complicated, *Big Daddy*." Cain smirked as Damon's head twisted in his direction.

"You're *not* calling me that. That's never going to be a thing."

Cain hummed thoughtfully. "Too late. Pretty sure it's already a thing." When Damon didn't reply, he shrugged and continued, "Bas feels bad for the way things happened after the accident. He's decent at the core, even if he seems like a total asshole."

"I guess," Damon said dubiously. Then a minute later, he added, "And what did you tell him?"

"That he needed to stop being a hypocrite and pull his head out of his ass when he's dealing with Drew," Cain admitted. He grinned and glanced at Damon again. "It felt really good."

Damon's lips kicked up. "I bet. So Cain Shaw lost his temper and the world didn't end? That's twice in one day," he noted.

Cain opened his mouth, then shut it again, grateful when the GPS reminded him to take the next exit so he could concentrate on driving and not have to reply. The truth was, it did feel really good. Not because he'd lost his temper, but because he hadn't. He'd stood up for himself and he'd stayed in control the whole time.

He'd no sooner had that revelation than his phone began to ring from the holder on the dashboard.

Mom calling.

He glanced at Damon, who'd obviously read the display. He'd missed two calls from her already when they were at Drew's house, but he really didn't want to have this conversation while Damon could hear him. Phone calls with his mother always followed a certain script, and this was not going to be pretty.

"I'll take that later," Cain said.

"Take it now," Damon disagreed. "You don't know when you'll get another chance."

True. Cain licked his lips. "Okay, I can put it on speaker while I'm driving, but... she can't know you're here. You have to stay silent."

Damon flipped his hands out, as if to say this was obvious. Cain took a deep breath and accepted the call.

"*Cain Edward Shaw,*" she said, before Cain even had a chance to say hello. "I'd like an explanation, young man."

Cain could feel Damon's gaze on him and his face went hot. *Kid, kid, kid.*

"Good morning, mother." He forced himself to sound calmer than he felt. "I'm feeling much better this morning, thanks for asking."

His mother's snort of disbelief resonated through the speaker. "You were no more sick than I was! And you have no idea what you put your father and me through when we couldn't find you."

"I texted to let you know I'd gone back to the hotel," he reminded her. "You couldn't have been worried for long."

"I most certainly was! There was a security incident at

the fundraiser just after you left! Some… big *thug* tried to force his way into the party."

Cain and Damon exchanged a glance. "That sounds awful," Cain told her. "Did the security people arrest him?" *Did they tell you I helped the man get away?*

"No! They let him go, and no one even mentioned it until after the fact. Your father is very upset!" she cried. "*Very* upset. You know how hard he works to keep us safe."

His father liked to keep *himself* safe, that much Cain could agree with. He made a non-committal sound that his mother took for agreement.

"I think we'll all feel a bit more relieved when he's finally eligible for Secret Service coverage," she sighed. "Real professionals who understand how security should work."

Cain lifted a hand from the steering wheel and ran it over his forehead, imagining a world where his father was a presidential candidate. He'd never survive it - figuratively and possibly literally, as well.

"But *none* of this excuses *your* behavior, Cain. I'm very disappointed in you. We didn't provide you with that phone so you could ignore my calls, and we didn't provide you with your education so you could abandon your father when he needed you."

Cain felt a familiar curl of humiliation and anxiety in his gut. Even after nearly a quarter of a century of dealing with his parents, even knowing the terrible things his father had done, hearing his mother speak like that triggered something that compelled him to soothe, to please.

"I'm sorry," he told her. "I really wasn't feeling well. I didn't want to ruin the evening for everyone, or to make anyone question why I was acting strangely. It was better that I left."

His mother would never admit he was right, but he

could tell she'd been somewhat mollified when she continued, "You know these gatherings aren't just for your father's sake. They're an opportunity for you to meet influential people, to grow your own name so you can be just like your father someday."

Be just like your father someday. He could feel Damon flinch at those words, could almost sense when he began to withdraw into himself, to sever the easy connection they'd had. His own chest clenched. But what could he do? What could he say without making things worse, without giving things away, without his father getting back at Jesse?

His mother sniffed. Having successfully completed the angry portion of the call, he predicted she was about to move into the guilt-inducing phase instead. The part where she laid out exactly what he'd do if he wanted any hope of erasing his mistake.

He wasn't disappointed.

"I didn't even have a chance to finish telling you all the details about Mr. Fassbender's ski party."

Oh, God. Skiing with the Fassbenders. If he could bang his head on the steering wheel while still navigating down the two-lane highway, he would.

"Mr. Fassbender has a daughter, Penny, you remember?"

His mother's eager voice made his stomach flip, and out of the corner of his eye, he saw Damon shaking his head in disbelief.

"Remember I told him you'd attend and gave him your number? They're leaving Monday morning. I'll text you his information, and you can contact him to make arrangements. It's the least you can do, after disappearing so rudely before I'd even introduced you to Penny."

Anger and self-loathing churned in his gut, but what could be do? "I'll call him," he whispered.

"Do it soon," she instructed. Then, apparently pleased by the outcome of the call, not that there had ever been any doubt she'd get her way, she said fondly, "I am so pleased that things are turning out so well, Cain. You and Cady working alongside your father and I for the good of our family, knowing that we're all safe after everything that happened with Jack Peabody, and now knowing that you're making just the *right* sort of friends, socializing with young people who'll be good influences on you, like Penny Fassbender."

Cain swallowed, though his throat was dry. "I didn't think you'd met her until last night."

"Oh, but you can just *tell* about a person. Just like I could tell Camden Seaver was never a good friend for you, and that *Jesse* person would be a troublemaker."

He ground his teeth together. Jesse hadn't been the troublemaker, not ever. Without thinking, he snapped, "Just how much is Penny's father donating?"

Beside him, Damon snorted quietly, but his mother didn't catch his sarcasm.

"He's a huge supporter of the party!" she said happily. "He pledged a hundred thousand to various candidates and PACs just last night, and there's more where that came from!"

This explained Penny's charm.

"I've got to run," she told him. "I'm taking Marnie Fassbender to hot yoga with me. You'll call Mr. Fassbender?"

"Said I would," Cain muttered.

"Oh! Before I forget!" Cain could hear a muffled crackling as his mother moved the phone around. "Your father wanted me to ask if you'd been in touch with the Seavers recently. Cam and that *man* he's been seeing."

"I haven't seen Cam in weeks," he told her honestly. "And he hasn't contacted me."

"Ah. I didn't think so, but I wanted to be sure. Will you let me know if you speak to him?"

"Why?"

"Because he's being very rude in not answering your father's calls. I think he forgets that your father is his godfather and feels an obligation to help him!"

Right. No doubt that was why. "I don't expect him to call me, but I'll let you know," he agreed, trying to end the conversation.

"Turn left in two hundred feet," the GPS informed him, and it was too much to hope that his mother wouldn't hear through the speaker.

"What's that? Where are you?" she demanded.

"Out. Running errands. I'm nearly at the store. Gotta go."

"But I thought you were sick!"

Cain hung up, and the sudden silence sounded through the car like a gunshot.

Cain didn't know what to say, how to explain away all of the horrifying, embarrassing things his mother had just revealed. He was utterly mortified, and it didn't help that Damon wasn't speaking. Not a single word.

"That could have been worse," he said softly. "I mean, she could have talked about me running around the house naked when I was a kid or something. Or the time I drew myself a beard with permanent marker. She could have demanded to know where I was running errands... honestly, I'm surprised she didn't. She could have..."

"Cain," Damon said finally, thrusting out a hand. "Could you just... not talk right now?"

Despite his stomach shrinking in on itself, Cain nodded and shivered at the silent tension.

CHAPTER SEVEN

Damon was officially in hell.

"I want to get out of the car!" Molly screamed, kicking the driver's seat to punctuate each word. The vibration was making Damon's teeth rattle.

"What about if we sing a song, honey?" Cain said from the backseat, his voice full of the brittle cheer of someone who was at the end of his tether.

"The one time in her life she won't take a freakin' nap in the car." Chelsea's pissed-off whisper from the passenger's seat was pitched low, so only Damon could hear.

"No! I. Want. To. Get. Out. Of. The. *Carrrrrr,*" Molly wailed. Her tone was so high-pitched and frantic that Damon's eyes shot back to hers in the rear-view mirror.

The little dark-haired, dark-eyed minx had seemed perfectly angelic when they'd first arrived at Chelsea's apartment, sitting primly on the ruined sofa in their living room, tapping her feet together with three-year-old abandon. While Chelsea had raced around frantically packing a few last-minute things, Cain and Damon had stood in awkward silence, while the solemn child had watched them with brown eyes so intense, Damon had fought the urge to squirm under the close scrutiny. Finally, she'd tilted her head to the side, and opened her mouth like she was about to pronounce judgment.

"I'm three years old," she'd said importantly. "*Almost* four."

The words had been so comically similar to the way Cain had described his own age that Damon's eyes had flown to him of their own accord. And for a moment, the smile they'd shared had loosened some of the tension that had built up between them.

Molly had attached herself to Cain immediately when they'd gotten to the car, recognizing that he was definitely the friendlier of the two strangers. Cain had endured it all with a smile and way more patience than Damon himself would ever be capable of. She'd wanted *Cain* to sit next to her in the backseat, *Cain* to listen to her jokes, *Cain* to read her the story about a pink princess. Damon had needed to bite his lip to hold back a smile when he'd started doing voices for each of the characters.

But then Molly, in her innocent way, had turned to Cain and said, "My friend Adrianna has two uncles. Are you and him my uncles?"

Cain's eyes had met Damon's in the rear-view mirror. "Uh, no," Cain had told her. "Damon is your uncle, and I'm his…" He'd hesitated, so clearly wanting Damon to finish the sentence, but Damon didn't, and Cain couldn't hide his disappointment.

Really, what were they to each other, though? *Friends?* Damon had never had a friend whose mouth he wanted to pillage, who he wanted to hold down and *fuck through a mattress* before, which was pretty much where all his wayward thoughts had headed from the second they'd left his apartment this morning, even after bearing witness to Cain's conversation with his mother.

And he couldn't deny that hearing Cain on the phone had seriously brought the man's loyalty into question and made him regret his impulsive decision to let Cain come with him.

He'd recognized that Cain wanted a shot at redemption, a shot to help Damon without risking his own neck. *Kid*, he'd thought. *He's young and struggling to do what's right.* It would take a certain level of coldness to put his own father behind bars, and he didn't want to fault Cain for not being a cynical asshole like Damon himself.

But then Cain had agreed with every asinine thing that came out of his mother's mouth. She'd treated him like she owned him, and he'd let her. She'd made insane demands, and he'd agreed to them. So how was Damon supposed to trust that Cain wouldn't just crumple like wet cardboard the second anyone questioned his whereabouts or demanded to know more about Damon and Chelsea? It wasn't just about coldness, he'd realized, but about strength. How could he trust that Cain would be strong when he needed to be?

In the end, Damon's hesitation over the question hadn't mattered, because Chelsea had stepped in to deliver a killing blow.

"They're not your uncles, sweetie. Neither of them. They're just *drivers*, taking us someplace safe." She'd shot Damon a glare hot enough to roast a lesser man, then sat back with her arms folded over her chest. She'd been staring pointedly out the window ever since.

The tension in the car had reached stratospheric levels after that, with neither of his adult passengers meeting his eyes or speaking to anyone but Molly, and so maybe it was no surprise that now the little girl had decided to throw the world's most epic temper tantrum.

Molly struggled against the buckles of her booster seat, demanding to be freed. Cain's face was flushed and worn, his patience long since evaporated.

Damon made an executive decision and took the next exit off the highway.

"We're stopping now."

"Already?" Chelsea's posture unlocked as she glanced at the clock on the dashboard. "We've only been driving for five hours. We're not nearly far enough away yet."

"Don't argue with the *driver*," he snapped. When her teeth clicked shut angrily, he sighed. "We haven't been followed, as far as I can tell. And if anyone is trying to track us, they'll expect that we'll keep driving as far as we can. Varying our length of time on the road is a good thing. Tomorrow, we'll get up early and drive straight through the day. Okay?"

She shrugged, and he took it for grudging acceptance.

He pulled into the parking lot of The Stafford Motel, whose sign proclaimed, *'Best Breakfast in the Poconos!'* and found a secluded spot where the car wouldn't be visible from the road, then cut the engine. Molly's whining cut off at exactly the same time.

"I'll go get us a room," he said, opening the door.

"Two rooms."

He turned back to find Chelsea glaring at him. "One room. It's safer if we're all together."

"*Two* rooms. I don't know you, Damon. I'm sure as hell not sharing a room with you." The stubborn glint in her green eyes - so similar to his own - told him she wasn't going to back down.

He sighed. "Fine. Two rooms." He stood and stretched his leg, which had begun to throb dully. He'd been glad to drive this leg of the journey - grateful for the distraction, even. But his leg definitely couldn't handle an all-day-stint.

"I'm going with you," she told him, unbuckling her belt and sliding out her side.

"You fine with Molly?" Damon asked Cain, not looking him in the eye.

"Yeah. We'll be great."

With a nod, Damon set off for the office, Chelsea trailing behind him.

When they returned to the car, nearly twenty minutes later, Chelsea was no happier. "I said I could pay, Damon."

"And I said *no*. You're my sister, and I…"

"You are *not* my brother! *God!*" she fumed. "Do you know how many times I wished I had a brother or a sister, someone who could take me out of that shithole? But I didn't. Because you never bothered getting in touch with dad after you left. And now I don't want your help. I don't need it. The only reason I'm letting you help me right now is because I literally don't have a choice, also thanks to you."

She blew out a breath. "I need to cool down before I get Molly or I'll just upset her." She grabbed one of the keys from his hand and walked off in the other direction, taking the long way to her room.

Damon sighed, and went back to the car to get Cain and Molly. But when he got to the Acura, no one was there.

He panicked for half a second, before he heard laughter coming from behind a group of trees maybe a hundred feet away. He shuffled over, damning the stiffness in his leg once again. He'd purposely left his pain medication back in Boston, knowing that he'd need a clear head no matter how painful his leg was.

Another burst of childish laughter made him slow his steps as he got closer to the trees, and had him peeking around the side rather than yelling at them to hurry up. He was glad he'd been cautious. A pair of dark heads was bent over a picnic table, an open plastic container of crayons between them. A yellow-haired doll sat propped on the tabletop, supervising the art.

"Yeah, your mom must know coloring is your favorite," Cain was agreeing. "That's why she remembered to bring your supplies."

"Yeah. My Momma was running this morning," Molly told him matter-of-factly. "Hurrying around like..." She waved both hands in the air frantically and made a buzzing sound.

"Oh, yeah? And how were *you* feeling?" Cain asked. His tone was mild and he kept his eyes on whatever he was drawing.

"*I* was fine. But maybe... maybe Jenny was a bit scared, though." She nodded at the doll on the table.

"Hmm. I can see that. Jenny's just *little*. She's not almost-four, so she doesn't understand things like you do. Maybe you could explain to her that Damon is here now, and he's not going to let anything happen to any of you. And neither will I."

Damon squeezed his eyes shut tightly, and had to brace a hand against the tree trunk at the conviction in Cain's voice. It made his heart beat faster knowing Cain had that much faith in him. And it made him feel like an asshole, because he didn't - *couldn't* - have the same faith in Cain.

He almost stepped forward then, but Molly spoke again.

"Jenny maybe thinks Damon is... scary."

Cain huffed out a laugh. "He gets pretty scowly, doesn't he? Like this?"

He couldn't see what Cain was doing, but Molly started giggling. "Yes! His face is so pinchy, just like my Momma's when she's losing her mind."

"When she's *what?*"

"Losing her mind," the little imp repeated patiently, as though explaining a foreign language to Cain. "One time, I colored on the cabinets in the kitchen even though I was s'posed to know that *markers only color on paper for God's sake, Molly.*" Her voice as she imitated Chelsea was pitch-perfect. "And my Momma made me go to time-out in my room for like a *hundred* hours, or maybe even a *year*, because she was *losing her mind.*"

Damon shook his head, and Cain's voice was choked with suppressed laughter when he replied, "But then she came and got you?"

"When she found her mind again. Yeah," she agreed. "So, why is Damon losing his mind?"

"Uh. *Well.* He's very angry that somebody made your mom upset, for one thing. He loves you both, even though he doesn't know you as well as he'd like to. He was worried."

"He was?"

"Sure. So was I."

"Hey, can I have the purple one?"

They colored in silence for a minute, while Damon stood staring at the back of Cain's head through the low branches of a pine tree, wishing he could read Cain's mind. Was it really that simple for him?

Trusting people was such a weird and rare thing, Damon didn't totally understand it. There were people he trusted because they'd earned it, like Cort, who'd grown up with him, sacrificed for him. There were people he trusted because he couldn't help it, like Chelsea, who should have been his family all along. And there were people he trusted because he understood how their minds worked, like Sebastian Seaver, whose loyalty to Damon, such as it was, stemmed from guilt.

Cain didn't fit neatly into any of those categories, and even though Damon *wanted* to trust him, wanted to believe that the unguarded man hanging with Molly could never turn on them, even to please his father, he had no idea how to make himself believe it.

"Do you ever get scared?"

Molly's voice was so low, Damon could barely hear it, but he saw the back of Cain's head move as he nodded.

"All the time. Anyone who says they're not ever scared is telling a big, fat fib."

Molly nodded, and Damon could see her eyes widen.

"One thing I do when I feel bad or scared is to play a little game called *Worse.*"

"I never hearda that game."

"No. I made it up. It's just something that reminds me that no matter how bad things are, they're still pretty okay. Like, hmmm. What's your least favorite food?"

"Cauliflower, because it is nothing like a flower even though it says so in the name."

Damon could see Cain's shoulders shake with his chuckle. "You know, you're right! Okay, so, if you had to eat cauliflower with your dinner, that would be annoying, right? But what's worse than that?"

Molly's eyes narrowed. "Eating it for two dinners?"

"Yes, *exactly*! You're really good at this game. So when you have to do something yucky like eat cauliflower, just remember, it's not *so* bad. It could always be worse."

The little philosopher nodded sagely, her dark curls sweeping her shoulders. "Cain, you know what's worse than that? Eating nothing but cauliflower for the rest of your life."

Cain laughed. "Right? That would be awful."

"And know what's worse than that?" Molly said,

bracing her hands on the tabletop in excitement. "Would be having no food *forever*."

"Wow. That escalated quickly," Cain said. "But, uh. Yeah, I guess."

"You could go on *forever* thinking of worse things!" Molly told him as she resumed coloring, and Cain's voice was gentle as he replied.

"You could, princess. But I hope you don't have to."

"He's sweet with her." Chelsea's soft voice off to his side startled Damon.

"Yeah," he said, stepping back from the tree, but keeping his eyes on the pair at the table. "He's a good guy, I think."

"You're not together," she said. It was a statement, not a question, and Damon shook his head wordlessly. "Why not?"

He really didn't want to talk about Cain, not when he barely understood his own feelings about the guy, but the fact that Chelsea was talking to him at all about *anything* felt like a miracle. He forced himself to be patient. To be honest.

"He... I..." Damon brought a hand up to rake through his long hair. "For one thing, he's a kid."

"That's an excuse. He's an adult who's older than me, and I have a daughter. Try again."

Damon snorted. "He's rich and fucking gorgeous. Totally out of my league."

"And he looks at you like you hung the moon. Try again."

"How about he and I both dated and got screwed over by the same guy?"

"Weird," Chelsea agreed, arms folded across her chest. "But not insurmountable. Common experience brings people together."

Damon winced. "Aaaand there's the little fact that his

dad was probably the one who sent the goons to your apartment."

"What?"

Nodding, Damon confirmed, "His dad is…Well, better if you don't know. Suffice it to say, he's got money and power, and he's determined to keep both by whatever means necessary."

"Jesus, Damon. But you brought Cain along anyway?"

"I did." He shrugged. "It seemed like a good idea at the time."

"Why, for God's sake? Because you want to get together with him?"

"Not really." He forced himself to be honest. "Or not *entirely*. I'm attracted to him, yeah, which is pretty fucked up for all the reasons I just gave you, but more than that I actually *like* him. He hasn't done anything wrong, so I have no reason to judge. I mean, none of us is our father, right?"

Chelsea snorted. "That's true."

"But I still don't know if I trust him one hundred percent, even though I know that's not fair." He turned to look at the petite blonde woman at his shoulder, who was bundled up in a sweater and carrying a miniature pink sweatshirt for Molly. The sun had sunk low in the sky, and the air was chilly. "But I promise, I won't let anything happen to you or Molly."

Chelsea nodded, arms still crossed. "Well, to be honest, I don't one hundred percent know if I trust you, either, even though *that's* not fair." She sighed. "What I said before was uncalled-for. You didn't know I existed when I was a kid, and my shitty childhood isn't your fault. But even though I know that logically, it still doesn't change the way I feel. Trusting someone who has the potential to hurt you is just *hard*. Especially when you've been screwed over by somebody in the past." She gave him a look. "Or *several* some-bodies in your past."

"Exactly. So it makes sense to be cautious."

"Maybe. I don't know." She shook her head and her ponytail swayed. "I don't know how you're supposed to make yourself trust someone, but I guess I don't think it's fair to just go around treating everyone like a heartbreak waiting to happen, either. Sometimes you have to just trust your gut. Can't go through life waiting for the other shoe to drop."

Was that what he was doing? Was this one more way of distancing himself from Cain before Cain could hurt him?

"So, what's the solution then?"

"Hmm. I think choosing to give someone that chance is probably the first step." She gave him a wry look. "Which is how I've found myself somewhere in fucking Pennsylvania at a place that could be the Bates Motel but apparently serves great breakfast."

Damon laughed and pulled on a strand of her hair - the same light color his had been, before it had all gone gray. "You're pretty smart, you know?"

"Next you'll tell me it's genetic," she teased, but then she grew serious. "If I can give you a shot, maybe you can give him one."

"You're gonna give me a shot?" he asked, trying not to sound too hopeful. "A chance to be in your life and Molly's?"

"Yeah. Yeah, I will. I was thinking as I was walking over here that you're putting yourself out there for me, for Molly, and I can't let old fears and hurts weigh me down. Otherwise I'm letting all the shit I thought I got through just drag me back. You know?"

Yeah. Yeah, Damon knew exactly.

She took a deep breath, like she was shaking off the

weight of their conversation and called up a genuine, warm smile, then stepped forward and clapped her hands. "Hey, Molly-mine! Guess what? The restaurant next door has *chicken fingers*."

Molly's face lit up as she hopped off the picnic bench. "I *love* chicken fingers!"

"I know you do, baby!"

Cain turned around to watch mother and daughter hug, and his eyes snagged on Damon. He looked away.

Damn. Damon had been an ass.

Chelsea picked up the crayons and art supplies, but Molly took a paper on the stack and handed it to Cain instead. "I made this for you. It's a *tree*."

"Oh, that's awesome! But it's pink!" Cain sounded bemused.

"So?"

"Oh, nothing," Cain told Molly, backtracking quickly. "No, it's *awesome*. I've just never seen a pink tree before."

"It's a Molly-tree. Molly-trees are pink. Right, Momma?"

"Sure, baby." Chelsea gave Cain a wink over Molly's head, and the little girl shrugged, more self-acceptance in that one gesture than Cain had likely ever had in his entire life.

A lock in Damon's chest broke open with an almost audible *click*.

Yeah, Cain was gorgeous and rich, and yeah, he'd been raised in a lifestyle Damon couldn't imagine... but none of that had any effect on who Cain was inside because he didn't believe himself worthy of any of it.

Cain was constantly worrying, constantly pleasing everyone else, constantly hiding himself, and never realizing just how funny and caring and *good* he was. The very idea that Cain didn't know this about himself made Damon's chest hurt, and for the moment all the other very serious problems confronting them paled in comparison to this one. He needed to make Cain see how special he was.

He limped towards the table as Chelsea and Molly said their goodbyes, and hauled himself up onto the table top. They sat in silence for a moment, Damon enjoying the chill in the air, Cain staring at Molly's drawing.

"Don't suppose you're as excited about chicken fingers as Molly?" Damon said finally, and Cain looked up.

"Yeah. That's fine. Whatever you want," he said listlessly. His shoulders slumped, his eyes dull.

"*Whatever I want.*" That opened up a whole range of possibilities in Damon's mind - possibilities he wasn't sure he had the self-control right then to hold himself back from exploring.

He grabbed the collar of Cain's shirt and pulled him in towards the table, leaning over him. "*Whatever* I want? You sure?"

Cain's eyes widened and lit up instantly, like a switch had flipped. "What are you... what?"

Damon smirked as he stood, grabbing Cain's hand. "Let's go check out our room."

CHAPTER EIGHT

Cain's mind was a total black hole of confusion - thoughts went in, but they didn't come out. What the hell was going on with Damon? Why was Cain following him across the parking lot to their motel room, salivating like some blindly obedient puppy, after the man had not only ignored him but had actively frozen him out all afternoon? What had changed?

"Hey, slow down," Cain said, pulling back on Damon's hand as they passed the Acura. "We don't even have our bags."

As he'd been coloring with Molly, he'd pondered how he and Damon had gotten so off-track in the first place. Things had been going fine until that fucking conversation with his mother, where Damon had overheard every morti-fying word. After that, Damon had clearly been disgusted by Cain's spinelessness and decided Cain's epic passivity would be a liability.

The sad part was, as much as Cain wanted to help Damon, Chelsea, and Molly, he couldn't say for sure that the latter half of that assessment was wrong. In the end, would he sacrifice himself, sacrifice Jesse, to help Damon? He honestly didn't know. In this situation, the best and most helpful thing he could do for Damon would be to simply leave him alone, giving him one less complication to worry about. He'd decided, after Damon and the girls had left in the morning, he'd rent a car and drive himself back to Nashville.

"Leave the bags," Damon said impatiently, tugging at Cain's wrist again. "We can come back."

"We can get them now," Cain argued. "Open the car."

"Cain."

"*Damon.*"

Damon dug the keys out of his pocket, his eyes glittering, and opened the locks. "Happy?" he asked, as Cain grabbed both his own bag and Damon's from the hatchback.

"Ecstatic, *Big Daddy*," Cain said dryly, but the word ended on a little squeak as Damon slammed the lid closed and pushed Cain back against the car. Their bags hit the ground with a dull thud.

"You're just provoking me now, *kid*." Oh, shit. The growl. Cain couldn't help the shiver that ran up and down his spine. God, why did the man have to be so sexy?

"I thought I'd already provoked you earlier," Cain shot back. His voice was way breathier than he would have liked.

In the dream he'd had this morning, he'd felt so much more confident than he did right then, and he wanted to channel that version of himself. He struggled not to give in too easily. He still wanted an acknowledgment from Damon, an apology... *something.*

"Yeah, you provoke me every time I'm around you," Damon growled. "Sometimes I can't *think* because of it, can't focus on all the shit I *should* be focusing on, because the only thing on my mind is *you*."

Cain only had time to suck in a shocked breath before Damon leaned forward and took his mouth. He honestly wasn't sure which was more shocking, the warm slide of Damon's lips against his, or the words that had come before it. It wasn't an apology or an explanation for his hours of cold silence, but it was nevertheless something real and concrete, something Cain's mind could grab hold of before he lost himself in Damon completely.

Damon pushed him harder against the car, his right leg insinuating itself between Cain's as he assaulted Cain's mouth in a kiss that was deep and carnal and *perfect*. He pulled back to grab Cain's top lip between his teeth, biting and tugging, while his hand roamed up Cain's side, dragging up the edge of his shirt. The cold evening air hit Cain's exposed skin and made him shudder.

"Come with me," Damon whispered, and at that moment, Cain would have followed him anywhere. There was something about Damon that called to him - maybe the way Damon seemed to really *see* him - with all of his weaknesses and temper tantrums, all his flaws and inconsistencies, and unlike every other person in his life, he still wanted him...in one way at least.

"Yes," Cain said, because that was all he needed to say.

He wrapped his arm around Damon's waist, and they stumbled towards the two-story motel. It was a strange parody of their shuffle out of the fundraiser the previous night, but this time, Cain was the one leaning against Damon, and Damon was the one urging them forward, their luggage in his hands.

Damon unlocked the door and pushed it open so hard that it slammed back against the wall. Cain barely had time to notice the layout of the room - clean but dated, with a giant pink love seat against one wall and a double bed covered with a garish floral bedspread flanking the other - before Damon threw their bags on the floor with zero care, and pushed Cain back against the closed door.

"What do you want?" Damon demanded, his breath washing hotly over Cain's neck. His hands found the button of Cain's jeans and thumbed it open, then his hands slid back around Cain's waist until they rested against the top curve of his ass.

Want? What did he *want?* It was impossible to form thoughts. All he wanted at the moment was for this to never end, to stay lost in Damon for as long as he possibly could. And he wanted this to be something Damon couldn't ever forget.

"More," he whispered, and that seemed to be enough for Damon.

His hands coasted up Cain's sides, dragging his t-shirt with them, pulling it up and over his head. He felt goose-bumps chase across his skin in the cool air, until Damon stepped close again, blocking out the chill. In the dim light of the motel room, he saw Damon's hand come up to trace along his collarbone, then further back, skimming over his shoulder. It was a gentle touch, so different from their heated exchange.

"What?" Cain asked.

Damon's hot green eyes met his. "Freckles. I wasn't expecting the freckles." His finger tracked a path along the cord that ran from Cain's shoulder to his neck. "There's a constellation here. Like little stars."

Cain's head went back against the door and he moaned. And suddenly he knew what he wanted.

He grabbed the hem of Damon's t-shirt and hauled it up with even less finesse than Damon had used, throwing it somewhere on the floor near the bed. Then he pushed

Damon back a pace, and turned him around, pushing *him* back against the door instead.

"This is what I want," he said. Then he unbuttoned Damon's jeans and dragged them down with him to the floor.

He glanced up at Damon, at the molten green gaze that hadn't left his face. "This is what I want," he said again, as he reached for the band of Damon's boxer shorts. Damon's hand came to cover his, and his eyebrow raised in a silent question. Cain nodded, nuzzling through Damon's boxers at the junction of his thigh, running his nose along the coarse hairs of his leg. "Please?"

Damon moved his hands from his waistband to the back of Cain's head, and Cain felt a burst of joy so acute it made him lightheaded. *This* was what he'd been craving, though he hadn't known it - to have Damon want him, to make him as crazy and off-balance from wanting as he'd made Cain.

He slid Damon's boxers down slowly, like he was opening a present he wanted to savor. But when Damon's cock sprang free, Cain's mouth began to water and he couldn't wait. Damon toed off his shoes and Cain pushed his jeans and boxers off completely. He hesitated when he caught sight of Damon's injured leg. Was this going to be too much?

He glanced up to find Damon leaning against the door, watching him. He traced his fingertips up the patchwork of scars, much the way Damon had done with his freckles, acknowledging every mark. Damon's muscles twitched beneath his hand.

"Do it," he breathed a second later. "God, Cain. Now."

But Cain wouldn't be rushed, not now that he finally had Damon at his mercy. This moment, in this incredibly pink hotel room, literally part way between his old life in Boston and the new life his parents had created for him in

Tennessee, wasn't bound by the rules and limitations of yesterday and tomorrow. Just for tonight, Cain was going to take what he wanted, and by God he was going to savor the fuck out of it.

For a long time - ever since his affair with Jack - he'd denied himself this basic human connection. Hookups weren't a possibility for *the senator's son*, and he'd learned the hard way that trying to conduct anything approaching a real relationship in secrecy wouldn't be fair to anyone involved. Now he was like a man who'd been submerged for decades and was finally breathing air - he could feel the cells of his body realigning, feel his heart beating faster, feel a weight he'd been carrying disintegrate from his shoulders like it had never existed.

He nipped the skin at the junction of Damon's thigh and cataloged every second of Damon's shivering response, dipped his nose into the hair at the base of his shaft and appreciated the musky, inherently male scent, let his tongue caress Damon's sac and savored the salty sweetness. If this was a moment out of time, the only chance he and Damon would ever have, he would fucking enjoy it.

"Cain, what are you doing to me?" Damon moaned. His hips jutted toward Cain, as if drawn by an invisible tether.

Cain looked up and met Damon's hazel eyes, smoldering with golden fire. When he was certain he had one hundred percent of Damon's attention focused on him, he licked a broad, wet stripe up the man's cock.

Damon's head flew back with a groan, and Cain's entire being hummed with consciousness of his own power. *I made him do that. I can make him lose control.*

He grabbed the base of Damon's dick in his hand and let his tongue explore the engorged head, lapping and sucking, dipping inside the slit to taste the salty fluid. Damon's hands came down on his head, cradling his skull to hold him in place, but Cain held him back, bracing his hands on Damon's hips to prevent his thrusts.

"What do *you* want, Damon?" Cain demanded, tossing his words back at him.

Damon growled, as though his power of language had been stolen, and he looked nearly angry.

"Do you want to fuck my mouth?" Cain continued. "Hold my head and fuck me hard? Because I want you to. You can have anything you want, but you have to say the words if you want it to happen." *Make this real. Make this unforgettable.*

"Brat," Damon rasped, grabbing Cain's hair in both hands. The words and the sensation combined to make Cain's stomach somersault, and when Damon spoke again, his words were fierce. "You can't handle what I want to give you. Not when you've got me on edge already."

Cain's hands moved around to cup Damon's ass, pulling him infinitesimally closer. He loved the way his tattoos looked as his skin touched Damon's, like he was badass and strong, someone Damon could need. "I can handle your temper," he breathed. "I can handle whatever you give me."

"You think so, kid? *Yeah*, I wanna fuck your mouth. I want to push so deep down your throat you can't breathe anything but me, I want to hold you and choke you, make you take exactly what I want to give you. I want to ruin you for every other blowjob you ever give or receive." He pulled Cain's hair again, making his scalp ache from the sting. "You think you can handle that?"

Gorgeous and defiant, Damon stared down at him, like he expected Cain to renege on his offer, or he imagined Cain would tremble in fear.

He had no clue how much yearning had been built up in Cain, or how much he needed exactly what Damon was offering.

"Try me," he whispered. Then without taking his eyes off Damon's, he swallowed his cock to the root.

"Fuck. *Fuck,* Cain," Damon said. Cain's tongue swirled around the head as he popped off, then he lifted a hand to play with Damon's balls, pulling and tugging, feeling their solid weight, while the other hand kneaded Damon's ass.

"Is there a problem?" Cain asked innocently.

Damon clearly wasn't in the mood for teasing. "Suck me, Cain!" he growled.

But Cain shook his head. "Make me," he said simply.

He shifted up on his knees, wide eyes level with Damon's bobbing cock, and clutched his hands together behind his back. His own dick was rock-hard, but he was too focused on Damon to care right now. This moment *right here* - this epic, powerful moment - made up for every time he'd had to walk away from a relationship, every time he'd had to hide or pretend not to want what he wanted. This moment would provide the inspiration he'd need for the thousand lonely nights to come. He'd be damned if he'd yield right now.

Damon's hands tightened in his hair and he tugged again, as though he couldn't help himself. Cain could see his hesitation in the considering frown on his face - did Cain really want this? What were the implications? The man's innate need to protect was totally messing up Cain's plan, even as it made Cain's heart squeeze.

Still, their gazes held, and Cain tried to convey his want, his need. Apparently Damon got the message, because he sucked in a deep breath, exhaled the last of his resistance, and then groaned, "Open for me."

When Cain didn't comply as quickly as he wanted, Damon tugged his hair again, pulling Cain close enough to rub the head of his cock against Cain's wet lips. "Open, Cain," he demanded.

The second Cain's lips parted, Damon surged inside, taking control, *using* Cain, making Cain the instrument of his pleasure, exactly the way Cain wanted.

He gasped as Damon got rougher, gripping the back of Cain's head, yanking him forward until Damon's pubic hair tickled his nose, then forcing him roughly back. Cain kept sucking and swirling, groaning around Damon's cock as the man's body shuddered before him.

"Cain, Cain, *Cain*," Damon chanted, and it might have been the world's sappiest love poem for the effect it had on Cain. He swirled his tongue harder, forced his jaw to open wider, willed his throat to accept Damon's cock. His eyes watered as Damon's flavor exploded on his tongue, and Damon threw back his head and cried out as Cain swallowed every last drop.

Cain pulled off, panting, and rested his head against Damon's stomach. Damon slumped against the door and tried to bring his own breathing back under control, inhaling in short, shuddering gasps.

Fuck. That had been the single best sexual encounter of his entire life, and he hadn't touched himself at all.

Then Damon wrapped his hands around the back of Cain's neck, more tenderly this time, and snarled, "Get on the bed."

Cain stood on shaky legs - and Damon steadied him for half a second, before forcing him backward five paces to collapse onto the floral monstrosity. Eyes blazing, Damon reached for Cain's jeans and dragged them down, throwing them on the floor along with Cain's shoes, socks, and underwear. Without a word, Damon leaned down and caught Cain's nipple between his teeth, his silver hair falling around his jaw like a curtain.

"You are just full of surprises, baby," he said, while his hand brushed down the length of Cain's body.

His mouth trailed wet kisses down Cain's stomach, and then finally reached Cain's cock. Unlike Cain, Damon didn't need to play games in order to make Cain lose his mind. Just the sight of his dick disappearing between those lips, the feel of Damon's scruffy beard against his thigh, had him panting and ready. Damon's hands held Cain's hips in place as he writhed beneath Damon's mouth, and Cain threw his own hands wide, catching the scratchy bedspread in his hands to hold himself in place.

He heard someone wail, and realized it was him. Some distant, instinctive part of his brain warned him to be quiet, that anyone could hear, but he couldn't make himself care. No part of this pleasure could be denied or modulated, and he refused to try.

"Damon? *Damon*. Oh my God, Damon," he moaned, as his balls tightened. His neck arched, his head grinding into the mattress, as his heels dug into the edge of the bed. He was coming, and he almost didn't want to. Nothing had ever felt like this before and he was almost positive nothing would ever feel this good again after tonight. He wanted to draw it out as long as possible.

But he couldn't stop the need from building, couldn't stop the way his hips bucked futilely against Damon's hands, the way every muscle in his body locked down, or the cry of absolute surrender that came from his throat. He was lost to all of it. Lost to Damon.

A second later, Damon collapsed on the bed and curled around him, his face in Cain's neck, his hand resting over Cain's heart.

There were a lot of things Cain wanted to say in that moment - a hundred questions, a dozen thank yous, and one really shitty goodbye - but he kept his mouth shut. He was well aware this perfect peace would only last a few more hours and he wanted to spend them just like this.

It could be worse, of course. He could never have had this night to begin with. He could have died on the plane with Jack. He could…

His conversation with Molly earlier came floating back to him and stopped his little game with a sound like a needle scratching across a record.

You could go on forever thinking of worse things! she'd said, all excited about this new game, which was fine when it came to cauliflower. But was thinking of ways things could be worse really the best way to go through his entire life?

The bedspread was hot and scratchy beneath his ass, and his feet were dangling off the bed at an awkward angle, but Cain would have happily stayed right where he was forever.

Maybe, *maybe*, it was time to start thinking of ways he could make things better.

CHAPTER NINE

Damon slowly came to awareness to find weak autumn sunlight filtering through the motel's sheer pink curtain panels. His eyes opened in surprise. He couldn't remember the last time he'd woken after daybreak. He inhaled deeply and rolled over to find Cain sitting on the silly pink loveseat on the opposite side of the room, cradling his phone in his hand.

"Hey," Damon murmured, his voice even raspier than usual, pushing himself up to sit against the headboard. He pushed the hair back from his face with both hands.

"Oh. Hey, yourself," Cain said. He flushed as his gaze drifted from Damon's face down to his bare chest. The weight of his stare had Damon's cock stirring to life beneath the thin blanket, but he tried to ignore it. Damon didn't regret what had happened the previous night - far from it - but that didn't mean they could have a repeat, not until he and Cain had a rational discussion about what exactly this thing between them was or *wasn't*. And that wouldn't happen until he'd gotten Chelsea to the one place he could think of where she'd be safe.

He strove for a casual tone and ducked his chin towards the phone in Cain's hand. "You seem to have woken up more easily today, anyway. Something exciting happening in the world?"

"Huh? Oh. Nah." Cain turned the phone to show Damon the black screen. "I was trying to pack so fast yesterday, I forgot my phone charger. Stupid thing is dead." Cain pushed the phone into the back pocket of his pants, and only then did Damon notice that the man had clearly showered and dressed already, in a pair of slim, dark jeans and a long-sleeved t-shirt.

Damon shrugged and yawned. "That's fine. You can use my phone if you need to."

Deep blue eyes met his, then flitted away. "Actually," Cain said softly. "I'm thinking maybe I should just head out myself this morning. Rent a car. Get back to Nashville, maybe." He picked a spot on his pants. "Or, hell, maybe go skiing with the Fassbenders. Sure to be a rollicking good time." His lips twitched with the ghost of a smile.

Damon didn't want to think too deeply about why his stomach pitched at those words. He'd had pretty much the same thoughts yesterday as they were driving - that he'd be better off taking Chelsea to safety without Cain and his confusing loyalties, and that Cain was a complication he didn't need. Despite Chelsea's advice and his decision to let Cain prove himself, all of those factors were still true. Even so, he had to clench his hands around the sheet to stop himself from arguing, from convincing Cain to stay.

"That what you want?" he growled instead.

Cain nodded quickly. "Yeah. I think it's probably for the best. You drove most of the way yesterday and your leg was fine. If you need her to, Chelsea can drive, too." He licked his lips. "And I figure you want to spend some time with her and Molly anyway. Get to know them without distractions."

Damon exhaled sharply through his nose. "You're prob-ably right."

That ghost of a smile played around Cain's gorgeous lips again. "*Always am.*"

"Baby, that is the least-right thing you've ever said," Damon teased. The *baby* had come out naturally, without thought - probably a holdover from the night before. But when his gaze met Cain's, he knew they'd both registered it, and he saw the sadness in Cain's eyes.

They couldn't pretend things hadn't changed profoundly between them overnight, but that didn't mean they were in any position to have a relationship either.

"So, uh, this place has breakfast," Cain said with false enthusiasm, rubbing his hands on his thighs before pushing himself to his feet.

"Yep. Best in the Poconos, or so I've heard," Damon returned dryly, rolling to his feet.

"And you might have noticed I didn't get any dinner last night." He clapped a hand to his stomach dramatically. "Not even chicken fingers."

Damon rolled his eyes as he made his way to his bag and rummaged until he'd found clean clothes to put on.

"I made sure you got your protein," he reminded Cain with a smirk, biting his lip to keep from laughing at the way Cain's blue eyes widened and his mouth fell open in shock.

"Did you... did you just make a bad blow job joke right now?" Cain asked.

"Maybe." Damon shoulder-checked him as he passed by on his way to the bathroom.

"Has your sense of humor evolved at all since you were twelve?" Cain called, as Damon closed the door between them.

"Just tryna get on your level... *kid.*"

Damon pretended he couldn't hear the scream of frustration that was Cain's only reply, but he smiled the whole time he was in the shower.

"So, you're not coming with us?" Molly's dark eyes were more compelling than any puppy dog Damon had ever seen, and he could see Cain hesitate, forking up his last bite of pancakes as he shook his head.

"I'm not. I have... stuff to do," Cain told her lamely, and once again, Damon wrestled with the urge to convince Cain to stay. It would be stupid for them to get further involved, and possibly dangerous for Chelsea and Molly, which is why he *wouldn't* do it, but damn if he didn't want to.

"But, who'll color with me?" she demanded, somehow making her eyes even more liquid and pitiful.

Chelsea covered her smirk with her napkin. Cain shot her a pleading look, but Chelsea shook her head, an indication that Cain was on his own in this.

Cain huffed, but then smiled mischievously. "Maybe your Uncle Damon will color with you!" he said brightly. "Oh, and you should ask him to tell you some jokes. He's got some hilarious ones."

Molly looked at Damon expectantly, and he could feel his face turn red. Beneath the table, he aimed a kick at the man in front of him, but Cain shifted his chair back before his foot could connect and gave him a knowing grin.

"I'll get the check," Cain said. "Meet you guys outside to say goodbye."

Damon slugged back the last sip of his coffee - black and strong, unlike the melted ice-cream Cain drank - and stood, waiting for Chelsea and Molly to do the same. Chelsea lifted her daughter down from the bench, and

Damon was stunned when the little girl reached out and put her hand in his. He blinked down at her.

Molly's hair was in little braids today, and she wore a pink dress with the slogan *Undercover Unicorn.*

"Cain says you're only growly because you want to protect us," she confided, her forehead creased with a frown, and his heart lurched.

"He's right," Damon agreed.

Molly's other hand came around to trace the pink scars visible beneath the hem of Damon's long sleeves, and he held his breath, but she made no comment about them. Still, her next words floored him completely.

"Who's gonna protect Cain if you're not there?" she wondered, and Damon's gaze shot to the diner counter, where Cain stood paying the bill. He looked confident, a friendly smile on his face as he joked with the cashier, until you looked at the tightness around his eyes, the purple smudges that showed he'd had far less sleep than Damon had.

Fuck. Who *would* protect him?

It was easy to remind himself that Cain wasn't likely to be in any physical danger, but what about emotionally? Who'd made him so afraid to lose his temper, to show his personality, to be himself?

He swallowed. "He's a big boy, sweets, not a kid. He'd be the first one to tell you that."

"But he still gets scared, though. He told me."

Damon took a deep breath but didn't reply. He didn't know how. They walked toward the parking lot, Chelsea following close behind.

For a single moment, he let himself wish that Cain were walking out alongside them, that he'd be coming to the parking lot not to say goodbye, but to get in the car with them. He had a momentary image of showing Cain the place where he'd be taking Chelsea - one of his favorite places in the whole world - and he knew without a doubt that Cain would love it as much as he did.

And in his distraction, he failed to notice the black sedan.

The beast reversed from a parking space and headed right for them, tires squealing and engine roaring as the driver stepped on the gas. Damon heard someone scream, and saw from the corner of his eye as a bystander yanked Chelsea backward, out of the path of the car. He grabbed Molly's shoulder and threw them forward, between two other parked cars, twisting as he fell to make sure he cushioned her.

Fuck! His right leg screamed in agony and he could swear he heard the damaged tissue ripping as he fell. The pain in his elbow registered next - sharp and burning. He'd scraped the hell out of it.

"Uncle Damon?" Molly's voice was high and quivery.

"Yeah, sweets," he said, trying to temper the rough growl of his voice. "You okay?"

She nodded. He quickly moved her off him and started to stand, a red haze across his vision. *Where was Chelsea? Who the fuck had been in that car, and were they coming back?*

But suddenly Cain was running toward him, panic on his face.

"Down! Get down! They're coming back, and..." His voice cut off as he dove on top of Damon, shielding him and Molly as gunfire shattered the morning air.

Crack, crack, crack.

Glass shattered somewhere above his head, and there was a sharp, metallic *ping* as a bullet embedded itself in the door not far from his head. Cain's body jerked on top of his. There was another squeal of tires, followed by a single moment of ringing silence... and then the whole world burst into motion.

"They're gone!" someone shouted. "Did you see the license plate?"

"Call the police!" another voice cried. Then several pairs of feet came running toward them, demanding to know if they were okay.

"Moll?" Damon recognized Chelsea's voice, panicked and high.

"Momma!" Molly pushed herself out from beneath Cain and scrambled into her mother's arms.

"Damon, my God. Are you hurt?" Chelsea demanded. "Cain, are you?"

"No." Cain's voice sounded dazed. "Yeah, no. I'm fine." He looked into Damon's eyes, like he wanted to be sure Damon was okay, too.

Damon had no idea whether he was okay, and had no voice he could raise in reassurance. Cain had just jumped on top of him. Had literally thrown himself in front of bullets to protect him.

Maybe there was no way to be sure of someone's loyalty until they'd proven it, but Damon didn't need any further proof of what kind of man Cain was.

He lifted his hands, dirty and gravel-covered as they were, and cupped Cain's jaw. "Fuck, baby," he said, his voice barely intelligible even to himself. "Why?"

Cain shook his head like he didn't understand the question. "Damon are you hurt? Your leg!" he said, horrified, as he realized that he'd been laying on it. He stood up quickly. "Is it broken? Shit, did I hurt you? Are you okay?"

Damon braced himself on his good leg, holding his right as steady as possible as he grabbed the closest door handle and pulled himself up. Yeah, that leg was not going to be holding him anytime soon. *Fuck.*

He looked around the parking lot, quickly assuring himself that the black car, and whoever had been driving it, were long gone. He had a pretty good idea who had been behind the incident, but *how*? How could they have been found, when he'd been so careful to pay for things in cash, to drive an untraceable car?

But he couldn't think about that now. He had to get his family to safety.

He grabbed Cain by the upper arms. "Help me get…" He registered Cain's flinch a second later, and they both looked down at Cain's arm, where blood was seeping through his dark shirt.

"Shit, Cain!"

"Scraped it when I fell, I guess. Or maybe it was the broken glass?" He looked confused, like he couldn't remember how it had happened. He shook his head like he was clearing it. "It's fine," he told Damon firmly. "Really."

Damon peered at him closely, then nodded. "We need to leave as quickly as possible."

"Right. You need to get going! Get them safe. I can…" He looked bewildered for a second. "What can I do? Use the phone in the office? Call Bas and Drew?"

Damon grabbed him by the back of the neck and shook him gently. "You can help me to the car, baby. You're coming with us."

"But…"

"But *nothing*. They shot at you, Cain. You're not leaving my sight."

Cain blinked. "I didn't… I don't think they were shooting at *me*."

"Doesn't matter who they were aiming for," he whispered fiercely. "Come on. Before the police come, and start asking questions we don't have answers for."

Cain nodded, wrapping his good arm around Damon's

waist and taking his weight as he limped to the car. He got Damon to the passenger's seat, then made his way around the car to take the wheel.

"God, you're a pair, huh?" Chelsea said. Her voice was shaking as she climbed into the backseat and hovered over her weeping daughter protectively. "One good set of legs, one good set of arms?"

"I guess so," Cain agreed distractedly.

Damon directed him out of the parking space, ignoring the hotel manager who was trying to flag them down, and pointed out the sign for the highway they needed to take. His eyes scanning the road for any sign of the black sedan, he barely heard his sister murmur, "Guess that means you should stick together."

CHAPTER TEN

The day had long since turned to night by the time Damon directed Cain up a steep and narrow mountain road somewhere in eastern Tennessee. At a guess, he'd put them maybe two hours away from his parents' mountain cabin, but he was so turned around he could hardly tell.

Damon had insisted on them taking the longest possible route this side of the Mississippi, detouring into lots of deliberate switch-backs and local roads, turning what should have been a nine-hour trip from Pennsylvania to Tennessee into a two-day odyssey that had involved a stop at a crappy motel in West Virginia where no one but Molly had dozed for more than a few minutes at a stretch. It had been a pain in the ass and tiring as hell, but Damon had sworn it was necessary and Cain wasn't going to argue. The incident yesterday - seeing Damon and Molly on the ground, wondering for just one second if they were dead - had been scarier than anything Cain could remember.

For hours, Cain's head had been pounding in syncopated rhythm with the hot pulse of the cut on his upper arm. The initial adrenaline rush had burned off quickly yesterday, and the lack of sleep from the past two nights had caught up with him. He was running on Diet Coke and determination.

In the back seat, Molly was zonked out in her car seat, Chelsea still leaning over her just as she'd been since yesterday morning. It had been hours since their last rest stop - a five-minute pause at a drive-thru and a chance for Damon to check the bandage he'd tied around Cain's arm. Damon had looked grim. Though the blood flow had mostly stopped, the cut occasionally reopened when he moved too fast, and Damon thought he might need stitches or a tetanus shot. Unfortunately, heading to a hospital was too dangerous.

"Just a mile or so up the road," Damon said now, looking over at him in concern.

"M'kay. How's your leg?" Damon had managed to fuck himself up pretty thoroughly in his fall, and though he had been hobbling around somewhat, he needed Cain's help.

"Still attached."

"Want one of your pain pills?"

Damon snorted. "No thanks. I'd rather not pass out in the car." He looked at Cain. "I still can't believe you thought to grab those off my kitchen counter."

Cain shrugged tiredly. "I thought you might need them. I still can't believe you left them behind deliberately, or that you've refused to take them up to this point. Not sure why your stubbornness should come as a surprise, though." He shot Damon a glare.

"Funny. Speaking of stubborn, how's the arm?"

"Also still attached. It'll be *fine*."

"Hmmm. I want Eli to look it over when we get there, anyway."

Cain's ears perked up. Damon hadn't said where they

were going, and given the man's trust issues, Cain hadn't wanted to be too demanding. He'd resolved to just follow Damon's lead and help out as much as he could. But he was pretty fucking curious about the place Damon would choose to stash his sister and niece.

Cautiously, he asked, "Eli?"

"Yeah. Eli Davis. He's the man we're going to see. The man I'm hoping is going to agree to have Chelsea and Molly stay with him."

Cain frowned as he navigated the rutted, packed dirt. "Hoping? Why didn't you call him last night after you let Bas and Drew know what had happened?"

Damon chuckled. "Eli doesn't believe in phones."

Well. Okay, then. Curiosity surging wildly, Cain demanded, "Why not?"

"First of all, because the reception up here is for shit. And second of all, because that's how the government gets ya." Cain shot him a look that made Damon laugh softly again. "Oh, Eli's got a whole list of ways the government will get you. Internet, credit cards, banks, social security numbers, satellite imagery…" He ticked the examples off on his fingers.

"So he's, like, one of those separatist people? With a room full of guns and a plan to never pay taxes again?" Cain frowned at the innocent girl sleeping in the backseat. Was this really the safest place to take a three-year-old?

"No. He's not planning to declare his independence from America," Damon said, clearly amused. "But he doesn't trust the government either. He hasn't thinned the trees around his house at all, so drones can't get through, and he pays for everything in cash or by bartering."

"That's odd."

"It's actually pretty cool," Damon contradicted, and Cain shot him a glance again. He had a fond smile on his face, and he was shaking his head with amused exasperation. "Eli is… he's a special person."

Cain's stomach twisted sharply. "Special?"

"Yeah." Damon's eyes were focused on the road outside the window. "You're gonna want to bear right up here. Yeah, near the tree." He continued in a soft voice. "Eli's a stand-up guy. The Seavers' plane crashed into the mountain about twenty miles south of here. Eli saw the whole thing happen. Said he was in his truck before he even saw the smoke, and he was the first person on scene. He used to be in the military," he said, shooting Cain a quick glance. "Sniper. But he was discharged a couple years ago."

Cain nodded, the terrible twisting in his gut stealing his ability to speak. What would it feel like to be someone Damon thought was special?

"He's huge - taller than me and stronger, too. And it's a damn good thing he is," he mused. "The plane was on fire when he got there, but I'd been thrown a fair distance away. I was making a lot of noise, I guess. That's how he found me. Next thing I knew, I was waking up in the hospital."

There were many things Cain disliked in this story - the fact that it had happened to Damon at all was paramount, of course, because Cain wasn't a total asshole. But not far below that was a poisonous feeling he recognized as jealousy. Jealousy of this big, tall, strong man who'd saved Damon's life. Jealousy of the reverent way Damon spoke of him. Jealousy because this Eli person was someone Damon trusted absolutely, while Cain was… not.

"Eli's anti-government stuff might seem weird, but it saved my life." Damon shot Cain a glance. "When he took me to the hospital, he claimed he'd found me in a wrecked car on the highway, mostly because he didn't wanna get himself involved in any investigation of the plane crash. He took me in, then took off without giving them any other information. But he came back."

He shook his head, as if lost in the memory. "He happened to be at a diner in town a while after that. Saw my picture on the television and knew immediately I was the guy they were looking for, so he came back to the hospital, claiming to be my brother. When they discharged me, he took me home with him and kept me there for months while I recovered."

Cain squinted through the trees that lined the road, distracted. "Why, though? I mean, I'm glad he did. I'm glad he helped you. But why would a guy who hates to get involved… well, get involved?"

"If there's one thing Eli hates more than the government, it's the one-percent. Rich, entitled corporate assholes, you know? The preliminary investigation from the NTSB was placing all the blame on me, so he automatically assumed it was bullshit."

Damon was chuckling like he was recounting a fond memory, but Cain couldn't even summon a fake smile. His eyes burned, his arm throbbed, and his head pounded. He was hungry, thirsty, and exhausted. He was currently driving them to the house of a man who was apparently like The Rock and St. Michael all rolled into one big tinfoil-hat-wearing mountain man, and who would likely hate him on sight for being a) rich, and b) related to the biggest government asshole he could think of.

Wow. Awesome.

Cain tried to play the *Worse* game, tried to think of a way he could be more miserable than he was right then, but nothing sprang to mind, and that just made him feel shittier.

The road curved around to the left, and Cain slowed the Acura to a crawl. The branches of the trees were close enough to scrape the sides of the car, and he really hoped Drew was feeling forgiving when they brought it back.

A few seconds later, they entered what appeared to be a junkyard in the middle of the woods, and as the headlights played across the scene, Cain's heart sank further and further. There was a rusted blue Chevy pickup up on cement blocks to one side, and a graveyard of used appliances to the other - a refrigerator, a washing machine, and several rusted oil drums. The ground was boggy, which was odd since they hadn't had seen any rain, but perhaps the trees - enormous, towering oaks and pines - grew so thick overhead that no sunlight could ever seep through to evaporate the dampness.

It was every terrible redneck joke he'd ever heard, represented in one piece of property, and he could almost swear he heard a banjo playing somewhere nearby.

Please don't let this be the place. Please, please, please.

"Stop here," Damon instructed, confirming Cain's worst fears. And it didn't help when he cracked open the door, turning on the interior lights, and burst into laughter. "Cain! Oh my God, you should see your face!"

Right. Yes. My face is the problem here.

Cain reached for his door handle.

"No, wait!" Damon said, but the urgent words didn't register until after Cain's door was open and he was already twisting his cramped legs out of the car.

"I'm just stretching my legs," Cain complained. "I'll help you to the door so you can deal with- "

And then the dogs started barking.

"He has dogs?" Cain demanded.

Of course he did. Rottweilers, by the look of them, and not remotely friendly ones.

"Get back in the car, Cain!" Damon demanded. And

when Cain hesitated, he yelled loudly enough to disturb Chelsea and Molly. "Now!"

Cain twisted his legs back into the car and slammed the door just as the dogs reached them, snarling and barking as they pawed at the driver's side door. From the backseat, Molly screamed.

Damon, meanwhile, opened his door and whistled sharply. The dogs immediately silenced and dropped to the ground, going over to Damon to investigate. Within seconds, he was petting them, scratching them behind the ears. In the rearview mirror, he met Chelsea's glance and saw his own shock and dismay mirrored in her eyes.

"Ripper! Puck!" a harsh voice boomed, and the dogs obediently trotted over toward a giant of a man who stood halfway between the car and the shack, a shotgun cradled in his arms. "State your business," the voice demanded, and Cain would be lying if he said that voice didn't shake him to his toes.

Not Damon, though.

"I came for pancakes," Damon yelled.

The man appeared to squint through the darkness.

"Hooooleeeey shit!" the man said, stepping closer and holding the rifle at his side. "Damon? That you?"

"Who else would come to see you, Eli?" Damon demanded, and the man chuckled as he reached the door.

Handsome. Damon had forgotten that little adjective when describing Eli, but in the light from the car interior, Cain could see the man was tall and strong and *handsome as fuck*, with black hair, a full black beard, and blue eyes just a shade brighter than Cain's own. He was also young - maybe a few years younger than Damon.

"You brought friends," Eli said, as he looked from Molly to Chelsea to Cain. His eyes lingered on Cain's the longest, and it took all of Cain's focus to meet that intimidating gaze with a steady, blank stare of his own.

"My sister, Chelsea," Damon said, hooking a finger into the backseat. "And my niece Molly."

Eli nodded at each of the girls in turn, then his eyes were back on Cain. "And this is?"

Damon hesitated. "This is… Cain."

That introduction shouldn't have made Cain wince the way it did. It was simple. Accurate. It was also completely devoid of any claiming whatsoever. Not even *my friend Cain*. Ouch.

"I didn't know where else to go," Damon said, urgency in his voice. "I need your help."

"And you know I'll always help you." Eli gave Damon a smile that was way warmer than simple friendship. "Whatcha waitin' for? Christmas? Getcha ass inside!"

Damon shrugged. "'Fraid it's not that easy," he said sheepishly. "Messed up my leg again. Can't really walk."

"Course you did." Eli smirked. "Come on, then."

"Cain," Damon said. "Could you…"

But Eli pushed Damon's arm and motioned for him to swivel. He waited until Damon had swung his legs out of the car, then reached in and grabbed Damon under the armpit, lifting him to stand. He plastered Damon to his side, and his huge mass supported even Damon's bulky frame smoothly as he half-carried Damon to the house while the dogs trotted obediently behind.

Cain watched their backs disappear for a moment, then exhaled sharply through his nose and looked at the girls in the backseat. "I guess we'll follow." His voice was brittle, but he shut off the car, stepped out, and opened the back-door to help unbuckle Molly.

"I'll grab the bags," he said, and Chelsea nodded as she gathered her daughter into her arms.

Cain loaded himself up with luggage as best he could given his injured arm, and picked his way across the pitch-dark yard. With the headlights off, it was a little like navigating an obstacle course. His eyes still burned and he wanted to cry for reasons that had only a little to do with his sore arm.

Pull it together, Shaw.

He took a deep breath and climbed the rickety porch stairs, then stepped cautiously into the tiny house…

Except it wasn't so tiny at all.

Like some backwoods TARDIS, the house was enormous on the inside. It had, indeed, been built into the mountain, but rather than the cavernous, dank space Cain had expected, it was a huge, two-story room, with large windows carved through the stone at the far end that would no doubt provide spectacular views in the daytime, wide-plank oak floors, and an enormous fireplace complete with a roaring fire. It even smelled good - like cinnamon and grilled meat all at once.

"Y'all need something to eat?" Eli asked Damon as he got him arranged on a cushy blue sofa near the fire.

"No. We're fine. You and I need to talk, but is there maybe a place where we can sleep?" Damon suggested. "It's late, and it's been a long day. Two days, really." Then he caught sight of Cain standing there, and his brow lowered. "Cain, what the hell are you doing with those bags?"

Really? "Carrying them," Cain sniped.

"That's way too much for you to carry! Are you crazy?" Damon was leaning forward in agitation, like he wanted to stand up.

"Calm down there, chief," Eli said, bracing his palm against Damon's chest and easing him back in the seat. "I'll help the kid out."

Cain sucked in air through his nostrils and stared up at

the rafters, trying to figure out what the worst part of that exchange had been. Damon calling him weak? Or maybe Eli calling him a kid?

Neither. It was the proprietary way Eli had touched Damon, like he had the right.

"I don't need help," he said, dropping the bags on the floor. Then he added, "but thanks anyway," because it felt rude not to.

Eli shrugged. "Anyway. Damon, you can bunk right here on the sofa, just like when you first got here last time. No stairs to get to the bathroom." He gave Damon a wink. He told Chelsea, "I got two rooms upstairs, and one's got a pullout. I'll show ya." His brow puckered. "You need me to carry her for ya, missy?"

Chelsea shook her head. "No, I've got her."

Eli nodded and ushered her up the stairs.

"Your bags," Cain reminded her, and Chelsea shot him a grateful look as he handed off two of the bags to Eli.

When Eli and the girls had gone upstairs, he stood awkwardly at the entrance to the living area, staring around the fire-lit room. He tried to think back to the last time he'd felt so out of place and completely unnecessary, yet so completely stuck.

Oh, right. At the fundraiser. And every other time he was forced to interact with his family.

Didn't really matter whether it was a mountain cave-house or a Boston function room when you had nothing to offer anyone, but also couldn't leave.

He debated the wisdom of offering to sleep out in the car. He'd honestly prefer it, but he didn't want to sound like a petulant child.

His roving gaze came back to Damon, and found Damon watching him.

"I didn't think to ask," Damon said. "Were you hungry?"

Because he couldn't ask for food himself if he needed it? Cain rolled his eyes. "No. I'm good." He couldn't hold Damon's gaze. He was on the edge of some emotional precipice, one hard push away from going over. He rolled his shoulders, wincing as his injured arm pulled. "Tired, maybe."

Damon nodded slowly. "Of course you are."

Of course, weak creature that he was. Weak body, weak will. *Weak.*

"So… Eli, huh?" Cain said lamely.

Damon looked startled. "What about him?"

Cain shook his head. *Shut your mouth, shut your mouth, shut your mouth.* "I didn't realize you guys were so close."

Damon blinked, then frowned. "Well, yeah. In a way. I mean, I haven't seen him in months. We don't exactly keep in touch. But…" He shrugged. "He's a good friend."

A friend. *Right.* So Cain had just imagined the something-else he'd seen in Eli's eyes, the casual way they touched? He looked away.

"When Eli comes down, I'll ask him to look at your arm," Damon said, shifting in his seat to get more comfortable. "I didn't like the way it looked earlier."

"It's fine," Cain said. The very last thing he needed was to have the great and wonderful Eli tending his nicked arm. He'd probably tell Cain to stop being such a whiner and suck it up. Eli would probably have been able to carry a hundred bags from the car with both arms amputated, because he was magic like that.

"Yeah? You a doctor now, Cain?" Damon said, one eyebrow elevated and his arms crossed over his chest.

Somehow, even from this distance, even from a seated position, the guy managed to be intimidating and hot, which annoyed Cain, too. The injustices were piling up all around him tonight.

"I said it's fine."

"Don't be stupid," Damon said. He raised his voice and shifted forward, like he was trying to get to his feet again.

"But that's me, right? A stupid kid." Cain nodded, swallowing hard. There were actual fucking tears behind his eyes, and this day needed to be over, *now*.

Eli came down the stairs at exactly that moment, because *of course he did*. "Problem?" he demanded, looking back and forth from Cain to Eli.

"Nope. No problem. I just need a place to crash," Cain said evenly.

Eli's eyes narrowed and he flitted a look at Damon. "You can have my bed. Upstairs, second room down."

"No, I can't do that. Where would you sleep?"

Eli shrugged and flashed Cain a smile that showed even white teeth behind his beard. "Down here with Damon. Wouldn't be the first time."

And, there it was.

Cain looked at Damon to see if he had any objection.

Please object, please object.

But Damon just nodded, and the strands of gray hair around his face burned silver in the glow of the fire. "Yeah, that's probably good. Cain needs some sleep."

A pacifier, perhaps, and a warm blankie. Cain nodded once and grabbed his bag from the base of the stairs.

"Eli, can you take a look at his arm first?" Damon asked, and Cain paused.

"What's wrong with his arm?" Eli's skeptical gaze flitted over Cain.

"I scratched it. It's fine. I don't need help. But… thank you." Damn his ingrained manners.

"Cain," Damon warned, but this time Eli cut him off.

"He says it's a scratch, man. Leave the kid alone."

"Yeah, Big Daddy. Leave the kid alone," Cain deadpanned, pleased to see Damon's jaw tighten. "Thanks for the bed," he told Eli, and he walked himself up the stairs.

"Who the hell is that?" Cain heard Eli mutter, just before he closed the door to the bedroom. He hovered by the door to hear Damon's answer.

"It's complicated," Damon sighed.

And Cain shut the door silently. Maybe he was better off not knowing.

CHAPTER ELEVEN

"Explain it to me like I'm five," Eli told Damon, handing him a tumbler of whiskey before taking a seat on the opposite end of the couch.

Damon ran both hands through his hair and tried to figure out how to begin this story about his sister and niece, and how the hell to explain Cain without implicating him in his father's sins.

"Huh. That fucked up? Okay, then. How about I ask questions and you answer," Eli offered after a minute of silence.

Damon nodded. "Yeah, that's probably better," he agreed, taking a sip of his drink.

"You're fucking him."

Damon nearly choked. "What?"

"Come on, Damon. Don't bullshit me. I can tell just by the way you look at him. And I can sure as hell tell from the way *he* looks at *you*."

"What's that supposed to mean?"

"Don't tell me you didn't notice? Boy was flaying me with his eyes every time I said your name." Eli arranged himself on the sofa more comfortably and chuckled in a satisfied way. "It was fun messing with him."

Damon stared at him blankly. "I don't get it. Messing with him how?"

"He thinks you and I hooked up," Eli said. Smiling mischievously, he added, "Which is funny as hell."

"Since you're *straight* as hell."

"And ain't that a sad loss for the gay men of America?" Eli teased, patting Damon's good leg. "But the boy looked like he was gonna have kittens every time I laid a finger on you. Seriously, how'd you end up with him? He's young enough to…"

"Be my kid? I'm aware." In fact, there was roughly the same age difference between the two of them as there was between Chelsea and Molly. *Big Daddy and kid, indeed.* Damon chuckled ruefully as he stared at the drink in his hand. "But apparently that doesn't matter to my dick." He looked back at Eli. "And I like him."

Eli shrugged noncommittally. "Seems a little bratty to me, but okay."

"Nah, he's not. I mean, he is." Damon laughed again, thinking of the way Cain had acted in the dressing room at the fundraiser, and the little temper tantrum later in his apartment. "Sometimes. But in a good way. He's… good for me."

Eli's brows went up. "You think?"

"Maybe. I don't know." He stole a glance up to the loft area, wondered whether Cain would be able to sleep or whether, despite the long day, he was as keyed up as Damon. "He saved me," Damon said, thinking back to yesterday morning… and then further back to the fundraiser. "Actually, twice."

"Huh. Wouldn't've pegged him that way. Kid seems a little… entitled."

"Well, he's not," Damon said sharply. "And he's not a kid, either. There were bullets flying yesterday morning, and that *kid* jumped on top of me and Molly. Then he drove us here over two days, with zero complaints."

Somehow it was fine when he called Cain a kid, but that was different... or something. In any case, he'd be damned if he'd let Eli do it.

"Bullets?" Eli leaned forward and slammed his empty glass on the coffee table, his eyes sharp. "You're kinda burying the lede here, chief."

"Yeah. I guess I am." He took a deep breath and told Eli everything that had happened over the past few months - Jack Peabody and his confession, the fundraiser with Senator Shaw, the threats against Chelsea, and the incident the previous morning. By the time he was done, he was rubbing his stiff leg and wishing he'd taken one of the pain pills Cain had grabbed off the kitchen counter *because Damon might need them.*

It was a tiny thing, but Damon couldn't remember the last time someone had thought of his comfort that way.

"Fuck, Damon," Eli whispered, pushing to his feet and running a hand over his thick black hair. "You've got some asshole, power-crazed senator after you, and you brought those girls *here*?"

"I'm sorry, Eli. I really didn't know where else to go," Damon told him. "I didn't know who else would keep them safe while I figured out how to stop this."

Eli grunted. "And the kid? Jesus." He blew out a breath, obvious disgust on his face. "The senator is his *father.*"

"Yeah, and *my* father is an asshole who threw me and Chelsea to the wolves at every opportunity," Damon reminded him.

It was funny how Eli's thoughts so closely matched

Damon's own doubts, but when Eli voiced them, Damon felt compelled to defend Cain.

"I'm not gonna judge him based on his father," Damon told Eli - told *both* of them, really. "And once again, don't call him *kid*. It really pisses him off."

Eli gave Damon a pointed glance, clearly indicating that Cain's feelings weren't his priority.

"Can you protect them?" Damon asked. "I'm gonna leave in the morning with Cain. But I need to know Chelsea and Molly are safe."

"I'll take care of the girls," Eli said with a nod. "Don't worry about that. Fuckers better not show up here, or they'll find out exactly what I'm capable of." He hesitated, scratching at his beard. "You really trust the ki-, uh, *Cain*? You really trust Cain? *Think*, Damon, and not with your dick. How did they find you in the middle of Pennsylvania so quickly when you didn't use credit cards and didn't leave a paper trail? A hit like that, with pros like them… it's not the kind of thing they can just set up on the fly. They had to know where you were going practically the second you did."

"You're right." Damon let his frustration show. "And I don't fucking *know* how they figured it out. Hell, as far as I can tell, they didn't know I was alive until two days ago, and now suddenly…" He shook his head. "But it wasn't Cain."

Even from the first confused moment, he'd known that. The look of shocked horror on Cain's face, the determination in every line of his body as he'd shielded Damon and Molly.

Eli sighed. "I get that you don't want to believe it. He's cute, if you're into that kind of thing. But how else…"

"Those guys were shooting at him, same as me, E. He's the one who got hit with the flying glass or whatever in that shit-show." Even now, the very idea of it pissed him off - that Cain had been the one to get hurt, that Damon hadn't been able to protect him. "I don't know who they were, I don't know who sent them, but I don't believe Cain contacted anyone. Hell, his cell phone's dead. He's as much a pawn in all this as Chelsea and Molly and me."

"Alright, fine. Have it your way." Eli shrugged. "But what are you and *Cain* gonna do while the girls are here?"

"Cain had an idea that we could head to Nashville. We could search his parents' house, his dad's office. Apparently, the senator's a stickler for keeping physical records of things. Maybe we can find some evidence tying his father to the Seavers' plane crash, or some indication he knew what Jack was up to that we can present to the authorities."

"You're wading into a lion's den so you can steal its tooth? You hobbling on one leg, while he's got a bum arm. *Christ.*"

"If you've got a better idea, I'm all ears. I've considered and rejected every other possibility, and this is pretty much the only option I've got now." He rolled his eyes and tossed Eli a smile. "You remember my motto? Hard and easy don't matter…"

"Yeah, yeah. When there's no plan B. I remember." Eli sighed. "And you think he's going to turn that evidence over to the authorities, even though he won't go to them on his own?"

Once again, Eli's thoughts lined up exactly with Damon's own fears. Was he just being stupid here? Eli was rational, removed from the situation. If he really thought this was a shitty idea, should Damon listen? He glanced up at the loft once again.

Eli didn't know Cain. And yeah, maybe Damon didn't know him very well yet either, but everything he learned about the man made him *want* to know him, and want to trust him.

"I don't claim to understand all his reasons, Eli." He chuckled shortly. "Frankly, I don't understand my own fucking reasoning half the time. But my gut tells me I can trust him, so I'm choosing to do that."

Eli shifted his neck back and stared at the ceiling, one hand braced on his hip. "Alright," he finally said with a shake of his head. "You feel that strongly about it, I'll reserve judgment." He turned and speared Damon with a glance. "But promise me you won't let your guard down completely, Damon. Cain might be a pawn, but he's his *father's* pawn. And it won't matter what his intentions are when his father moves him around the chessboard."

CHAPTER TWELVE

"Just out of curiosity, how long is this silent treatment going to last?" Cain demanded as he negotiated the car down a twisty two-lane highway. They'd left Eli's cabin before daybreak, after saying a surprisingly emotional goodbye to Molly and Chelsea and obtaining Eli's promise to purchase a burner phone as soon as possible in order to stay in contact with them. That had been nearly two hours ago, but other than a few brief, barked directions and one stop to take a leak, Damon had been completely, *stubbornly* silent the entire time, which was not helping Cain's own mood. Not one little bit.

"Maybe when I stop being pissed at you for going to bed last night without letting Eli check your arm." Damon folded his arms across his chest.

Cain exhaled sharply as he pulled around a minivan full of children and got them back in their lane. "And how was I supposed to know it was a bullet wound? I figured it was a rock or glass or something, just like you."

"You *weren't* supposed to know!" Damon exploded, turning in the seat to face Cain. "That's the whole point of having someone trained in first aid checking out your injury, so you can have it treated properly before the whole fucking thing gets infected and your fucking arm falls off!"

Cain's eyes nearly rolled back in his head. "Right, of course. Not that Eli is a doctor or anything, but apparently his magic powers extend to medicine. If my arm falls off, why don't you just bring me back to Eli and he can reattach it?"

"What the *fuck* is wrong with you?" Damon cried, throwing his hands in the air.

"Not a damn thing! That's what I'm trying to tell you!" Cain roared back. His chest heaved, his breaths nearly audible in the sudden silence that rang through the car. He tried to regain his hold on his temper.

It wasn't Damon's fault that he and Eli were... whatever they were. Or, more to the point, it wasn't Damon's fault that Cain's stupid crush on him had grown all out of proportion. *Be an adult about this, Shaw. Hooking up means nothing.*

"Damon, chill," he said in a calmer voice. "The great and powerful Eli said I just have to keep it bandaged and cleaned."

"Chill? Are you kidding me? You were *shot*, Cain!" Damon crossed his arms and went silent again.

Cain didn't get Damon's mood at all. But then, the whole morning had been pretty fucked up, starting from the moment Eli had barged into his room - well, into Eli's *own* room, really, where Cain had finally fallen into a fitful sleep - with a glint in his eye, demanding to see Cain's injury.

"Damon says he wants me to look at it," Eli had told him when he'd refused. "And frankly, I don't give a good goddamn what you'd prefer."

After a quick assessment of Eli's height, bulk, and proximity to the door, Cain had grudgingly relented. Eli had pulled off the bandage Damon had placed there yesterday and whistled through his teeth, his eyes briefly lifting to Cain's. "How'd you say you hurt this again? Cause this wasn't caused by some chunk of glass, kid."

Because Eli was a wound-detective, too. Asshole.

"How do we even really know it was a bullet?" Cain asked Damon now. "Eli's not psychic, or anything. It just looks like a big cut."

"Really?" Damon shook his head in disgust. "Eli was in the service, remember? He knows what a gunshot wound looks like."

Cain pressed his lips together. He wanted to fire back with something snarky, like *"Is there anything Eli doesn't fucking know?"* He mentally patted himself on the back for withstanding the temptation.

Last night, he'd tossed and turned for hours, listening to the indistinct hum of the conversation happening down-stairs while his arm had burned like fire and his mind had whirled. He'd had no idea where things stood with him and Damon, but that was fine. *Really.*

He was here to help Damon get his sister and Molly to safety, and then to help bring his father to justice. The stupid crush he'd developed on Damon Fitzpatrick had nothing to do with it. And so what if he and Eli were fucking downstairs? Damon hadn't made him any promises, after all, so he was free to do whatever he wanted. Eli was enormous and gorgeous, and some kind of superhero. He wasn't a *kid.*

So, fine. Apparently there was no way for Cain to win here. His father was an asshole, which made Cain's every thought and action suspect. It fucking sucked, but Cain could almost understand it. Damon was making it quite clear that whatever they'd had two... or was it three? ... nights ago, and whatever strange emotion he'd seen in

Damon's eyes in the parking lot the other morning - had been a momentary blip.

Cain could hardly abandon Damon on the side of the road, but he wasn't going to take another mile of Damon's silent-treatment bullshit, either. He put on his blinker and pulled onto the grass verge at the side of the road.

"What the hell are you doing?" Damon demanded.

"Stopping."

Damon glared at him. "Any particular reason?"

"I'm on strike," he said coolly. "Until you explain to me exactly what you want me to do here. Am I supposed to apologize for being shot? I *am* truly sorry, if for no other reason than because it hurts like a bitch. But I sure as hell didn't do it as a personal insult to you, so could you maybe stop being an asshole?"

Damon blinked, scowled, then blinked again.

"I didn't say you did it as an insult to me," Damon said, though his peevish tone indicated Cain's words hadn't been too far from the truth. He darted a look at Cain. "I'm pissed that you got hurt. And I'm more pissed that I didn't insist on you having it checked last night."

"But it was my choice," Cain reminded him reasonably.

"A stupid choice."

"Fine." Cain rolled his eyes again. "But it's *my* arm, and *my* stupid choice, right? You're *not* responsible for me."

Damon's jaw locked and he looked stubbornly out the windshield, like he wouldn't argue the point.

"Right, Damon?" Cain persisted.

Damon turned to face him. "I feel pretty damn responsible. Why wouldn't you let Eli look at it last night?" he demanded before Cain could reply.

Cain's teeth clacked together, and it was his turn to look at the endless blue sky and road laid out before them. "I was tired. I... didn't feel like it."

"Really? That's why?"

"Of course. Why else?"

"I dunno." Damon shrugged. "Eli seemed to feel there was some personal issue."

Cain glanced at him quickly. "No."

"It wasn't that you thought there was anything happening between Eli and me?"

"I-I mean, no. That's not… It's none of my business if there is," Cain said adamantly. "That had nothing to do with… anything."

"Huh."

"*Huh?* What do you mean, *huh?*"

Damon shook his head, but Cain could see a strange light dancing in his eyes.

"Eli is straight," Damon said.

Cain scowled. "Yeah, well, so am *I* if you go by popular opinion."

"No, Cain. Like, we've had a conversation about it. He has zero interest in men. And there has *never* been anything between us but friendship."

Cain blinked. *Alright, well… Good. That was good.*

"None of my business," Cain said dismissively, but Damon reached over and grabbed his chin, turning Cain's face toward his.

"Isn't it?" Damon asked.

"Is it?" Cain whispered, and Damon shrugged, but the smile on his face made something bright and warm flare to life in Cain's chest. Oh, this was dangerous. This was so, so dangerous. He was way too happy about the fact that Eli and Damon had never been anything but friends, and way, *way* too happy about the idea that Damon thought this was his business.

"I don't like you being hurt," Damon whispered. "Just… for fuck's sake, don't get hurt again." Damon moved his hand from Cain's chin to cup the back of his neck, his thumb dragging along Cain's jaw.

Cain laughed shortly. "Oh, says *you*, Mister Drop-and-Roll with the fucked-up leg."

"That's different," Damon insisted.

"*Sure*," Cain said, but he glanced at Damon and both of them burst out laughing.

Damon dragged his hands up and down his face, and Cain could hear the scratch of stubble against his palms. "Alright. I'm sorry. I've been an asshole. I'll be better, okay?"

Cain nodded shortly. "Apology accepted," he said magnanimously. "And I guess... I guess I haven't been particularly mature, if we're being honest. Now we can—"

But before he could move to shift the car back into gear, Damon was reaching a hand over the console, dragging Cain toward him by the back of the neck. Their lips met in a drugging kiss.

Momentarily startled, it took Cain a second to respond, but when he did, he surged forward, pushing Damon back against his headrest. Cain poured every ounce of his hurt, frustration, and annoyance into the kiss, and Damon took every bit, threading his long fingers through Cain's hair and groaning into Cain's mouth. It was hot, frantic, and perfect - tongues dueling, teeth clacking. But then Damon tugged his hair and pushed back, taking the kiss deeper and gentler - calming, soothing, and reassuring.

When they broke apart a minute later, Cain's head was spinning and his breath was coming in pants.

"You... you apologize well," Cain told him, and Damon grinned.

"Drive, Cain," he said, shaking his head.

And after a deep, steadying breath, Cain did.

THE MORNING PASSED QUICKLY, and despite Damon's insistence on backtracking and taking detours at every opportunity, they found themselves an hour south of Nashville shortly after lunchtime.

"Oh, shit, not this song again," Cain complained.

"Thought you Nashville folks lived for country ballads."

Cain gave him side-eye. "There are so many things wrong with that statement."

He reached for the radio control, only for Damon to bat his hand away. "Navigator picks the tunes," he said.

Uh, what?

"Bullshit." Cain threw him a scowl. "Driver is the DJ. Everyone knows this. It's road trip law."

"Well, you lost your opportunity the first two times this song came on and you did nothing. You're fired."

"Fired… as DJ?" Cain clarified.

Damon shrugged and spread his hands out in mock apology. "Cain, I don't make the rules."

Cain burst out laughing and shook his head. "By all means then, please make a selection." He waved his hand at the radio like a game show hostess.

Damon scrolled through all of the pre-set stations on Drew's satellite radio, his frown getting deeper each time. "Drew listens to Sports Radio, NPR, and classical music?"

Cain shrugged. "This doesn't surprise me."

Damon kept punching buttons, and the sound of classic rock filled the car. "There we go," he said.

"Aerosmith?" Cain said dubiously, and Damon turned to look at him.

"Okay, pause. Whatever you're about to say right now, I want you to think about it carefully," Damon warned. "This could have a significant impact on our… friendship."

Cain's lips quirked. He'd almost swear that Damon had been about to say relationship, but honestly, *friendship* was pretty fucking cool too.

"Nothing wrong with Aerosmith," Cain allowed. "If it makes you feel comfortable."

"Comfortable?"

"You know, older people need their routine. They like things a certain way. It's cool," Cain said quickly, loving the scowl on Damon's face. "We can totally listen to this."

"Listen, *sonny*, respect your elders. These are the Bad Boys of Boston. They're kings."

Cain rolled his eyes. "I mean, they *were*," he agreed. "Two decades ago."

"Oh, tell me you didn't just say that. Tell me you did not just shade Aerosmith."

Damon sounded truly shocked, and Cain bit his lip. In truth, he probably owned every Aerosmith album available, but the opportunity to needle his *navigator* was too good to pass up.

"Don't get agitated, Big Daddy," Cain said in his most placating tone. "I'm not arguing with you."

"You know," Damon said, and despite having his eyes on the road, Cain could feel Damon's gaze burning his cheek like a laser-beam. "You're right. I really shouldn't be selfish. I'll pick something you'll like better, kid."

"Oh. Well thank you! That's thoughtful," Cain said. "I like Alt Nation, or maybe…"

The strains of children's voices shrieking tepid pop filled the speakers.

"What the fuck?"

"It's the kids' station," Damon said, his growly voice placid and his face blank.

Cain gasped. *This was war.*

"I wish I had my phone," he grumbled, giving a look to

the backseat, where he'd stowed the bag containing his dead cell. He'd have to try to find a charger when they stopped for the night. "All my music is on there. I could find you some screamo you'd love. Reminds me of you when you're cranky."

"Oh, check it out. *Opera.*"

"What? I don't like opera!"

"When they hit the high notes, it reminds me of *you* when you're cranky," Damon countered.

And Cain couldn't help but laugh.

The whole world - well, *his* whole world - was burning. The past two days had been a shit-show from start to finish, he had a gunshot wound marring the tattooed sleeve on his arm, he had no idea what the hell this evening's search of his father's office would bring, and for over twenty-four hours, his mind had been dancing around the knowledge that someone - probably his own father - had sent men to track them down and shoot at them — himself, Damon, Chelsea, and a *three-year-old*, for God's sake.

It was pretty fucked up that at this precise moment, he was still happier than he'd been in months.

And then Damon had to go and open his mouth. "So. Tell me about you and Jack."

Cain flinched. He couldn't help it. He'd actively avoided thinking, let alone talking, about the fact that both he and Damon had been involved with that asshole at roughly the same time. He focused on the road in front of him for a silent moment, then exhaled a long breath.

Yeah, okay, so maybe this issue was like a splinter beneath the surface of his *friendship* with Damon, just sitting there festering.

"What about him?" he asked flatly.

"How'd it start?" Damon's voice was gentle, and when

Cain darted a glance in his direction, he was steadfastly looking out the window.

"Can we turn Aerosmith back on instead?" Cain pleaded.

Damon didn't reply.

"Fine." Cain took a deep breath. "I guess… I guess it started maybe three years ago?" He tried to do math in his head, and shrugged. "Something like that."

"Christ, Cain! You were, what? Twenty-two?" Damon's outrage made him smirk.

"Still twenty-one," Cain corrected. "I remember because one of the first and only places he ever took me was to a rodeo on my twenty-second birthday." He shot Damon a glance. "For the record, I do not enjoy the rodeo."

"Noted."

Cain shrugged. "He just… started being friendly to me, you know? He'd been working for my dad for years, and he had to know I was gay. I mean, I never officially came out to my parents, but I never hid my sexuality among my friends. Not when I was younger. It was kinda like my family's version of Don't Ask, Don't Tell, but anyone who looked at the pictures on my bedroom walls had to know." Cain gripped the steering wheel more tightly. God, he hated talking about this stuff.

"Yeah? Hot guys?" Damon asked.

"Mmm. Gerard Way." When Damon stared at him blankly, Cain added, "My Chemical Romance? *Helena? I'm Not Okay?* No?" Damon shook his head, and Cain pressed a hand to his chest. "You're breaking teenage Cain's emo heart here, you really are."

Cain shifted in his seat and continued, "Anyway, I dated a couple of guys. Had a boyfriend for a while." He didn't want to talk about Jesse right now. He couldn't. "But then my dad's political ambitions became a thing, and suddenly I was back in the closet. Got a respectable haircut, the posters came down, and I moved to Nashville where I didn't date. *At all.* But then the summer after my junior year in college, Jack started paying attention to me."

He swallowed, sickened by his own stupidity. "He'd smile at me, laugh at my jokes, ask about the classes I liked and what I wanted to do after graduation. My family was... I dunno. They never gave a shit how I felt about things or what I wanted, and I felt like... like I could be myself with Jack." He chanced a glance at Damon's profile. "Dumb, huh?"

"Not even a little," Damon said sadly.

Cain drummed his fingers on the steering wheel. The last thing he wanted was Damon's pity, for fuck's sake.

"Anyway, I was a dumbass. He would blow hot and cold, all over me one day and then cold-shouldering me the next. It was one of those things where he was happy to ignore me until the second he had any inkling I was going to hook up with someone else, and then suddenly he'd call me again, or stop by my apartment at school out of the blue and we'd end up sleeping together. I always... I always just assumed it was because of my dad. He didn't want to get too close because he was worried about getting caught."

Damon frowned. "Don't you think it was?"

Cain shook his head and finally put words to the thought that had been nagging him more and more often these days, as he realized just what his father was capable of. "I think he was getting close to me because my father asked him to. To keep me quiet and contained, just in case I ever considered doing something truly terrible, like defying the family and coming out."

Damon inhaled sharply, and Cain noticed that his hand was clenched into a white-knuckled fist. "Jesus. Just when I think I understand just how awful your father can be..."

Cain shrugged, because what was there to say?

"It was never a dating thing. Looking back, after the first initial bit it was just a series of hookups. We never went out, we never talked about anything serious. I was naive, and Jesus, I was lonely." He laughed. "I made it into something it wasn't." Cain raised an eyebrow at Damon. "Guess Jack was getting his needs met elsewhere, too?"

Damon rolled his eyes and gave an exaggerated shudder, and suddenly it was okay again. Not quite funny, but... less awful. Not the shameful, horrible thing he'd tormented himself with.

Cain ran a hand through his hair before putting it back on the steering wheel. Eli's shampoo smelled like mint and medicine, and now Cain's hair had the same scent. Damon's too. Was it weird to be excited because he and Damon smelled the same?

God. Would he ever learn not to make things into a bigger deal than they were?

He cleared his throat. "So, uh. Maybe you can tell me your shitty story now and make me feel a little less stupid?"

Damon huffed and reached over to run his knuckle down Cain's cheek. No doubt Cain's face was tomato-red.

"You weren't stupid, baby" Damon said, and Cain glanced at him. "Believe it. You were young and he took advantage of you. I didn't have that excuse." Damon's hand dropped to the center console, and he wiped absently at a line of dust there. "You know I'm a pilot and a mechanic?"

Cain nodded.

"I worked at Central, the little regional airport your dad liked to fly into whenever he came to Boston on business, and I flew most of the charter flights. Jack introduced himself to me as your dad's pilot, and we became friends. We'd go out for drinks whenever he was in town, which was pretty often. Hell, we'd commiserate about how shitty our employers were. It took a month, or maybe a little longer, before we slept together."

From the corner of his eye, Cain could see Damon darting a glance at him.

"I'm sure he was working on your father's orders, then, too. But I was almost forty, so if either of us should have known better, it was me."

Cain's heart twisted at the pain in Damon's voice.

"He's a shithead who knows how to say exactly what you want to hear," Cain spat.

"Well, if that's true for me, it's gotta be true for you, too."

"Both of us just got played by a pro, then?" Cain mused. "Yeah. I guess. I can accept that."

"He was the last person I had sex with," Damon said. "Until the other night with you."

Cain's eyes widened. "Really?"

"Yep."

"Me too," Cain admitted, then he started laughing again and Damon joined in. "This is so fucked up."

"*So* fucked up," Damon agreed, rubbing his fingers across his eyes. "But you know what? I don't give a shit."

Cain kept his eyes on the road. "You don't?"

"I don't," Damon said. "I'm done thinking about him." He reached over to squeeze Cain's hand where it rested on the steering wheel.

Cain grinned and put the directional on, pulling into the parking lot of a fast food restaurant and sliding the car into Park.

"What are we doing here?" Damon asked.

"We're getting close to the city," Cain told him. "And it's time to finalize our plan."

"Okay."

"Okay," Cain repeated, biting his lip. "So, my dad has

an official office downtown. It's relatively new. He has staffers who work there full-time, doing fundraising and handling calls from his constituents and stuff. I-I mean, I guess it's possible that he might have kept things there, but I really doubt it. It's not nearly private enough, and he doesn't have enough control over it."

Damon frowned. "What's the other option?"

"His home office," Cain said promptly. "I mean, I would think that's where things would be since it's more private. Nobody's there except when he is. Also, I've gotta say, it's gonna be easier to get in there, since I have the access codes." He rubbed a hand over his face, suddenly exhausted and unsure. "Or, *Jesus*, I don't know, Damon. Maybe he'd keep the stuff at the public office, just because no one would think to look there? I'm like that guy in The Princess Bride who keeps overthinking which cup is poisoned. I'm trying to outsmart the master plotter, and I'm really not sure I'm up to this task."

Damon's hand slid over once again to touch Cain's, but this time he threaded their fingers together, and held Cain's hand on top of the center console.

"Trust your instincts, okay? Because, I trust you, Cain," he said slowly.

Cain's throat went tight. He hadn't realized just how much he needed to hear those exact words from him. He looked into Damon's bright hazel eyes.

"You sure? Remember, the guy in the movie ended up dead," Cain deadpanned.

But Damon just squeezed his hand again and smiled. "Positive."

"The home office," Cain said more confidently, and Damon's smile turned into a grin.

"Then that's where we're going. But first we're going to

get a hotel room. And before we do *that*, we need to stop at the pharmacy to grab some supplies."

"Supplies?" Cain repeated in surprise. *Like, condoms and lube?* Not that Cain had any objection, *at all,* but he'd really expected they'd talk more first, or…

"Bandages for your arm, Cain," Damon said, shaking his head. Little laugh lines exploded from the sides of his eyes when he smiled and Cain would gladly be embarrassed a million more times if he got to see those crinkles again.

"Right," Cain agreed. "Totally. I knew that."

CHAPTER THIRTEEN

"What's 089208?" Damon asked, watching as Cain put a passcode into the keypad that controlled the massive black iron gates outside Senator Shaw's sprawling suburban home. "Anniversary? Birthday?"

After Cain had made a quick stop at a pharmacy and another at a hotel where they'd rented a room, dumped their meager belongings, and quickly changed Cain's bandage, they'd gotten back on the road to the senator's house, about thirty minutes outside of the city. When Cain had turned onto his street, Damon's eyes had widened. He'd seen mansions before, but the concentrated wealth of the area, literally glinting in the setting sun, was pretty stunning.

"No. Neither," Cain sighed, turning to give him a look as the gates slid smoothly open. "It's the date they broke ground on the headquarters at Seaver Tech."

"You're kidding," Damon said, but Cain shook his head. "You're telling me your father types that passcode in every time he comes home?"

"Yeah, that's what I'm telling you," Cain agreed, but he shook his head again. "I'm not saying I understand it."

God. Damon's stomach clenched at the idea of someone who could murder his best friend, but still use the date they'd co-founded a company as his security code. Were there any limits Emmett Shaw wouldn't go to?

Cain pulled the car around the semi-circular brick-paved driveway and parked directly in front of the house. "You ready?"

"I guess."

Cain jogged up a short flight of stairs to the front door and paused to wait for Damon. Though not quite as bad as it had been yesterday, Damon's leg still hurt like a bitch whenever he put weight on it. Still, when Cain had suggested buying a pair of crutches at the pharmacy, Damon had refused. Coddling himself wouldn't speed his recovery, and it sure as fuck wouldn't make him feel better either.

When Damon got to the top step, Cain entered another passcode. "This one's the date my father was elected, with the numbers 9–4-9 at the end." He looked over his shoulder at Damon and explained. "It spells out W-I-N."

Damon wasn't sure what expression he had on his face, but whatever it was made Cain laugh softly. "I know. I know, it's gross."

They stepped into the house, which seemed unnaturally hushed.

"Nobody working?" Damon whispered. "No staff?"

Cain shook his head and answered in a hushed voice, "My parents are gone on a fundraising tour for various politicians for a couple of weeks. Because *nothing* says *Happy Holidays* like promising millions to your local politicians, right? Usually the staff stay here to take care of the house, but not this time. My parents gave them the week off for Thanksgiving."

"No security guards? No cameras?"

"No guards when my dad's not here, which means the outside cameras are recording, but aren't being monitored. Unlikely anyone would check them unless an alarm was set off. And there are no cameras inside the house at all. That's one thing my mother put her foot down about." Cain rolled his eyes. "She'd rather be caught dead than have someone leak a photo of her in her bathrobe, sans makeup."

Damon nodded. "So, if no one is here," he muttered. "Then why are we whispering?"

Cain shrugged. "I don't really know, except... I think I'm conditioned not to attract notice in this house." He grinned. "Hard to break the habit."

He led Damon up an enormous curved white staircase to the second floor, and then to an imposing set of double doors. "This is his office," Cain said.

Damon wrapped his t-shirt cuff around his hand then pushed at the knob. *Locked.*

"No worries," Cain told him. He went to the doorway of the room across the hall and stood on tiptoe so he could run his fingertips along the top edge of the doorframe. "Aha. Gotcha."

"That's where he keeps the key?" Damon demanded.

Cain chuckled. "Nah. That's where I keep the skeleton key." He jimmied the locked door, and a second later, the latch popped and the door swung inward. "I had to rescue my cell phone on more than one occasion when I was younger," he said. He took a second to put the key back atop the door, and Damon smirked. Putting everything back in its proper place was such a fucking *Cain* thing to do.

"Lead the way then, Secret Agent Shaw," Damon told him.

Cain rolled his eyes and shouldered his way past Damon into the office.

Dark wood and brown leather were the first things Damon noticed, as though it was an old English hunting lodge. The air inside the room was still and chilly, with an air of disuse. Damon limped forward, being cautious not to leave fingerprints on anything.

Cain paused in the middle of the room, looking around. "I have no idea where to even begin," he said. "There's a file cabinet, but… Maybe it would be hidden?"

"Does he have a safe?" Damon asked.

"Nah, not here. Not that I know of, anyway." He moved to a large painting of a horse suspended on the wall next to the door and lifted the edge to peer behind. "Nothing here."

"Check behind the other paintings and maybe in the closet," Damon instructed. "Since you're more mobile. I'll sit at the desk and check the file cabinet."

Long minutes ticked by, and neither of them made a sound. Damon diligently sorted through bills and receipts, but he'd already known when he'd found the cabinet unlocked that he wouldn't find anything useful in here. He huffed out a frustrated breath, and let his eyes track Cain, who had found a cardboard banker box at the bottom of the closet and was determinedly searching through it, as though his father might have absently chucked evidence that could implicate him in a felony into a random box and shoved it in a closet.

Still, the utter absorption on the man's face and the graceful movement of his fingers were soothing and maybe a little bewitching. Damon had to force himself to look away.

Behind Shaw's desk was an enormous window that looked out on what had to have been two or three acres of manicured lawns burnished pink-gold in the evening light. It was pretty, but empty… much like the house itself.

Damon's eyes drifted down to the credenza below the window, where several perfectly-posed family portraits rested. His eyes caught on one of Cain, back when he must have been seven or eight. His dark hair was longer and neatly parted to one side, his deep blue eyes huge and innocent, and Damon had the strongest urge to grab this younger-Cain and take him to safety, far away from Emmett Shaw and his bullshit. He shook his head. There was another of a blonde girl who must have been Cain's sister, and several more of a young Senator Shaw standing with his wife. But the middle picture caught his attention and held it.

"Cain? What's this?" he asked.

Cain came toward him, feet hushed on the plush carpet, and paused at his elbow before picking up the frame to look at the picture more closely. "Oh," he said softly, the single syllable sounding both fond and sad. "These are the Seavers, the McCanns, and my family. You probably recognize most of them. See? The tall, thin one is Bas, and Drew is the one with his arm around his shoulder. They both filled out a lot, huh? The scrawny one there is me," he chuckled. "And the slightly-less-scrawny one with the cowlicks is Cam. That's his dad behind him. And my parents. Mrs. Seaver with the blue headband, and then the McCanns, before their divorce. Mrs. McCann was a stunner back then, wasn't she? And the girls on the stairs trying to look like grownups are my sister Cady and Drew's sister Amy. They were best friends."

He sighed and sank back against the desk. "I remember when this picture was taken - the first time we all got together at my parents' cabin in the Smokies, not long after they bought the place. The first of, like, a hundred times we all vacationed there. My parents gutted the whole cabin and added on a third floor - it's all modern now. It's still one of my favorite places in the world, but I liked it better before," Cain mused.

"Does your family still own the cabin?" Damon asked, his heart racing.

"Oh yeah. But we haven't been there much since Amy McCann and the Seavers died. It's just not the same, you know? It was a family place back then, and the Seavers and McCanns were part of our family. My father's gone maybe three or four times this year for the fishing, and maybe a month ago, the whole family went, along with a couple of my dad's donors." He made a sour face. "That was the first time my dad brought strangers there. Though, you know, if anyone officially asked, I'd probably have to lie and say the Stornoviches were old family friends, too, not campaign contributors." He rolled his eyes, but when he looked up and his gaze met Damon's, he frowned. "What?"

"Your dad has a secluded cabin that hardly anyone has been to?" Damon asked sharply. "Don't you think it's possible whatever evidence he kept could be *there*?"

"I… I mean, I guess? Shit." Cain ran a hand through his hair, tousling the strands to inky spikes, and Damon couldn't help but cup his hand around the back of the man's neck, pulling him in for a short kiss.

"What was that for?" Cain asked when Damon pulled back. Cain's fingers traced the contours of his own lips, like he still felt Damon's imprinted there.

Good.

"How about because you're fucking adorable? How about because I *can*?"

Cain's eyes flashed with something Damon couldn't name, then he lifted himself to his toes and threw his arm around Damon's neck, pulling him down for another kiss.

Damon's injured leg twitched, but he steadied himself with a hand on the desk and returned the kiss enthusiastically.

He pulled back a second later, and they both smiled.

Christ, they did not have time for this, but Damon wouldn't do anything to stop it. If the past year and a half had taught him nothing else, it was that life could change on a dime. He'd take his happiness wherever he could find it.

Cain set the photograph precisely back on the credenza, and giving one parting pat to Damon's abs, he went to put the banker's box back in the closet.

"Wait," Damon said, his distracted brain finally catching up to something Cain had said earlier. "Did you say Stornovich?"

"Yeah. Uh, Adam and Ilya, I think. Father and son. They're in real estate investments, which is not particularly exciting, but whatever." Cain shrugged as he straightened and dusted his hands off. "They weren't exactly friendly, but then hardly any of my father's donors are. With the exception of the Fassbenders." He grimaced as he joined Damon. "Shit. I really need to call them, and I totally forgot to pick up a charger at the store. The damn thing is back in Boston and I don't have a spare. Remind me later?"

"Cain," Damon said, interrupting him with a hand on his arm. "Have you ever heard of SILA?" He could hear that his voice was rougher than ever, with a combination of excitement and worry.

"I don't think so?"

"It's a crime syndicate. The word is Russian for *power*."

"Oh! Wait, yeah. This reporter at my dad's fundraiser did a whole big story on —." His eyes went wide. "Wait, are you saying—?"

"What I'm saying is that the Stornoviches are a pretty well-known family inside SILA. They were nearly indicted by a grand jury last year, but managed to skate. It's not hard evidence, but it's a damn interesting coincidence."

"Wait, no. These guys weren't criminals. They were, like, short, portly, balding dudes who liked golf. One was old enough to be my grandfather. No guns, no… leather trench coats."

Damon raised one eyebrow.

"*Whatever.* Trench coats seem like a mobster thing to wear. My point is, these dudes were super normal. They looked like bankers… or like what they *are*, real estate investors." His voice was begging Damon to agree, to say that the men Emmett Shaw had invited into his family home hadn't been criminals, that such a thing was impossible. But they both knew it wasn't.

"And what would you say your father looks like, Cain?" Damon asked gently.

Cain squeezed his eyes shut, and once again, Damon wrapped an arm around the back of his neck, this time lending him support.

"I remember thinking, back at his fundraiser, that my dad looked like this normal guy who liked to tailgate and eat Cheetos." His eyes flew open. "He *is* that guy, you know, Damon? God. He used to make model cars with me when I was five or six. We watched football. Though, granted, I wasn't usually paying attention." He gasped out something that was a cross between a laugh and a sob. "How can he be a normal person and an evil mastermind at the same time?"

"It's gonna be okay, baby," Damon said, pressing his lips to Cain's hair. In truth, he had no idea if it would be okay, or even what *okay* looked like in this situation. He led Cain out onto the second-floor landing and jerked his head down the hall. "I kind of wanted to see your room while we were here," he teased, hoping to make Cain crack a smile. "Check out all your soccer trophies or whatever."

But Cain shook his head. "I don't have soccer trophies. And there's not a single thing here that I want to claim as mine," he whispered. His eyes swam with pain and confusion. "Just... get me out of here, Damon."

Despite his earlier tease, Damon couldn't have agreed more. This seemingly innocuous house - the perfect facade hiding a multitude of dirty secrets - chilled him to the bone, and he couldn't wait to get Cain out of there. He wrapped an arm around Cain's shoulders, squeezing gently so as not to disturb his injury. He only wished he could shield Cain from the other painful things in his life just as easily.

CHAPTER FOURTEEN

"You sure you don't want any more?" Damon asked, eyeing the sandwich in front of Cain at the small table in their hotel room.

Cain nodded woodenly. He'd taken two bites of the turkey sub, but it tasted like sawdust and the idea of eating another bite made him nauseous - perhaps not an uncommon reaction to finding out your father, who you already thought was pretty much the embodiment of evil, was actually even more evil than you'd thought.

His hands were cold, despite the warmth of the room, and he shivered as he chafed them together.

"Want me to fix your bandage again?" Damon asked, but Cain shook his head. Damon had already redone it when they'd first checked in and nothing had changed. It still ached, but not nearly as badly as it had the day before.

Damon stood, using the table to lever himself up, and he tugged Cain's hands until he was standing, too. He guided them both to the end of the bed, then tore off the bedspread and sat down, tucking Cain in next to him and wrapping him up in his strong arms. He rocked them both quietly for a minute, and Cain was grateful for the silence. He had no framework for processing what he'd learned tonight.

"Tell me something about your father," Damon said, like he was asking for a weather report.

Cain stiffened. "Damon, please. Not now."

"No, I don't mean something that's going to help us investigate him or lead us to evidence. Tell me a good thing, Cain. Any good thing."

"I-I can't think of any right now," Cain said crossly. "All I can see is that he has been a selfish, manipulative asshole for years. He's murdered people. He knows fucking mobsters. In the grand scheme of things, does it matter that he volunteered as Cady's soccer coach, or that he sang in the church choir?"

"Did he?" Damon asked. "In the church choir?"

Cain sighed. "Yeah he's a tenor and my mom and Cady are sopranos. They used to sing solos sometimes at Christmas."

"And what about you?"

"I sound like a cat whose tail's been stepped on," Cain said wryly.

"I don't believe it," Damon said, sounding like he could *very easily* believe it.

Cain chuckled. "Oh, believe it. I was better at debate team." He remembered himself as a scrawny high schooler, nervous in front of the podium. "My father used to coach me in debate stuff. Like, give me pointers on my speeches, and show me how to refine them. And then he used to listen to me practice a dozen times, until I had it down."

"That's a really good memory," Damon said.

"But is it?" Cain wasn't so sure. "All I can think of now is what his real motivation must have been, you know? Why did he want to help me? Was it because he wanted me to follow in his footsteps, or lie for him?" He exhaled and felt Damon's arm squeeze him more tightly.

"You can't think like that," Damon said. "You'll drive yourself crazy. Remember, Cain, nobody is just one thing, you know? Nobody wakes up in the morning twirling their mustache and saying, 'How can I be *eeevil* today?' And that includes your father. He's a bastard, but he also enjoys Cheetos and football. And he loves you, I'd put money on it, even if it's not in the way you want or need him to love you. I'm sure he thinks he's doing the right thing for you and the rest of your family."

"You're talking about a man who *paid* someone to *have sex with you*, to make sure you were implicated in a *crime you didn't commit*," Cain reminded him. And just saying the words made Cain feel like he was going to heave. How could Damon be so calm?

"Yeah. I know." The pressure of Damon's arm didn't ease or hesitate, even for a second. "I'm also talking about your dad, Cain. Those things aren't mutually exclusive."

Maybe. Maybe it was okay to believe there was something decent lurking somewhere inside his father. But... "All I can think is, he's out there condemning people for being gay like it's this huge fucking sin, a crime against God. And meanwhile..."

"Yeah," Damon agreed. "There is that. The hypocrisy is strong."

"But thank you," Cain whispered, letting himself lean against Damon's side a little more fully.

"For what?"

"For not expecting me to hate him."

Damon shrugged. "Come on. It's not that easy. It's not black and white."

"It's taking me a long time to figure this stuff out, I guess."

"But you'll get there eventually," Damon assured him, pulling him more tightly against his side. "I swear."

Somehow, when Damon said that, Cain almost believed him.

It occurred to him that this was usually the time when his mind would start to focus on all the ways this situation could be worse, but tonight he had no urge to play that game. Not when he could focus on the warm weight of Damon's arms around him, and almost imagine a future out there that might actually be *better* than what he had now.

Damon shifted and winced, stretching his injured leg out in front of him, and Cain stood quickly. "Oh, hey, I bought something for you at the pharmacy today."

He grabbed the white paper sack he'd left next to his bag of clothes and removed a bottle.

Damon squinted. "Lotion?"

"Yeah, lavender and something else. Something that's supposed to be good for easing muscles," Cain said, giving the label a cursory glance. "I got it so I could rub your leg for you."

"Rub my leg?"

"I notice you digging your fingers into the muscles all the time when you don't think I'm watching," Cain informed him, plopping down beside him once more. "And I figured it'd be even better if I did the whole leg, you know? Since you won't take the stupid pain pills."

Damon blinked, his face a total blank, and Cain shrugged to hide the pang of rejection that squeezed his chest. "I mean, I don't have to. Or you could use it yourself, maybe. I can leave it in the bathroom for you," he said, pushing to his feet.

Damon grabbed his wrist before he'd taken a step.

"You… bought that earlier so you could rub my leg," he

stated slowly, like he wanted to get the facts straight in his mind.

Cain turned beet red. God, it sounded so *stupid*. He was no massage therapist. He had no clue what he was doing, or whether it was even a good idea. Dumb, dumb, dumb.

"Sorry," he whispered.

Damon's right hand came up to capture Cain's left. He removed the bottle of lotion and set it carefully on the bed. "What. The. *Hell*. Would you be sorry for?" Damon asked softly.

Cain squeezed his eyes shut. "I wasn't thinking. I don't really know what I'm doing, obviously. And I-"

Damon's hand came up to cup Cain's jaw. "I can't believe you thought of it," he interrupted in a whisper. "I legitimately can't remember the last time someone thought of me that way, except for yesterday when someone remembered to bring my pain pills because I'm a stubborn ass, and that was you, too."

"Well, that's… dumb," Cain blurted. "Why wouldn't they? You're… you're… amazing."

"Amazing?" Damon's eyes crinkled at the corners again, and he looked so happy Cain couldn't even be embarrassed. He rolled his eyes instead.

"Well, when you're not picking music, calling me kid, or giving me the silent treatment," Cain clarified. "Then, yes. Amazing."

Damon's hands found Cain's hips and pulled him closer until he was standing between Damon's spread knees. His face moved forward to nudge the hem of Cain's shirt with his nose, planting a kiss just above the button of his jeans.

"You can't just add qualifiers after the fact," Damon told him, nuzzling higher. "You said amazing."

Right then, Cain wouldn't fight Damon on *amazing* or any other adjective he wanted to use to describe himself.

His breath hitched as Damon's lips moved around his stomach and up to his chest, dropping small kisses like scattershot wherever he could reach.

It was just... *sweet*, Cain realized, his heart kicking up. He'd never experienced anything like it, and he found himself responding to it way too quickly, his heart thumping harder and his cock thickening behind the seam of his pants.

Damon noticed, and his hands curved further around Cain, holding his ass while he moved his kisses further south.

But Cain didn't want to simply get lost in Damon again.

"Hey. Do it my way first." Cain stepped back abruptly and dropped to his knees, working to remove Damon's shoes and socks, and then throwing them toward the door. He opened the button of Damon's jeans and pulled down the zipper. Damon stood, his hand braced on Cain's head for balance, so Cain could yank his jeans to the floor.

Of course, once the jeans were down, Damon didn't let go, which meant his boxer-covered crotch was directly in line with Cain's mouth. Cain looked up to find green-gold eyes latched onto his and he leaned forward, pressing a kiss to Damon's half-hard dick.

Damon shuddered, and Cain took that opportunity to push him gently back onto the bed.

"Shirt," he told Damon. His eyes still locked on Cain, Damon pulled his long-sleeved t-shirt off and threw it on the floor near his jeans.

"Lay on your stomach," Cain said huskily.

Damon raised one eyebrow, but complied, pushing himself up so his injured leg was supported by the bed. He twisted his neck so his eyes stayed on Cain's face.

Cain hastily stripped off his own shirt, and threw it on the pile with Damon's... but something about the sight of it there made him pause. His shirt tangled with Damon's, his life tangled with Damon's… God, he wanted that.

He shook his head to clear it. What he had was *right now*, and Damon willingly at his mercy for a second time.

He grabbed the lotion and pumped some into his hand, enjoying the clean scent. He rubbed his hands together to warm the liquid, then climbed onto the bed next to Damon's leg.

The first press of his fingers had Damon groaning lavishly, his back arching, and Cain had to focus to keep his massage slow and steady. He gently but firmly kneaded the muscles of Damon's lower leg, taking care with the pink scar tissue, and then slowly moved up to the larger muscles in his thigh. It occurred to him that Damon's other leg had to ache, too, from carrying extra weight all the time, so he pumped out more lotion and rubbed that leg also. When he got to Damon's ass, he paused. Although Damon didn't say a word, Cain could sense the electric hum of anticipation in the air.

He bit his lip and decided that waiting would do the man good.

Cain crawled up the bed and lifted a leg to straddle Damon's waist, then pumped out more lotion and began his massage again, this time at Damon's neck, smoothing his hands down the expanse of Damon's back and shoulders. He loved the way his pale arms and the dark ink of his tattoos contrasted with the honey-tan of Damon's skin. Damon had freckles, too, just like the ones he'd noticed on Cain, and Cain resisted the urge to trace them with his tongue.

He'd do that next time… if there *was* a next time. He forced the sad thought out of his mind.

He moved lower, digging his knuckles gently into the

small of Damon's back, and Damon moaned again, pushing his hips into the mattress.

"Lower," he whispered, his face muffled by a pillow. "Lower, Cain."

Bossy. Even buck naked and flat on his stomach.

Cain's fingers did knead lower, almost like they were responding to Damon's command without Cain's authorization. He toyed with the skin beneath the waistband of Damon's boxers, then pushed the fabric down three inches until just the top curve of Damon's ass was exposed.

Damon's back rose and fell with each intake of breath as Cain's hands found the dimples at the base of his spine. Cain smiled just a little, feeling his face warm.

He loved the sounds Damon made, the way his muscles tensed and clenched in pleasure, even as Cain loosened them.

And the biggest turn-on of all? Damon wanted him. It was true and obvious. There was no ulterior motive for him to be in this room - in fact, he showed *faith* in Cain just by being there.

He lowered Damon's underwear further, and Damon lifted his pelvis slightly so Cain could reach around and pull them down completely. His fingers lightly brushed the tip of Damon's erection - no longer only half-hard, but lying fully formed against his belly, thick and pulsing with heat - and Damon hissed in pleasure.

"More. More, Cain," he demanded.

Trust the man to try to take control, even with Cain straddling his back. Cain's lotion-slicked fingers gripped his cock more tightly and Damon thrust into his fist once, then twice. But Cain smoothed his hand up over Damon's hip and eased him back down to the bed.

"I haven't finished your massage yet," he said, his voice

no louder than a whisper. His own cock was rock hard behind his jeans.

He pumped the lotion again, this time directly onto Damon's naked ass, just so he could enjoy the way Damon shuddered and hissed at the coldness.

"You'll pay for that," Damon threatened, but it wasn't any kind of a threat.

"Yeah? I can't *wait* to see how you'll make me pay," Cain teased, his voice husky.

Cain's fingers glided through the lotion, smoothing it over Damon's hot flesh, before he kneaded the firm muscles of Damon's ass. He moved lower and lower, spreading Damon's cheeks apart. And then he brushed one slick finger over Damon's entrance.

Damon froze.

They hadn't discussed anal sex. Cain knew some guys weren't into it at all, especially when it came to receiving, so he slowly and carefully ran just his fingertip back and forth over the sensitive skin, before moving even lower to cup Damon's sac and play with his balls.

"H-higher," Damon said, and Cain blinked.

"What?"

"Higher," Damon instructed, no hesitation in his voice this time, and Cain's breath came faster.

Oh, fuck, yes.

He moved his finger higher, rubbing his finger slowly over Damon's taint, and then further back, toying with his ring.

"I..." Cain began, but his voice came out as a reedy squeak. *God.* He swallowed and tried again. "I bought condoms. At the pharmacy. And lube. Other *supplies* besides the bandage stuff. I just thought maybe you... and we... but I mean... I expected I would bottom, and I can... if it's what you want," he concluded in a rush, biting his lip in embarrassment. Had he assumed too much?

"Cain?"

"Yeah?"

"I swear to God, if you apologize to me for something else right now, I'm going to…" He paused, like he was thinking of an appropriately dire consequence. "I'm going to hold you down and make you listen to classic rock all night."

Cain smiled, the frantic butterfly-winged thrum of his heart settling into something slower and deeper. Damon's rough voice was garbled, like he was drunk on pleasure, pleasure Cain was giving him. And in the face of that, Cain's doubts vanished.

Well, most of them.

He could count on one hand the number of times he'd topped, and most of those had been a lifetime ago. Before Jack. Back when he and Jesse…

No. Those memories had no place here.

He trailed his fingers down Damon's ass once more, then lifted himself off the bed, taking care not to use his injured arm. He grabbed the little pharmacy bag with lightning speed and upended it onto the bed. Two packages of condoms and a little tube of lube spilled out, right next to Damon's naked leg, and the sight made him pause for half a second.

Concentrate!

He shucked his shoes and the remainder of his clothes, then climbed back onto the bed to crouch beside Damon.

Shit. Fuck. Damon's leg. He bit his lip and thought for a moment, considering the logistics, vaguely aware that Damon had twisted again and was watching him.

A large, long-fingered hand came to rest on his thigh. "Cain?"

"Yeah?"

"Stop thinking."

Cain lifted his eyes to meet Damon's gorgeous hazel ones.

"I mean it," Damon said. "This is fine. This is perfect. I want this."

"But your leg…"

Damon turned over all the way and sat up. His golden skin gleamed in the weak light from the single fixture mounted over the table. "My leg is just fine. Better than it's been in a couple of days, thanks to you." His voice was warm, and his hand trailed up the inside of Cain's thigh, making Cain shiver.

He wrapped his other arm around the back of Cain's neck, a move Cain was already coming to think of as *Damon's* signature hold. And just like it always did, the small claiming steadied something inside him.

"Kiss me," Damon said, and Cain blinked. Damon's hand at his neck was so warm, and his clever fingers trailed up and down Cain's leg - closer and closer to his erection, which had flagged just a little thanks to his worry, but was now raging back to life once more. "Stop thinking and just kiss me."

So Cain did, leaning forward into Damon, letting his hands spear into the long strands of Damon's hair. Damon's hand on his thigh moved to his back, pulling their chests flush, and then Damon sank back down onto the bed, pulling Cain with him.

All of Cain's rational thoughts, all of his doubts, burned to ash in the fire of their kiss. Damon let him take charge - there was no doubt in Cain's mind that it was intentional on Damon's part, that he could have grabbed control at any moment, but he was giving this to Cain.

Cain stretched out fully atop Damon, bringing as much

of their skin as possible into alignment, and he thrust their cocks together. They moaned into each other's mouths, and it was glorious. Damon's hands roamed across Cain's back and over his shoulders, like he wanted to claim every inch he found, and Cain pushed himself harder into Damon, as though Damon could somehow take him over completely.

Damon, Damon, Damon.

No other thought in the world, no other star in the sky.

The simple friction of their bodies was the greatest pleasure Cain had ever imagined, but he was driven by the idea that he needed to make this as amazing as possible for the man beneath him. Without breaking their kiss, he fumbled for the lube on the other side of the bed. He pulled back for just a second and opened it - *Christ, what were they thinking when they designed these packages? Did they really think people had time to mess with this shit?* - then he drizzled some into his palm.

Damon had lifted up onto his elbow and was watching Cain, his eyes glimmering with amusement and something harder, something hotter. *Want.*

Cain leaned over him again, smearing the lubricant over both of their cocks, before gripping them together in his hand. He looked down, and the sight almost had him spilling himself then and there.

"Oh fuck." Damon's eyes rolled back in his head. "Not enough. I want your skin on mine. Get down here," he growled, pulling Cain down by the neck.

Within seconds, Damon was hipping up, fucking Cain's palm. "Jesus, Cain," he hissed. "It's too good. Too good."

No such thing. Not for Damon. Cain moved his hips even faster, squeezed his fingers even tighter.

"No!" Damon growled. "Stop!"

It took Cain a second to process the words, and in that

time, Damon pushed him gently back. "Not like this," he growled. "I want to come with you inside me."

Fuck, fuck, fuck. Those words, in that tone of voice.

He sucked in a deep breath and sat back, his knees next to Damon's thighs. He grabbed a pillow from the head of the bed with shaking hands, and Damon lifted his hips so Cain could slide the pillow beneath him. He reached for the lube once more, giving Damon one last questioning glance - *Are you sure?*

Damon's response was to widen his legs, bending his good leg until his foot was flat on the bed, giving Cain unrestricted access.

Cain shuddered as he squirted lube onto his fingers, onto Damon's ass... so much lube, possibly too much, but Damon didn't seem to care, so Cain wouldn't either. He dragged his finger across Damon's pucker, and while Damon was still gasping at that sensation, he pushed his finger inside.

"*Fuck*," Damon said, his ass clenching around Cain. He was so hot, so fucking tight, and Cain was almost a tiny bit jealous of Damon. He couldn't wait for Damon to do this for him. But in the meantime, he was determined to blow Damon's mind.

Cain drizzled more lube, added another finger. Damon's neck bowed and his fists clenched at his sides.

"More," he whispered, his voice wrecked. "Another one, Cain. Now."

God, the look on Damon's face. Cain added a third finger, bending his knuckles slightly as he withdrew, and Damon's back arched off the bed. "Fuck, yes!"

One of Damon's fists uncurled and traveled up Cain's thigh, to his cock, pumping slightly. "Fuck me, Cain. Please. Now. Don't think, just do it."

Cain whimpered, biting his lip as Damon's thumb glided

over his slit, spreading the moisture over the head of his cock.

What was he doing? Fuck. *Fuck!* Condom, right.

He grabbed the little box and liberated a foil-wrapped packet, but before he could open it, Damon's hands were there, tearing it open and rolling it down Cain's erection. He grabbed the lube, too, spreading a copious amount.

"Go slow," he instructed. "But fuck me *now*, Cain. *Please.*"

Cain nodded, his eyes locked on Damon's as he crawled into position. He fucking loved that Damon was still so in control, that Damon was guiding him. He didn't have to worry about what Damon wanted or whether this was good.

But at the same time, he couldn't wait to make Damon lose his mind. He lined himself up with Damon's hole and pushed forward just slightly. Just enough to make Damon freeze. Then he leaned forward and captured Damon's mouth in another frantic kiss.

"I'll do it when I'm goddamn ready, Damon," he teased.

Then he pushed forward again, grunting as he felt Damon tense… and then relax.

Holy shit.

"Christ, Damon. You're so fucking tight," he moaned, squeezing his eyes shut as he gave several more tiny thrusts, until he was seated fully inside.

Damon didn't reply - it seemed he couldn't. Cain opened his eyes to find Damon's head thrown back, his mouth open, his eyes tightly shut. "Damon?" He panted and held himself still.

A second later, Damon opened his eyes and lifted one shaking hand to Cain's face.

"It's been a long time," he growled. "And I… I forgot."

Cain braced himself above Damon, elbows locked, and

fought to keep his body still and his mind on Damon, when every instinct in his body told him to thrust *hard*.

"Forgot how fucking good it could be," Damon said. His voice was slurred and warm with lust. His hands locked around Cain's waist, then trailed back to cup his ass, pulling him forward. "Do it, Cain."

Cain pulled back, nearly to the tip, then sank back into Damon with one smooth thrust.

He couldn't believe this was happening. Couldn't believe Damon was giving himself over this way. He had no idea what the next day would bring, or what the future held for them, but this moment was incredibly perfect. He simultaneously wanted it to last, and wanted to race to the finish.

Damon didn't give him the choice. "Harder," he yelled, his fingers digging ten tiny bruises into Cain's ass, marks he hoped he'd still have in the morning, just to remind himself this hadn't been a dream. "Harder. Give it to me, Cain. Give me everything."

Cain was helpless against the curl of need that threaded through Damon's voice, helpless against the tidal wave of hunger that swamped him. He pumped his hips harder and harder, wanting to imprint himself on Damon, to take possession of him as surely as Damon possessed him.

Damon's hands splayed out, grabbing at the pillow above his head and squeezing it tight. Their rhythmic panting breaths were curiously aligned. Cain felt a bead of sweat fall from his forehead and land on Damon's chest, mingling with Damon's, and it felt incredibly erotic and so fucking right.

He reached down for Damon's cock, wanting to ratchet his pleasure up even higher, and Damon cried out at the sensation. It only took two fast pumps, and then Damon was coming, his seed spilling out all over his stomach and chest, making a sticky mess between them.

Fuck, yes.

Cain lowered his chest to Damon's, then reached out and grabbed Damon's hands, threading their fingers together.

It only took a second before his own release hit, and he cried Damon's name when it did, his vision whiting out and his muscles seizing as he came, and came, and came, filling the condom inside Damon.

Holy. Hell.

Utterly wrung out, he collapsed fully atop Damon. Without thinking, or even *overthinking*, he laid his head in the crook of Damon's shoulder, his ear directly over the pounding of Damon's heart.

He floated like that for minutes or hours or eons, before sensation penetrated the beautiful, white-noise hum of his brain and he had to reach down and deal with the condom as he pulled out.

"Sorry," he said as Damon winced.

He tied off the condom and threw it in the bucket next to the bed before resuming his position against Damon, who hadn't moved. It was so serene he wanted to... *fuck!*

Damon slapped his ass, one firm crack that rent the stillness.

"What the hell?" He lifted his head to find Damon's eyes twinkling.

"No more apologizing for shit that doesn't require apologies. Understand?"

Damon grabbed the back of Cain's neck and pulled his head down again, nestling him even more firmly into the curve of his neck.

Cain bit his lip and smiled. No more apologizing. He really, really liked the sound of that.

CHAPTER FIFTEEN

The autumn leaves skittered across the road in the morning sunshine when Damon flicked on the directional. Another road, another switch-back, another way of trying to confuse the men the senator had sent after them - if they were still after them at all.

Still, this morning, Damon couldn't bring himself to mind taking the long way. Not when he had Cain next to him in the passenger seat singing along to the radio. Not when his ass was still pleasantly sore from last night. Not when he felt stronger and more positive than he had since before the crash, like he could almost see a future where the senator was in jail and he was free to resume a normal life.

He glanced over at Cain, who had stolen one of Damon's clean t-shirts to go with his jeans this morning, and was calmly sipping the mostly-milk-and-sweetener confection he liked to call coffee.

"You should not be humming along to this trite shit when you're wearing a Sabaton t-shirt," Damon said. "It's disrespectful."

As expected, Cain turned to glare at him. "Who the fuck is Sabaton?"

"Who are… Are you kidding me? Did you even look at the shirt before you put it on?"

"Uh, nope. Didn't look. Also, not kidding. Never heard of them." The brat was totally dismissive.

"They're only one of the greatest Swedish metal bands in *existence*," Damon informed him.

"Hmm. If you say so." Cain shrugged. "I picked it because it was the smallest t-shirt you had, and I'm still swimming in it. No disrespect to Swedish metal intended."

"Clearly your musical education has been sorely lacking."

"You gonna educate me?"

So fucking saucy. "I could pull over and educate you right now," Damon threatened, and Cain smiled wickedly.

Fuck. He was sorely tempted. Partly to distract himself from giving in to temptation, and partly from a desire to know more about Cain, he said, "Tell me about your tattoo." The lines of tiny swirling text interspersed with colorless tongues of flame and skulls that seemed to dance down his arm were as beautiful and mysterious as the man himself.

Cain stuck his arm out, and looked down with a furrow between his brows, like he was somehow surprised to see the ink still on his skin, or maybe just surprised that Damon had asked him. "Oh. Uh. It's from a poem by T.S. Eliot," he said simply, then he closed his eyes and quoted:

"What we call the beginning is often the end
And to make an end is to make a beginning.
The end is where we start from….
Every phrase and every sentence is an end and a beginning,
Every poem an epitaph. And any action
Is a step to the block, to the fire, down the sea's throat
Or to an illegible stone: and that is where we start."

He cleared this throat when he was done, looking slightly embarrassed. "It…it's only part of that stanza, but it was important. A reminder."

Damon blinked. He wasn't sure what he'd expected to hear, but likely something more along the lines of song lyrics. Some ephemeral life motto. He wasn't sure why he kept wanting to believe that Cain was somehow younger than he was, less mature than he was. Like the tattoo, Cain was complex - half-shaded and with pieces left unfinished, but that did nothing to detract from his beauty.

Or from how much Damon wanted him.

While Damon was lost in his thoughts, Cain had resumed his soft singing, his eyes drinking in the lavish mountain views, now stained with the golden fire of turning trees, and Damon found himself appreciating them, too. One last blaze of glory at the end of a growing season, one last punch of gorgeousness before the blanket of cold fell over this corner of the world. But they held so much promise, too. A reminder that even when stark winter came, it too would fade away into lush green. A cycle.

An end that was also a beginning, just like Cain's tattoo.

The strains of the alt-rock song on the radio faded into silence and Cain stopped singing.

"Hey!" he grumbled, trying to pick another station. "That was an awesome song."

Damon hadn't recognized the track and hadn't understood a single lyric. If anything, he'd been focused on Cain's voice, which had sounded happy and peaceful…and not at all like an injured cat, as Cain had claimed. Although maybe Damon was biased. He was beginning to realize he was pretty pitifully gone on Cain.

"I don't think you're gonna find any of the stations come in, baby. It's satellite radio, and we're out of range," Damon reminded him, and Cain leaned back.

"Oh, hey! Then will you stop at the next rest area so I can get a charger for my phone? We can listen to my music."

"Oh joy."

"Shush." Cain whacked him playfully on the arm. "And there's all that other bullshit I need to deal with, like the fucking ski trip that left *yesterday*, which apparently I'm not making." He sighed gustily. "Probably a good idea for me to check in with my parents, too. I forget where they were heading to campaign this week, but I'm pretty sure they're headed to DC for the holiday. I should make sure they're not going to be anywhere near the cabin. Do you mind?"

Damon set his jaw. Yeah, he very much minded the idea that Cain was going to check in with his parents, but he kept his mouth shut. He couldn't keep the man from his family, no matter how shitty that family might be. When they came upon a sign for a welcome center a few silent miles later, Damon pulled in so Cain could make his purchase.

He came back to the car with the cable, along with a bunch of food and a red baseball hat that he plopped onto Damon's head.

"What the hell is this?" Damon demanded, taking the hat off his head while Cain messed with the charger, plugging in his phone.

"A souvenir," Cain said, not meeting his eyes. "They were having a fundraiser to create some new hiking trail, and lots of businesses had tables set up. One of them was this barbecue place." He cracked open one of the white Styrofoam containers he carried, and the tangy, smoky scent of barbecue filled the car. "They were practically giving the hats away."

"And you had to get one, *why?*"

"Because it reminded me of you. It was fate."

Damon ran his finger over the embroidered design on the front of the cap. *Big Daddy's BBQ.* He raised his eyebrow in Cain's direction, but Cain smiled innocently.

Damon stuck the hat back on his head and reached for a fork. It turned out to be damn good BBQ.

A few minutes later, Cain had tossed the containers into a trash barrel and they were back on the road. Cain played with his phone for a few minutes, and Kings of Leon's *Waste a Moment* came over the speakers.

"Who says you get to pick the music?"

"Uh, *you* did. Remember yesterday? *Navigator picks the tunes*," Cain sing-songed, punching buttons on his phone. "I'm just obeying your silly rule."

Damon grabbed the phone from his back pocket and handed it to Cain. "Connect my phone instead."

In his peripheral vision, he saw Cain cock his head mulishly, like he wanted to argue. Damon pointed to the hat. "Don't piss Big Daddy off, Cain."

Cain snorted and tossed Damon's phone in the center console. "Don't take the hat literally, dude."

Damon laughed.

"Fuck," Cain said softly, looking at his screen. "Guess we just drove back into a patch of cell service. Twelve missed calls from my mother, three from my father, two from Drew. A text from Mrs. Fassbender, who's looking forward to seeing me Monday, which was actually *two* days ago. And an email from Gary North." He sighed, and Damon could practically see the tension charging his frame from one moment to the next. "Guess it was too much to hope the whole world would lose my number, huh?"

But Damon's attention was caught on one of the names Cain had mentioned. "Gary North?" Damon asked. "Why does that name sound familiar?"

"He's a reporter." Cain tapped the phone against his leg.

"The one I told you about, who wrote the piece on SILA. My dad wants me to do an interview with him. Some human-interest piece for the fucking campaign."

Damon's eyebrows shot up. "The guy who reported on SILA wants to do a piece on your dad."

"Yeah. And my dad instructed me to agree. Weird, eh?"

It was more than weird, it was downright bizarre, and possibly suspicious. But Damon wasn't sure whether he should tell Cain his suspicions or not. "When is the interview?" he asked instead.

"At my convenience, or so Gary says. He wants me to set up a time that he can meet with me, either in Boston or wherever we are on the campaign trail. Time and place of my choosing."

"Sounds eager."

"Yeah." Cain thunked his head back against the headrest. "I don't know how the hell I'm supposed to do this interview without giving something away. This may be my father's stupidest idea yet."

"You could always say no," Damon reminded him.

"Yeah, right." Cain turned his head without lifting it from the seat. "If it were just the guy wanting the interview, I'd have said no when he first talked to me at the fundraiser. But according to my mom, this is all part of my dad's strategy. Or something." He sighed. "Maybe we can do it by phone."

"Hmmm."

"What's that mean, *hmm*?"

"It means you have no problem arguing with *me*."

Cain frowned at him in surprise. "Should I?"

"Nope. Though, you know, I am apparently the Big Daddy. But I'm wondering why you have a hard time saying no to your parents."

Cain froze. "It's different."

"Well, yeah. Clearly. But you're one of the bravest men I know. Christ, Cain, you threw yourself in front of a *bullet* for me. Why can't you stand up for yourself when it comes to your parents?"

Cain said nothing, so Damon pushed on. "I'm not saying you want to come out, either privately or publicly. If you're not ready for that, you're not, and I would never push you to do something you're not ready to do. But why not tell your dad to fuck himself when he tries to run your life? No more campaign rallies. No skiing with the Fassbergers."

"Fassbenders," Cain corrected. "And it's just... not that easy." He rubbed a hand over his head.

"So explain it to me, then," Damon said, trying to mask his frustration. "I want to understand. I really want to know how you can be so strong sometimes, and then so..."

He bit his tongue before he finished the sentence, but not quickly enough. Cain laughed, but it was a bitter sound that didn't mask his hurt. "So *what*, Damon? So weak? Say it."

"That's not what I was going to say," Damon lied. "I just don't get it."

Cain looked at the ceiling, his arms folded across his chest and his lips pursed. For a second, Damon was afraid Cain was going to cry, and he cast around for something to say, some way to distract him.

But when Cain began speaking a moment later, his voice wasn't sad, but absolutely livid.

"Back when I was in high school, I was mostly out. I told you that."

Damon smiled. "Emo gay boy. My Chemical Romance. Yeah, you told me."

Cain nodded once. "Well, emo gay boy had a boyfriend. Another gay boy like me, but a jock. Big, built blond guy with a perfect GPA and a soccer scholarship. His name was

— or *is*, I should say, since he's still alive, even if I haven't seen him in years — Jesse Porter."

That Jesse person, Damon remembered Cain's mother saying during that truly horrifying phone call. Someone she'd always known was a troublemaker.

Cain's hand clutched at the handle above the passenger window, and he stared resolutely at the mountain road that rose and fell in front of them.

"I had a crush on him for the longest time. My second-ever real-life crush, after Cam Seaver."

Damon's eyebrows went up, and he saw a smile play at the corner of Cain's lips. "Surprised you, huh? We dated a couple of times, too. But I wasn't his type. For one thing, I wasn't out, and Cam pretty much always was."

Cain cleared his throat, and Damon said nothing, understanding that Cain needed to get this out, however long it took. "Jesse, though… he knew I was never going to want him to bring me home to his parents, and he sure as fuck knew I was never going to bring him home to mine. He had a reputation to uphold, you know. Super jock scholarship kid from a middle-income family. He needed a full ride to school, and he definitely did not want to be the token gay athlete. So, things started slowly. We flirted at a party, hooked up on a spring-break ski trip." He darted a glance at Damon. "Proof that not all ski trips are bad."

"Right."

"And before I knew it, we were spending all our time together. He flunked an English test on Transcendentalism - I swear he did it on purpose - and the teacher asked me to tutor him. So the two of us had every excuse to spend our afternoons up in my bedroom with Emerson's Essays open on our laps. Not that we read them," he added.

Damon smirked. "Uh huh. I was that age once," he reminded Cain. "I get it."

"He was my first at almost everything. I was pretty sure I was in love with him. And then that summer… I kissed him outside."

Damon blinked and tore his eyes from the road to glance at Cain. "Outside?"

"Yup. In a semi-public place."

"Oh," Damon said, as facts began to click into place.

"We were at a pool party at my parents' house." Cain's voice was a miserable whisper. "I made him kiss me behind the pool house. Just kinda grabbed him, and—. My father saw us."

"Oh, damn, Cain. I'm so sorry."

Cain shook his head, looking lost. "Don't feel sorry for me. Believe me, I don't deserve one second of your sympathy."

"What happened?" Damon demanded.

"What do you think? My father threatened to out Jesse - to take away his scholarship, to get him kicked out of school."

"Fuck." It was no worse than Damon had been expecting, the tip of the iceberg in terms of the senator's sins, and yet the bleakness in Cain's voice made him wish the senator was standing right in front of their car right now.

He stepped on the gas harder.

"I told Jesse…" Cain licked his lips. "I told him it didn't matter. You know? *I have a trust fund! We can get jobs! We can be together!*"

Damon winced and Cain caught it. He chuckled darkly.

"Yep. Yeah, you know what happened after that. And I mean, I can't blame him. We barely knew each other, and it was *way* too early for that Romeo and Romeo shit. Besides, it was my fault we got caught in the first place. I accepted all that. What killed though, was that he couldn't distance himself from me fast enough. Told me I needed to get over this stupid shit, use my head. This was just a phase he was going through, and I'd taken advantage of his inexperience. The whole nine."

"Taken advantage of *his* inexperience?" Damon sputtered. "Are you fucking kidding? When you were no more experienced than he was? This guy sounds like an asshole, Cain."

Cain shrugged. "Maybe. But we weren't even eighteen yet, you know? He was young, and so was I, and he was scared because my father had threatened him."

"None of that was your fault. Your father threatened *you* every bit as much."

"Maybe," Cain agreed. "But it was still my fault. *My* father, right?"

He gave Damon a pointed look, and Damon sighed. Yeah, he'd fallen into similar guilt-by-association thinking where Cain and his father were concerned.

"And I was the one who'd wanted to mess around, to take a chance." He sighed. "I haven't talked to Jesse since then. We haven't kept in touch, not even on Facebook."

"Well, yeah! Why *would* you?" Damon demanded, still annoyed. Big blond asshole jock could line up in the middle of the road along with Cain's father so Damon could mow them both down.

"Apparently, I'm the only one who didn't keep tabs on him. My father's known exactly where he's been. Penn State undergrad, just like he planned, and then on for his MBA. And Jesse managed to land a coveted entry-level job at one of the biggest advertising agencies in Manhattan. He's engaged now."

Damon frowned. "And that bothers you?"

Cain laughed shortly. "That he's graduated and gotten engaged? Fuck no. I'm glad for him, and whoever the woman is."

"A woman."

"Yep. Turns out it *was* a phase." He waved a hand negligently in the air. "Or whatever. No, what bothers me is that my father knows all this because he's been monitoring Jesse this whole time. Know how Jesse managed to land that prestigious job? One phone call from my dad to an old friend of his." He turned to look at Damon. "And with one phone call, he could take it all away."

"Right. Well, sucks to be Jesse, and I mean that sincerely. But what does that have to do with you now?"

"*What?*"

"I don't understand what that has to do with why you won't stand up to your dad now."

"He could destroy Jesse's life. Hurt him. Kill him," he whispered.

"He could likely get Jesse fired," Damon allowed. "From a position that Jesse may or may not have earned in the first place."

"But…"

"No, wait. Cain, seriously? Is this the way he's been controlling you this whole past year?"

One look at Cain's ravaged face confirmed it was.

Damon put on his blinker and pulled into a scenic overlook by the side of the road. The view of the valley beside them was gorgeous, but he barely noticed it. He twisted in his seat and grabbed both of Cain's hands in his own.

"Seriously, is this what you've been torturing yourself with?"

"Yes! God, Damon. Imagine my father ruining things for Jesse, hurting him just because *one time,* like, six years ago the guy kissed me! I can't let that happen."

"Cain. Cain, that's *crazy.*" He grabbed Cain's shoulders and shook him lightly. "You're not a high-school kid anymore, baby. You can change things."

Cain shook his head, clearly locked into his own inner story. So freakin' stubborn.

Damon slammed a hand on the center console, and Cain's eyes flew to his.

"This is fucking ridiculous, Cain. Call Sebastian Seaver right this second. Find out if he needs some new marketing expert on his team. I will fucking guarantee you that he will say yes in a heartbeat. In *less than a heartbeat.* Christ, he made up a whole new *division* so he could give Cort a job. He'll do whatever it takes to get you to come forward about your father. And then he'll get Jesse round-the-clock protection, or relocate him to Timbuktu."

"Damon, you still don't get it. I can't ask Bas to do that."

"Why the fuck not?"

"Because it's *my fault*! It's on *me*! I am the one who needs to fix it."

"That's stupid, Cain."

"Damon…"

"You're telling me it's more important for you to handle this than for me to get my life back?" he demanded. "Because I don't think you really believe that. Not anymore."

Cain's eyes widened and filled with tears. "I know. I *know*. I have already thought of that so many times. Your freedom or his, your life or his. You have every reason to hate me. I don't blame you."

"I don't hate you! Christ Almighty, Cain. I don't hate you, I fucking… I *care about you,*" he said, mentally backing away from the word he had been on verge of blurting out. It was way too early for the L-word to make an appearance, especially when so many things were unresolved. "I care about you, and I don't want you torturing yourself when it would be so easy to let people *help*."

Tears tracked down Cain's cheeks and Damon caught

them with his thumbs. "How is that possible? How is it possible that you can care about me when all I've done is mess things up for you and make your life harder?"

"Chelsea told me the first step to trusting someone was *deciding* to trust them," Damon told him, leaning forward to press a soft kiss to Cain's lips and another to his temple. And he was really, really glad he'd listened to her.

"I just… I am so tired, Damon."

"I know you are, baby," Damon said, leaning over the fucking stupid console as far as possible so he could take Cain in his arms, cradling Cain's head against his shoulder. "I know you are." He ran his hands up and down Cain's back in a soothing motion.

"I will help you protect Jesse, even though he's an asshole," Damon promised, and Cain's watery chuckle made his arms squeeze tighter. God, he wanted to protect Cain from everything. "But you have to trust me to help you. And believe that you deserve better than to torture yourself this way. You've done nothing wrong by being gay, Cain. Nothing wrong by falling in love with a boy who didn't deserve you. It's not your fault your dad is the way he is. It's not your fault Jack conned you, because he did the same fucking thing to me. Do you hear me? Do you *believe* me?"

Cain nodded, a soft bump of his cheek against Damon's chin. But then he added more firmly, "I believe you."

"Okay. Okay then. Here's what we're going to do…"

CHAPTER SIXTEEN

By late afternoon, Cain was exhausted, even though he'd barely moved from the passenger seat all day. He'd made several phone calls - one to Drew, who was still with Bas, and who'd promised to look into the Jesse situation, and another to the Fassbenders, apologizing for the sudden, terrible flu that had *-gosh darn it!* -prevented him from going on their *super-fun* ski trip. But he'd put off the last phone call he'd needed to make as long as possible… until after they'd stopped for lunch, and then for groceries, until the car had started climbing up and up the side of the mountain and until Damon warned him they'd lose reception again if he didn't do it soon.

Even then he'd hesitated, his fingers like lead as he'd located the number and hit Send.

"Cain Edward!" his mother had answered on the first ring. He'd had to squeeze his eyes shut, not because her tone was scolding - he was somehow beyond that now - but because ever since he'd left the Nashville house, he'd found it impossible to think of her without wondering how much

of his father's schemes she'd known about, and how much she'd gone along with.

"Hello, Mother," he'd said, and he hadn't had to fake the way the words came out slow and tired.

"What's this I heard from Marnie Fassbender? You're not going on the ski trip? And you didn't have the courtesy to call her until *today*? For God's *sake*, Cain."

"Did she tell you why?" Cain had asked.

"Something about a flu," Lucy Shaw had said dismissively. "But you were fine last time I saw you."

"Things changed. It would be far worse to get the entire Fassbender clan sick simply because you didn't want to lose out on an opportunity to solidify a connection."

"No, this is your way of defying me," his mother had argued. "You're no more sick than I am. There's still time, if you leave…"

"Enough," Cain had interrupted, rubbing his hand over his forehead. "I'll assume you send your best wishes for my speedy recovery. I will *not* be going skiing. In fact, I only called because I wanted to know where you'd be spending Thanksgiving in case I felt well enough to join you."

"Cain!" His mother had been shocked, and he couldn't blame her. When was the last time he'd defied her more than once in a single phone call? Possibly never… No, *definitely* never. "Why are you speaking to me this way?"

He'd heard his father's voice in the background, asking questions, soothing his mother. "Leave him be, Lucy. He's a grown man." And then his father was holding the phone, speaking to him. He couldn't remember the last time they'd spoken directly - it had been months, for sure.

"Cain?"

"Yes?" He didn't, *couldn't*, add a "dad" to the end.

"Be respectful to your mother."

"I always am," he said, and then he fell silent, feeling no need to defend himself the way he always seemed to.

Was this what adulthood was like?

The senator seemed nonplussed by his deviation from their script. He sighed. "We'll be heading to D.C. tomorrow for Thanksgiving. Will we see you?"

Not if he could help it. "If I'm feeling better, yes. Otherwise I'll stay away." Far, far away.

"Fair enough, son." His father hesitated, then added, "Love you. Feel better."

Cain disconnected the call and sat staring at the blank screen of the phone as Damon's GPS guided them through the hilly terrain and into the driveway of the Shaw family cabin high in the Smokies.

Love you, feel better.

Damon cut the engine and unbuckled his belt, listening to something on his phone, but Cain just sat staring at the house for a long moment. The cement-and-glass house stood three stories tall, two floors of living space above a garage that had been carved into the mountainside. Steel balconies ran around three sides of the upper floors, facing out over the valley below, but from here, there were only four oval windows visible, making the house look vaguely like a giant rectangular spaceship that had crash-landed in the middle of the woods.

It was funny how the house looked so different now than when they'd first bought it - no more cozy log A-frame, no more wide front porch complete with rocking chairs. But although the structure of the house no longer resembled anything Cain remembered from his childhood, there were so many familiar things, too - the topography of the mountains that had been unchanged for millennia, the tall trees that still curved across the long driveway. There was a strange sort of symbolism in it. Despite the effort and buckets of money his parents had poured into making a showplace of something that should have been a haven, all of the essential things remained unchanged, for better *and* for worse.

He opened his car door and stepped outside. Pine resin and the wood smoke from some unseen neighbor's fire lent an acrid tang to the air that was welcoming and comfortable. Though the sun still shone, the air was much cooler this high up, and he shivered slightly, until Damon made his way around the car and wrapped Cain in his strong embrace.

Damon was a little bit like the mountain. The fanciful thought took root in Cain's brain, and he turned to bury his face in Damon's chest. Damon was solid, unyielding. A comforting hope that had lived in Cain's mind for far longer than Cain had even known he existed. A *home*.

Which was silly, really. He and Damon were... *well*. That was a damn good question, really. Lovers, but not. Friends, but not. He hesitated to put a label on it, because that implied a sort of permanence, and whatever they were, nobody had ever said it was permanent.

He pulled away to stand on his own.

"So how do we get in?" Damon asked, and Cain chuckled.

"There's only one way in, besides the fire escape. Come on." Cain's feet crunched across the leaf-strewn gravel and typed in the code on the keypad next to the garage while Damon grabbed their bags from the trunk.

"Let me guess," Damon said, coming up behind him and nodding at the keypad as they watched the door slide up. "The date of the next presidential election? The date he became a vampire?"

Cain blinked. "What? No. Uh... This one *is* birthdays

actually. Mine, then Cady's." A vise squeezed around this heart.

Damon grabbed his hand. "Cain," he began. "I heard your conversation in the car. Are you — ?"

But Cain shook his head. "I'm *fine*," he said, trying to convince himself as much as Damon. "It's like you said before. He's not all one thing or another. He loves me in his own way. But he's not a good dad, and he's not a good person."

Damon said nothing, but he didn't let go of Cain's hand, even as they made their way through the garage, past an old blue pickup truck and a low-slung black convertible parked there, and up the carpeted stairway to the main floor.

The air inside was still and chilly, but unlike the stale, cold feeling of the Nashville house, here the stillness was expectant - a weird buzzing in his brain that told him they were in the right place and they'd find what they were looking for, in one way or another.

Cain grabbed the grocery bags and moved into the kitchen, tossing food haphazardly into the nearly-empty fridge, but Damon had stopped by the stairs for a moment.

"Wow," he finally said, dropping the suitcases and moving into the open living area.

Cain tried to see the place through Damon's eyes. Gleaming cherry floors covered the entire expanse, from the kitchen and bathroom that faced the driveway, all the way through the living and dining area to the giant sliding glass doors that led to the deck. Beyond the doors, a leaf-strewn steel-and-glass balcony held an enormous built-in grill, along with several chairs and tables.

"Yeah, I guess it's pretty wow," Cain agreed quietly. Damon paused at the doors and cocked his head, a silent question, and Cain came forward to slide the doors open.

"We can sit out here later, if you want. After we, you know, search the house."

Damon wrapped an arm around his waist and pulled him out onto the deck. "Maybe the searching can wait a minute."

"No. No, we should get started before—"

"Cain. It can wait."

Cain took a deep breath of the crisp air. He let Damon tow him over to a dark wicker love seat strewn with comfortable cushions, where he pulled him down, and wrapped him tightly in an embrace that already felt comfortable and expected.

"Talk," Damon said softly.

"About what?"

"Oh, I don't know. The Patriots' playoff chances? What you want Santa to bring you for Christmas? What the hell possessed you to buy me a hat that says *Big Daddy*?"

Cain snickered. "I already told you. It was too perfect, after I'd already given you that nickname."

"*Uh huh*. Or maybe," he suggested gently. "You could tell me about your phone calls this afternoon. I overheard some parts."

With a sigh, Cain nodded. He'd already known that Damon had heard almost everything. "You really think Bas and Drew will be able to keep Jesse safe? Make sure he keeps his job and nobody talks about his past?"

"Drew already told you he was going to take care of everything, and Jesse never has to know you were ever involved." He paused, hesitated. "Unless you want him to know."

Cain shook his head. Memories of Jesse were some of the fondest, happiest ones he had. He'd hung onto those memories, hung on to *Jesse*, for that reason. But now, everything with Damon was so brightly colored, so much *more* than anything he'd ever experienced, that he saw just how pale and washed out those memories of Jesse really were.

"I can't think of a single reason I'd want him to know," Cain said firmly.

Damon nodded, like this was no big deal, but Cain could feel the muscles of his arms relaxing where they wrapped around Cain's shoulder.

"And we didn't ask Drew this, but I'm pretty sure they'll make sure you're taken care of too, Cain. If you don't want to live with your parents anymore, you have places to go. Remember? Friends. Whether you want to testify against your dad or not."

Cain didn't reply, just sank more deeply into Damon's side, grateful for Damon's words and the calm acceptance in them. Cain didn't want to think about what they would find when they searched, what the proof to convict his father would look like. But more than that, he didn't want to think about what would happen if they found nothing at all.

All along, Cain had been determined not to come forward about his father in order to protect Jesse. Now that Jesse was safe, he had to confront the fact that he really didn't *want* to come forward. He should and he *would*. But he hated that circumstances had decreed he'd be the one to bring the gavel down on his own father.

Love you. Feel better.

Cain was weak. As always.

But Damon seemed to read his mind - or maybe to read the clench of his belly and the tightening of his shoulders. "You know, I was angry this morning. When we were talking about this stuff in the car."

"I know. I don't blame you. Anyone would—"

"No, let me say this," Damon argued gently. "It wasn't fair of me to say that you were putting Jesse's life before mine, or to suggest that not confronting your dad made you weak." He exhaled slowly. "Things were different for me growing up. My own dad is generally recognized as a piece of shit - a total womanizer, an addict, a thief, and a bully. After my mom died, I was a foster care kid for a long time. I had no… *legacy* to uphold, or whatever you want to call it. If I ever thought of my dad, it was to make damn sure I didn't turn out like him. I don't have any loyalty to my dad."

Damon picked up Cain's hand and toyed with his fingers. "And even though I hated him? I still think I probably would have turned out just like him, if not for Cort. I mean, when you don't love anyone and you don't have anyone who loves you, how can you help but turn into a self-absorbed asshole? If Cort hadn't come into my life when he did, if he hadn't *needed* me, I don't know where I'd be now. And I ask myself, what would I do if I believed Cort had committed a crime? If he'd killed someone, or hurt someone? Would I turn him in?" He shook his head. "Like you said before, it's not that easy."

"Cort's different," Cain whispered. "He loves you, and you know he's a good guy. My father… I don't know how or when his priorities started changing, but I can't say the same about him." It fucking killed him to accept it, let alone to say it aloud, but he did. "He's just not a good man."

"You never really know why people make the choices they make, Cain. You know, just as we pulled into the driveway this evening, I got a voicemail from my brother." He winced. "A pretty loud, furious voicemail."

"What?" Cain sat up slightly, pulling away. "Why? Is everything okay?"

"Yeah. He and Cam are fine, I think. He didn't really say." He chuckled humorlessly and drew Cain back down. "He was too busy taking me to task for the fact that I left town without telling him, that I went to Drew and Bas for help with Chelsea instead of asking him, that I called Drew about helping Jesse." He ticked off the list of grievances on his fingers. "And worst of all, he had to find out about the whole people-shooting-at-us thing second-hand from Bas."

"Oh." Cain could see how that would be... pretty terrifying, actually.

"Yeah, *oh*," Damon said, shaking his head ruefully. "And he's right. If the shoe were on the other foot, I'd murder him for not telling me. But it's not just about what's happened the last few days. I mean, Cort was the most important person in my life for a long, long time. And then, after the crash..."

He paused to look out over the mountains, and Cain pushed himself more fully against Damon's side, trying to share his warmth, his presence. Trying to comfort Damon the way Damon comforted him.

"After the crash, I abandoned him. That's how he felt, anyway. But from my perspective, I was convinced that keeping my distance would save him, and having me around would only drag him down."

"What? That's crazy!" Cain poked Damon in the ribs, and Damon's eyes flared in response.

"It's not." Damon grabbed Cain's offending finger and bit it gently. He stretched out his leg, and Cain began to knead the muscles with his fingertips. Damon squeezed his shoulders in appreciation. "When I first woke up from the accident, I believed everything they said about me was true," Damon told him. "I believed I'd missed something in my pre-check. Jack and I had only had one drink apiece the night before, so I didn't think it was possible that I could be hungover, right? But I was tired, groggy. Jack offered to help me with the pre-check, to go over everything again in case I'd missed something, while I went and got some coffee. And I was *grateful*. I was wide awake when we took off that day, but for the first couple of weeks after the crash, I was convinced I had somehow been negligent. I thought I was toxic, and I wanted to protect Cort from, well, *myself.* Later on, when I saw Jack on TV lying about how I had been drinking, I recognized that I'd need Cort's help to bring Jack to justice, but even then I thought I was doing him a favor by keeping my distance and only communicating as little as possible."

Cain shook his head sadly. "I get it. It sucks that you felt that way."

"But the thing is, did I fix it? Did I stick around and make things up to Cort?" His fingers closed more tightly over Cain's and he pressed a kiss to Cain's temple. "Nope. I decided since he had Cam, he didn't need me and my drama hanging around. And then I left to take care of Chelsea without even consulting him."

"You were protecting him."

"I was," Damon agreed. "But I'm kinda starting to realize that in my quest to protect him, I've hurt him a lot."

"Maybe so, but if you're trying to compare your behavior with Cort to my father's behavior with… everyone in the world, you're missing the point. Actions aren't the only thing that matter. Motive matters too."

"Spoken like a future lawyer, Mr. Shaw," Damon teased, and just like that, the weight on Cain's chest lifted.

He slapped Damon lightly in the stomach. "Spoken like a smart and mature individual," he corrected.

"A smart-ass, immature individual?"

Cain sat up and looked Damon in the eye. "Just for that, you don't get to see the hot tub."

"Wait, hot tub?" Damon squinted. "I was not aware this was even on the table."

"Uh huh. That's because you haven't been upstairs yet." Cain stood and planted his hands on his hips.

"You can't just dangle those words in front of a man after you've taken it away, Cain," Damon said with mock anger.

"And yet, I have," Cain told him sadly.

"Reconsider," Damon growled, pushing to his feet with one hand on the arm of the sofa. "Remember who's the… the… *Big Daddy*."

Oh, it was too perfect. "I'm not sure. I see no hat."

"I left it in the car. A king is still a king without his crown." Damon grabbed Cain by the belt loops and drew him closer until their chests were brushing.

"Okay," Cain relented.

"Okay?"

"Yeah, okay. We can use the hot tub after dinner. Because you saying the words *'Remember who's the Big Daddy'* just made my *life*, so I'm giving you a pass. Use it wisely." He pointed a threatening finger at Damon.

Damon grinned and pulled Cain even tighter. "I think we should probably use the hot tub *now*. Just in case I say something else at dinner that makes you change your mind," he said, and all Cain could do was laugh, because it was so true.

They did manage to wait until after dinner, mostly because Cain's stomach had started to growl just then. Damon cooked rice and reheated the chicken they'd bought, while Cain ran their bags upstairs, got the hot-tub set up, and assembled a salad. They worked together in a coordinated way, shuffling around each other with a prac-ticed ease that Cain wouldn't have thought possible. While the chicken was in the oven, Damon hefted himself up onto the counter and occupied himself by alternately stealing cucumber slices as fast as Cain could cut them, and trying to read the script of Cain's tattoo. Not a second went by when Damon wasn't trying to touch him or tease him into laughter. *"That cutting board too high for you, kiddo? Big Daddy's got it."*

Maybe it was odd that the simple act of assembling a meal with someone was somehow imbued with meaning, but it seemed that way to Cain. He loved how they'd been able to have a serious discussion out on the porch, one where Damon had allowed himself to be vulnerable and validate Cain's feelings about his father, and all that good, important stuff… and then devolve into teasing over stupid jokes.

He'd never experienced a connection like this - sure as hell not with his family, and not even with his friends. The fact that he'd found it with someone so sexy, so *kind*, was damn near unbelievable.

Cain was a pretty fatalistic person - he knew this about himself. Bad shit happened all the time, scales were balanced one way or another. But rather than wasting his time wondering how this thing with Damon would all come crashing to an end, he found himself wanting to just enjoy their time together. This crazy, shitty, wonderful adventure that he and Damon were on could end tomorrow… probably *would* end tomorrow, when they found whatever evidence they were looking for, or pretty soon after, if there were no evidence to be found. Either way there was no way Cain's life would ever be the same, and there was no way *Cain* would be the same, either.

If he ended up alone a month from now, laying in the single bed in his parents' house, thinking back on this crazy step out of time with Damon, he wanted to have plenty of good memories stored up to fight the inevitable bad.

And that was why, when the last bites of dinner had been consumed, the last of the dishes washed and put away, Cain took Damon by the hand, and led him upstairs.

CHAPTER SEVENTEEN

Damon followed Cain up the steps, their fingers threaded tightly together, his breath catching with every stride in a way that had nothing to do with the climb or the strain on his leg, and everything to do with the sexy man in front of him.

Christ. Had he ever wanted someone so badly? He couldn't remember it, if he had. In fact, he couldn't remember ever wanting *anything* so fucking badly - not his hard-won education, not the job he loved, not even getting his name and his life back.

And *that* knowledge was terrifying as hell. How had this guy become so important to him so quickly? How had Cain managed to get under his skin and somehow, with his sweetness and his sly humor, with his strength and his submission, take the neatly-ordered list of Damon's life-priorities and rearrange them all?

Cain paused when he reached the top of the stairs and turned to face Damon, who was one step below. "So, um, the hot tub is out there." He hooked a thumb over his shoulder, where a small sitting area led to another sliding glass door and what appeared, in the dim exterior light, to be another deck just like the one downstairs. "This is the room where I usually sleep," he said, pointing to the door opposite the stairs. "The other bedrooms and my dad's office are down there." He gestured down the hall.

He bit his lip when he turned back to Damon. "I'm pretty sure we have bathing suits around here somewhere, if you want?" His voice was husky, his eyes were glowing with desire, but he was strong enough to put his own needs aside and make sure Damon was totally comfortable, that he wasn't imposing or assuming too much.

Fragile and strong and *sweet.* Maybe the better question was how he hadn't fallen for Cain even sooner.

Damon took the final step, bringing himself flush against Cain, then kept advancing, walking Cain into the wall behind him. "Cain?"

"Y-yeah?" Cain's deep blue gaze fluttered from Damon's eyes to his lips and back again.

"We *won't* need swimsuits."

"Oh—" Cain began, but then Damon's lips met his, and anything else he'd been about to say seemed irrelevant in the face of the overwhelming fire that seemed ready to burn them both up.

He was dimly aware of Cain's fingers sifting through his hair, grabbing onto it as if Damon was the only point of stability as the world shifted around them. And maybe he was; Damon was holding onto Cain just as tightly. His tongue plundered Cain's mouth, cataloging every note of his sweetness, every sensation of his tongue, placing them all in a treasure box in his mind where everything about Cain was stored.

Damon broke away just long enough to strip Cain's shirt off, carefully avoiding his bandage, and throw it on the floor of the landing. He turned them so he could back Cain across the seating area to the sliding door, kissing him all the while. It was not the safest course, given the furniture directly in their path, but when the back of Cain's leg hit a coffee table and he stumbled, Damon was there to pull him back up, laughing as he claimed Cain's mouth once again.

Damon broke away to wrench the door open while Cain's hands reached for the hem of Damon's shirt, then that, too, was on the sitting room floor. Damon grabbed Cain around the waist as they tripped their way outside, the skin-on-skin heat of their embrace sending a shock through his body as surely as the cold night air.

"Jeans," Cain whispered against his lips as his feet hit the edge of the tub. The steam from the frothing water lent the night a foggy, mysterious air. He toed his shoes off, and Damon followed suit, but when Cain would have stepped back to remove his pants, Damon pulled him closer, pulling Cain's bottom lip between his teeth.

"Do you know how badly I want you?" he whispered, loving the blush that climbed Cain's cheeks.

"Yeah?" Cain asked, breathless and hopeful.

Jesus, how could he doubt it? Damon was rock-hard, not a single thought in his head besides how to pull Cain so far inside himself, meld them so firmly together, that none of the bullshit in their lives would be able to tear them apart. He'd imagined it was obvious.

But apparently Cain needed convincing.

He pulled back slightly, and Cain looked confused. "Wha-?"

"So handsome." Damon pushed both of his hands through the thick fall of Cain's dark hair, rubbing his fingertips along Cain's scalp as Cain arched helplessly toward him. The pink scars crisscrossing Damon's arms were silver in the dim light, and it should have looked strange or wrong for his hands to be touching Cain's perfection, but instead it looked incredibly *right.* "I love touching you. I fucking *love* the way you respond to me."

He moved his hand to cup Cain's jaw, running his thumbs along those high cheekbones, the clean lines that seemed like they'd been carved from marble, and stared into Cain's eyes. "Those eyes. So blue, baby. And always so open and honest." His voice was hushed, deep and shadowy as the night around them. "I sometimes wish I could see the world the way you see it - like everything is better and more important than it is, like *I* am better and more important than I am." Those blue eyes softened, wide and almost bewildered, and Damon lifted one corner of his mouth in a smile. "Wish you could see yourself the same way."

He traced his fingertips over the perfect cupid's-bow curve of Cain's lips. "Remember the first time we kissed?" God, that mouth. So lush and expressive, fascinating to watch even when Cain was giving him shit. Hell, *especially* when he was giving Damon shit. "Even before our lips touched, it was like… an earthquake, an electric shock." He shook his head at his own corny metaphors, but Cain didn't laugh or roll his eyes.

"I thought you didn't remember it," he whispered.

"I remember every single second," Damon promised him. "It was like this moment of clarity in the middle of the haze." He smiled. "To be honest, every time I'm with you is like that. You take me out of myself, cut through all the other stuff and remind me what's important. You remind me there's a future out there for me, and you make me believe I can find it." He could feel himself blushing. Forty years on the planet, and he'd still rather take a beating than spill his guts like this.

"You *can* find it," Cain lifted his hands to Damon's shoulders, then ran them up his neck. His gaze was calm and steady, reassuring, and Damon found himself speaking another truth.

"I think I already have."

He held steady while Cain looped his arms around his neck, let Cain draw his head down to kiss him, hot and sweet, like he'd put his entire soul into the kiss.

And then the heat that swamped him every time he was with Cain flooded his veins again, burning up all his words and all his control.

"Cain," he groaned, reaching for the button of Cain's jeans and stripping them down his legs so quickly that Cain laughed helplessly. Cain's boxers soon followed.

He pushed his own jeans and boxers down the same way, then stepped on the fabric that pooled around his ankles, gracelessly attempting to free his feet as he claimed Cain's mouth over and over again.

Braced on his good leg, he grabbed Cain around the waist - ignoring his cry of surprise - and moved him above the tub.

"Ready?" he asked, grinning.

"Damon Fitzpatrick!" Cain said breathlessly, as Damon set him gently in the water. "You can't just pick me up whenever you feel like it!"

"Why not?" Damon teased, stepping into the tub. The water was perfectly warm and he felt his whole body flush.

"Uh, because you're gonna give me a heart attack?" Cain pressed Damon's wet hand to his chest just above his heart. "Feel that? It's still hopping like a bunny on crack."

Damon smiled. "Let's see what we can do to keep that going." He dragged Cain atop him so he was straddling Damon's lap, then leaned back to allowing Cain to take the lead.

Cain didn't disappoint. He laced his hands behind

Damon's head pulling their lips together and bringing his cock into contact with Damon's stomach.

"*Fuck!*" Cain moaned, throwing his head back and rocking himself against Damon.

Damon's hands made tracks up and down the damp skin of Cain's back and over his freckled shoulders. He lifted handfuls of hot, frothy water, pouring them over Cain's chest and then following the paths of the rivulets with his fingertips.

God, those freckles. They fucking killed him. He traced them with his fingers, finding patterns in the scattered dots. He *wanted* in that moment - wanted unhindered access to that skin, wanted more light to see by, wanted to trace the shapes with his teeth. He vowed to himself that he would have it. This was only their beginning.

Cain's hands slicked over his chest, past his tense abs, to find his erection, stroking him firmly, and Damon gritted his teeth. It was so fucking good. Every single time with Cain was so perfect.

Cain had a mischievous look in his eye and he bent down to lick Damon's nipple... and then bit it gently.

"Aaaah!" Damon's hands clenched on Cain's ass, his fingers digging in. "Feels so fucking good, baby. I'm not gonna last."

Cain's face was beautiful, his desire so stark he seemed to nearly be in pain. "Damon, I want you inside me. Tonight."

Fuck. Fuck, yes. He wanted to claim Cain, finally. To make him his in every way.

"Then get out of this tub," Damon commanded.

Cain rocked one final time, as though he couldn't help it, and his frustrated whimper nearly made Damon lose himself. He braced his hands on Cain's hips and pushed him back. "In the house. *Now.*"

Cain pushed himself up in a rush of water and carefully stepped over the edge of the tub, his eyes burning into Damon's. Damon levered himself up and followed directly behind as quickly as he could, taking care not to slip in the water puddled on the deck.

"Holy fuck, it's freezing!" Cain said. His teeth were chattering before they'd made it to the door. "I can't believe I forgot *towels*!" He scurried inside, water sluicing down his body and leaving soggy footprints on the carpet.

Damon followed him in, pulling the door closed behind them, and took a moment to stare. Shivering, ridiculous, and still Damon knew this man was the most beautiful thing he would ever encounter, in this world or the next.

He grabbed Cain around the waist and pulled their bodies flush, pressing their kiss-swollen mouths together. If they froze to death, they'd do it locked this way. "Bed, Cain."

"Yeah," Cain sighed, like it had been a suggestion. Then he cleared his head. "Right, come on." He led Damon across the hall and into his bedroom, flipping on the light as he went.

Damon had the vague impression of dark oak furniture, a blue plaid bedspread - all the mountain-cabin warmth that was conspicuously absent in the rest of the jaw-droppingly modern house. It didn't surprise him that this was the place Cain had claimed.

Then Cain flopped himself down in the center of the bed, sprawled on his back, and Damon couldn't see anything but him.

"You're soaking wet," Damon reminded him as he stalked closer, stopping to grab his duffel bag and throw it on the end of the bed by Cain's foot. He wrenched the zipper open and searched for the condoms and lube.

Cain grinned, splaying his arms up and down like he

was making a snow angel, naked except for one extremely damp bandage on his arm. "I feel like the bed is only going to get wetter," he teased, his hot eyes raking up and down Damon's chest. "Anytime you're ready, Big Daddy."

"No." He paused in his search and pointed one stern finger at Cain. "No. That's just… *no*. It's not funny. Not in bed." He found the opened box of condoms and threw them on the mattress, then dug his hand in again. *Jesus, he'd swear he'd put the lube at the top of the case. Where the hell was it?*

Cain pushed himself to his knees and walked his way over to Damon. "You sure?" he asked, his voice husky. "Because I think it could be pretty fucking hot, *Daddy*."

Damon paused again to glare at Cain, but when their eyes met, he forgot what he was going to say. *Christ.*

"FYI, I'm about ten seconds from taking you without lube or prep, *kid*, so don't test me," he warned, but Cain only laughed at the empty threat. He reached his hand into the case and managed to extract the small blue tube of lubricant in two seconds flat.

"This what you're looking for…" He added in a whisper. "*Big Daddy?*"

Saucy brat. Damon was caught between laughter and lust - had he ever laughed this much while he was in bed? He hadn't known what he was missing. And it seemed like a tragedy that he could have gone his whole life without knowing how good it could be.

Damon grabbed the lube and pushed Cain back with one firm hand on his chest. He fell back against the bed laughing, and Damon climbed on top of him.

"I don't think you'll be laughing for long, brat."

"Wow. *Brat. Kid.* You're sure about the daddy thing? Because it sounds like…"

"It *sounds* like you want your ass spanked." Damon

straddled Cain's waist and grabbed his hands, pinning him against the mattress.

Cain blinked - actually fucking blinked, like he was considering it. He caught his lip between his teeth and his eyes burned up at Damon. "Maybe I do," he said slowly, and Damon had to take a deep breath.

His erection, which had subsided slightly thanks to the cold, roared back to life as he envisioned Cain's ass spread in front of him, rosy-pink from his palm, and...

Fuck. "You're determined to make me come before I get inside you," he growled. Cain glanced down at Damon's cock, and all traces of mischief fled from his face. He swallowed hard as his eyes met Damon's again.

"No, I'm not. Hurry," he whispered.

But Damon was realizing that he had his man right where he wanted him. He gave Cain a wolfish grin and sat back just far enough to take Cain firmly in hand. "You know, I'm actually thinking I should take my time."

He stroked Cain gently, *too gently*, in a way he knew would drive him crazy, gliding his thumb over the damp head of Cain's erection.

"Don't tease," Cain whispered urgently. "Please, Damon. Not now."

Damon leaned forward, bracing one hand on the bed as he bent his head down. "Let *me* do this," he whispered against Cain's lips, stroking him again, and Cain whimpered, but didn't argue.

Damon sat back and uncapped the lube, pouring some out onto his fingers. He stroked a single slick finger over Cain's hole, and Cain's back bowed off the bed. *God.* Damon wasn't sure which of them he was torturing. But he wanted to make it good for Cain. No, not good... *perfect.*

He continued his relentless stroking as he prepped Cain to take him, giving him one finger, then two, then three.

Cain was hipping up into his hand, his whimpers coming faster and faster until they morphed into one long keening wail. "Damon, I'm going to…"

He grabbed the base of Cain's cock. "Not yet," he breathed. "Together."

Cain's pupils were blown, his cheeks flushed, but he nodded. Damon ripped open the condom and covered himself, slicking lube down his length.

The muscles of his injured leg protested as he crawled on his knees between Cain's legs, but he firmly ignored it. Nothing, *nothing*, was going to interfere with this.

He lined himself up, and glanced into the deep blue gaze he couldn't get enough of. "Ready?"

Cain nodded seriously, lifting a hand to trace Damon's cheek. "More than."

Damon turned his head to plant a kiss on Cain's palm… and then slid home.

They moaned together, the sounds of their pleasure in total harmony as Damon seated himself completely inside Cain, and then he stilled.

"This is…"

"Perfect," Cain said, his voice coming out as thick and gravelly as Damon's usually was.

And it really *was* perfect.

He grabbed Cain's hand from his face and pushed it down to the mattress, then grabbed his other hand and pinned that down too. He'd never really noticed how large his frame was compared to Cain's, how much broader he was, but now it seemed totally right and perfect. Meant to be.

And with that thought ringing in his head, he began to move.

"Oh!" Cain cried. "God, Damon. *Harder*."

Harder, yes, and faster, too. That's what they both

needed. He wanted to embed himself inside Cain - tattoo himself into Cain's skin the same way the poem was.

He pistoned his hips, rocking them closer and closer to the end.

"Cain," he growled, and Cain's eyes swiveled to his. Gorgeous blue, fathomless and indomitable, they caught and held him.

There were so many things he wanted to say - I want you, I need you with me, *I love you* - but all that came out was a shuddering, raspy, "Oh fuck, baby. Fuck, Cain!"

But maybe it didn't matter, because Cain was with him, as always, his shining eyes reflecting back everything Damon was feeling: want and need and... yes, love.

"Damon!" Cain cried, tossing his head back. "So close!"

Damon reached between them, finding Cain's cock and stroking in exactly the way he knew Cain needed, and Cain went off, hot cum shooting between them. The feeling of Cain's release - the deep, hot clench of it, set Damon off, too, and in just two more thrusts, his end raced toward him and he came hard and long.

Heart pounding, skin prickling, he carefully lowered himself on top of Cain, and the words of the poem Cain had quoted came back to him. *The end is where we start from.* He lay cocooned with the man he loved, and let himself be content for the first time in as long as he could remember.

Cain threw another folder in the stack on his father's desk and ran a hand over his tired eyes, leaning back in the desk chair. "Anything?"

"Nah, nothing here," Damon replied, blowing out a long breath. He tossed his own stack of folders on the coffee table in front of him and leaned back on the sofa, turning his head to look at Cain. He dragged a hand through his messy hair - hair that had dried every-which-way after their shower the night before - and Cain had to resist the urge to cross the room and jump him. He looked good *always*, but the morning-after, messy-hair, barefoot, unbuttoned-jeans look was probably Cain's favorite. Plus, he admitted to himself that after last night, he wanted nothing more than to curl up against Damon's skin.

He lifted the collar of his borrowed t-shirt - another black band t-shirt he'd stolen from Damon's bag, this one emblazoned with the name Greta Van Fleet - and sniffed it surreptitiously. It smelled warm and delicious, like Damon himself, which was why he hadn't bothered to go through the old clothes left in his closet this morning, but had immediately claimed one of Damon's instead.

"You find anything?"

"No," Cain admitted. He gestured to the stack. "Not a damn thing here but a bunch of utility bills and an enormous bunch of receipts for the work on the house." He shook his head ruefully. "*Holy fuck*, I have no idea how they spent that much on renovations."

"There goes the inheritance?"

"Yeah, right. No sugar daddies around here, I'm afraid."

"Damn," Damon said sadly. "There goes my plan."

"Still a Big Dad—"

"Oh, God, *stop with that*," Damon grumbled, pushing to his feet, but he was smiling as he said it. He walked slowly to the desk, his limp more pronounced this morning.

"Your leg okay?" Cain asked carefully, but Damon shrugged.

"It's fine. Just overused it a little yesterday. Mostly last night." His smile turned smug as he began idly leafing through Cain's discarded folders. "Worth it."

Cain felt his cheeks grow hot. Last night had been the absolute best night of his life. Every hour, every minute. And not just because of the sex, but because of the laughter, the acceptance. There hadn't been a single moment when he'd felt ashamed of wanting Damon, not one second where he'd been focused on whether Damon really wanted to be with him or questioned his motives.

Yeah, this fucked-up road trip with Damon was like a journey into an alternate reality where the rules of his regular life didn't apply, but last night had been something beyond even *that*. He'd been a whole different person- a better, truer version of himself, and…

Jesus. Yeah, okay. Gross. He had a little bit of an emotional hangover. He could practically see the hearts and tweeting birds flying around his own head. And while he'd felt closer to Damon than he'd ever felt to anyone, there was still the enormous question of *how the hell they'd get Damon's life back.*

"I don't know where else to search," Cain said in irritation, eyes to the ceiling. "Maybe... I mean, he has his official office back in Nashville, but I still don't think he'd keep anything there, you know?" He pulled at his own hair, frustrated beyond belief. "I really felt like something would be here. When we walked into the house yesterday, I got this... I dunno, kind of weird sixth sense, like something would be here. Silly." He shifted his head to gauge Damon's reaction, and found that Damon wasn't paying attention to him at all. He was absorbed with the file of home remodeling bills.

"What are you looking at?" Cain demanded.

"Uh. Was I out of it yesterday when we pulled up? Is there a lawn around the property that I haven't noticed?"

"We're in a cabin in the woods, babe," Cain reminded him. "On the side of a mountain. There's no grass at all. Trees, bushes. Flowers in pots on the decks, when my mom feels like it."

Damon glanced up. "Then why did your dad pay $25,000 for lawn sprinklers? And why is he continuing to pay for monthly maintenance?"

"What?" Cain jumped out of the chair and ran around to the front of the desk. "Let me see that!" Damon handed over a sheet of paper and Cain read aloud. "Rabinov Mountain Landscaping and Design? I saw this one, but I didn't really look at the services listed."

"And what about this one for house painting? Just over sixty thousand last year."

Cain grabbed that paper too. "There's nothing to paint

in this house. Not outside, anyway. And the inside hasn't been painted since they remodeled years ago."

Damon leaned over and pointed to the header. "Color Home Professionals say differently. And the bill is marked Paid."

Cain's heart started beating harder. "Fuck, I need to grab my phone! It's downstairs."

"One step ahead of you," Damon said, sliding his own phone out of his pocket. He leaned his hip against the desk and started tapping furiously at the screen while Cain practically vibrated in place.

"There's the website for Color Home Professionals," Damon said, and Cain rested his head against Damon's shoulder to get a better view. It seemed pretty standard, if fairly light on actual info.

"Huh. Well, there are lots of pretty pictures of houses, alright."

"But that's pretty much all there is," Damon agreed. "That and a contact phone number."

Fuck. This had to be it. Had to be.

And honestly, what had Cain expected? An invoice from Jack labeled Airplane Tampering? He was so out of his depth with this. But he knew someone who wouldn't be.

"Send it to Bas."

Damon looked over at him and grinned. "Just what I was thinking."

"We need someone who can look into this and figure out whether these companies are real."

Damon put the invoices on the desk and snapped pictures with his phone. "I'm copying Drew, too. He'll understand the legal shit."

"Definitely." Cain took a step back. "Is… is this enough? If we can prove these companies don't exist, and he paid out thousands to them, do you think it would be enough to implicate my father?"

Damon shook his head, looking through the remaining invoices. "I honestly don't know. It looks damning, but your dad has a whole team of lawyers who'll jump on this and find a hundred innocent ways to explain it. Maybe he's just shitty with money, maybe he doesn't read his bills."

"You don't believe that, though."

"Well, no." He shrugged. "It's pretty fucking shady. But we don't know if it has anything to do with the crash, either. These invoices are all more recent." He grabbed the sheaf of papers. "If he's palling around with Russian crime syndicates, these could be for anything. We need to figure out exactly where the money went in order to prove there's anything criminal on your dad's end. And I imagine he's smart enough that it'll be really hard to find that info."

Cain drifted toward the window and looked at the rugged mountain profile in the distance. He lifted a hand and rubbed at a knot of tension in his neck. *Figures.* They'd found just enough to reinforce their own belief that his father was a criminal, but not enough to prove it to anyone else.

"So, what next?" He was afraid he knew exactly what the next step would be — Cain testifying to the authorities about his dad. And he still wasn't totally sure about that.

Feel better. I love you.

But if he didn't, what would happen to Damon?

"Cain?"

"Yeah?"

"Look at me."

Cain turned to find Damon watching him, ass propped against the desk, hands folded over his chest. "This changes nothing."

"What?"

"I told you before, I don't expect you to come forward with information about your father. We'll find another way." Damon looked fierce, even against the backdrop of the shiny wood desk and its ultra-modern accessories, a silver-haired warrior prince in a band t-shirt and jeans.

"Yeah, but..."

"There's no *but*. What's between us is not dependent on you doing *anything*. There's no requirement, and I don't want you to feel like I'll look at you differently, whichever way you decide. Okay?"

"I hear what you're saying." Cain turned back to the window and braced his hand on the glass. "But how can you not, Damon? We're talking about your life, about getting your identity back! And, okay, let's say you really don't care about that," he continued, holding a hand up when it looked like Damon would interrupt. "Though, I've gotta say, I don't believe it for a second. Let's say you let Bas and Drew pull strings, and suddenly you've got a whole new identity as Dave Fitz-something, a mechanic from Topeka."

"Topeka?"

"Whatever! The point is, nothing goes away, and you know it. My dad knows you're alive. He knows who Chelsea and Molly are, and they can't stay in hiding forever. He's gotta know who Cort is, too. And I'm guessing he hasn't gone after Cort because he's ex-FBI and dating one of the richest guys in Boston, but how long will that last? He went after *Levi Fucking Seaver*."

"Cain."

"No, Damon. I'm being real here. What about Bas and Cam? You think they're fine knowing the guy who wanted their parents dead is still running around free? You think they'll be all understanding about my moral dilemma?" He was beyond frustration, near tears. "This shouldn't be so hard," he whispered.

"Come here."

Cain shook his head. He could barely maintain his composure as it was, and he didn't want Damon's compassion. He wasn't sure he deserved it.

"I'm not sure I can live with myself if I let him keep doing the shit he's been doing." He dug the heels of his hands into his closed eyes, letting his vision fracture into a hundred tiny kaleidoscope pieces against the back of his eyelids. Broken pieces, just like his thoughts, just like his heart. "Essentially, either way this works, I'm going to feel like shit. I need to man up and do the thing that keeps people safe."

"Come. Here. *Now*."

Cain opened his eyes, expecting to find Damon looking at him with pity, or maybe even annoyance, but he wasn't. His smile was patient, his eyes firm but kind, and Cain didn't know if it was conscious thought or subconscious obedience, but he found himself crossing the room to stand between Damon's legs.

"There are a couple of things you're not considering, babe," Damon said softly, running his hands up and down Cain's forearms, brushing his thumbs lightly over Cain's wrists in a way that felt soothing and thrilling all at once. He felt like a captive, and like he was guarded and precious at the same time.

Cain huffed. "I'm sure there are a million things I'm not considering." Sniffing, he continued. "I'm not sure if you've noticed, but I'm kind of a mess."

"You're not a mess. You're brave, Cain. You're so fucking brave. Don't let anyone tell you that you're not."

"Yeah? Cause I don't feel so brave."

"Then trust me when I tell you. Okay?"

Cain snorted and looked away.

"*Cain Edward* don't be disrespectful."

Damon's imitation of Lily Shaw at her most outraged was so spot-on that Cain glanced back at him in shock. Damon grinned like a loon and gripped the back of Cain's neck. The Damon Hold.

"Listen, you idiot. You love your father, even though he's kind of an asshole. You feel an obligation to your family, to not see their lives destroyed by association. That doesn't make you weak, it makes you loyal." He lifted his other hand to run it over Cain's cheek, and the look in his eyes made it hard for Cain to breathe. "But Cain, your first loyalty has to be to yourself. Not to your family, not to me or the Seavers. There's no guilt here, okay? No obligation. You need to do what is best for *you*. You need to figure out what you can *live* with. And there are no right or wrong answers."

"How can you just stand there and be fine with this?" Cain sputtered.

"I am far from fine with this, Cain," Damon said, and for just a second, Cain could see the deep anger in his eyes. "I would give pretty much anything to get the information we need to end this. Every dollar I have, every possession I own. God, I'd give this fucking leg if I thought it would do any good." He pounded his fist on the thigh of his injured leg. "But this is what we have. This is the reality we live in. You beating yourself up over it changes jack shit."

"Before, you were so angry. And I understood that. Still understand it. You said…"

"Yeah, I know what I said. I didn't get where you were coming from, and I didn't want to. I can be a self-absorbed asshole sometimes, you know?" Damon grinned again, but then his smile faded. "And there's something else to remember here, too." He waved a hand at the papers spread on the desk behind him. "If those are dummy corporations, if your dad is mixed up with SILA, this goes way deeper than just stopping him. Even if we found a smoking gun that would get a United States Senator arrested and convicted, it wouldn't keep any of us safe. In fact, it might just make us even bigger targets. And that includes *you*, Cain."

"I don't care—"

"Yeah? Well, I *do*." Damon's hands were back on his wrists, no longer soothing but imprisoning. Constricting. "Did you hear what I said about where your first loyalty needs to be? You don't risk your life for this. Ever. Non-negotiable."

"So then… what the fuck do we do?" Cain let his head fall against Damon's broad chest. "I just want this over. I just want all of us to move on."

Damon's muscles tightened. "That eager to get back to school?"

Cain shook his head. "I don't even know if I want to go back to school. That's my dad's thing, not mine."

"So what do you want?" Damon asked softly.

Cain lifted his head and promptly drowned in the green-brown eyes staring down at him. Helpless, he answered with the first truth that came to his mind. "You. Damon, I want you."

Damon's hands slid up his arms, over his shoulders, to cup his neck in the familiar hold that made Cain feel strong and small all at once. "You've got me. Question is," Damon challenged, "what are you gonna do with me?"

Blood rushed behind Cain's ears, his pulse so loud he could hear the frantic syncopated rhythm of his heart. *You've got me.* What did that even mean? His mind whirled, trying to parse the complicated calculus of that deceptively simple sentence. Did it mean exactly what Cain wanted it to mean? Nothing in his life had ever been that easy. Promises like that carried expectations, but Damon was telling him there were none. It simply didn't add up.

"Stop thinking so hard," Damon said, brushing a kiss across his lips that did nothing to clear Cain's confusion. "You've got time to figure it out."

"I do?"

"Yeah, babe." Damon's strong fingers kneaded the muscles of Cain's neck. "Here's what I'm thinking for the short term. Ready?"

Cain nodded dazedly. He was ready for anything, as long as Damon's hands were on his skin, his raspy voice in Cain's ear.

"I'm thinking we are going to photograph the documents in this folder and send them to Bas and Drew." He handed Cain his phone, and Cain gripped it hard. "We're going to go through the rest of these papers again, now that we have a better idea what we are looking for, and see if we can find these company names listed anywhere else, and then we'll send that information on, too. We're going to go about this the smart way, and not rush in with a half-formed plan. Great advice this really smart guy gave me the other night." His lips quirked into a smile.

Cain snorted. "What about Chelsea and Molly?"

Damon's brow furrowed for a moment. "I need to talk to Eli and to Chelsea. If we can figure out a way to access the money Bas sent them without tipping anyone off, Chelsea will be covered for a good long while. She can stay with Eli, or we can relocate her somewhere more permanent if she wants. Maybe we can head back there tomorrow for a belated Thanksgiving and figure stuff out."

Cain's stomach flipped. "Yeah?"

"Yeah. Be nice to spend it with loved ones for a change. You in?"

Cain swallowed hard, trying not to read too much into *loved ones*. Danger, danger. "Totally. Eli and I forged a deep bond while I was there. We're besties now." *When he's not putting his fucking hands all over you.*

"I could tell," Damon said dryly. "So. Documents. Then email. Then head back to Eli's. But before we go…"

"Yeah?"

"Maybe we could take an hour to use the hot tub again," Damon suggested, one eyebrow raised like this was a question or a suggestion, when there was no question in Cain's mind that this was a perfect idea. "It is Thanksgiving, after all. That hot tub makes me very thankful."

"This time I'll bring some towels," Cain said.

"This time I'll bring the condoms and lube."

Cain laughed, because he couldn't help it. Even though nothing had been settled, things felt so positive and hopeful.

And maybe Damon was right - maybe he didn't need to decide everything today. Maybe he had time to figure things out.

"You make great suggestions," Cain told him, and when he lifted on his tiptoes to press a kiss to Damon's lips, Damon bent his head and met him halfway.

As their kiss turned hotter, Cain's hands went around Damon's waist beneath his t-shirt. The warm strength of him was the dictionary definition of reassuring, and Cain surrendered himself to the magical pull of the kiss. It went on for a long while, no hurrying and no demands, just all-consuming pleasure strong as gravity, unfightable and unstoppable by…

"*Cain Edward!* What is the meaning of this?"

Cain sprang backward like he'd been electrocuted,

pressing the back of his hand to his kiss-swollen lips. There in the doorway stood his mother, his father, and his sister, all staring at him with identical expressions of shock and horror.

And just like that, his time had expired.

CHAPTER NINETEEN

Oh, shit. Damon's head swiveled to the doorway to find three pairs of eyes locked on Cain.

Cain's sister - a blonde, tanned, negative image of her brother - seemed surprised more than anything, her jaw dropped open like she'd never seen Cain before. Cain's mother looked ready to explode, whether in anger or in tears, Damon wasn't sure. And Cain's father, the powerful, evil Senator Shaw who by all rights should have been twirling his mustache like some cartoon villain, just seemed befuddled and a little overwhelmed. His sandy hair was thinning, his stomach was paunchy beneath his Tennessee Volunteers t-shirt and neatly-pressed khakis, and he blinked slowly, not like he was calculating the next step in his plan for world domination, but like a dad who'd just seen incontrovertible evidence that his son was still very much gay, despite his attempts to coerce him into being otherwise.

Cain, meanwhile, was doing a good impression of a concrete wall. His milk-white face had flushed beet red, but he stood tall and said absolutely nothing to break the fraught silence that descended on the room.

Damon surreptitiously lifted a finger to touch Cain's hand, a subtle reminder that he was here if Cain needed him, but Cain jerked his hand away and straightened his spine, clutching Damon's phone so tightly in his far hand that Damon wondered if it might crack. The man was an island, cutting himself off from the censure he knew he was about to receive, desperately trying to wall himself off from everyone in the room, including Damon. It broke Damon's heart just a little to witness it, and it made him angry, not at Cain, but at the circumstances.

Cain had been outed to his family twice - once to his father in high school, and now again to his whole family. He hadn't gotten the option of when or where or how to come out, or *whether* he wanted to come out in the first place.

"You're *gay*?" Cain's sister — *Cady*, Damon remembered — spoke two words that shattered the silence like a grenade, and suddenly the suspended animation of the moment squealed into fast-forward, everyone talking and moving at once.

"Cain, my God, what are you *thinking*?" his mother cried, while his sister demanded, "How did I not know this? Cain, why didn't you tell me?" His father raised a hand to his face and rubbed his forehead.

Meanwhile, Cain stood like a statue, calm and composed, though from this distance Damon could see the tiny shudders that wracked him, like miniature earthquakes beneath the surface of his skin. But Cain was courageous, and Cain was strong. The hands at his side flexed for a moment, like he was unconsciously reaching for Damon, and Damon stood upright bringing himself closer, lending Cain his support.

"There's nothing to discuss, Mom. I'm gay. I think you and Dad have known for quite a while."

Damon sucked in a sharp breath. Those words carried such power, and they came at such a cost, whether you were saying them to yourself for the first time, or saying them to someone you cared about, or even when you were saying them to someone who had just caught you mid-kiss. Maybe especially then. Cain was claiming his identity, stating it clearly, making it so it was no longer a shameful secret.

"*No.* I did not know any such thing, and I don't know it now either! This nonsense was supposed to be over in high school, Cain," she informed him. "Your father took care of it. Moved us away from that boy who'd been leading you in the wrong direction."

Now all eyes darted to Damon, and he resisted the urge to wave. *Bad influence, right here.*

The senator's eyes flared with recognition, and then confusion. He glanced around the room and noticed the papers and files spread all over the desk and coffee table, then looked back at Damon. His jaw hardened, and Damon's blood went cold.

Until that second, he'd almost forgotten the stakes here were even higher than Cain coming out to his family. Now the senator knew exactly where Damon was, and soon he'd know just how much they'd figured out about his involvement with SILA. And still, Damon couldn't force himself to grab the folder of invoices and make a dash for it. In fact, he couldn't take a single step away from Cain, who was standing so close Damon could practically hear the cogs turning in his man's head as he absorbed this new blow.

Was it worse that his mother hated Cain being gay? Or that she denied he was gay at all?

Both, Damon decided.

"I cannot understand why you would do this *now*, when you *know* that your father is on the brink of announcing his candidacy!" Lucy continued her tirade, and Damon couldn't keep from rolling his eyes even though no one was paying attention to him.

"Wait, what happened in high school?" Cady demanded. Like an animal with no sense of self-preservation, she stepped further into the thick tension of the room, stopping halfway between her parents and Cain and looking back and forth between them like the chair umpire in a tennis match. "Cain?"

"Dad caught me kissing Jesse Porter." Cain's voice was tight and high, a combination of hurt and anger threading through the simple statement. He stared at his father without flinching, and the senator didn't move or speak.

"The kid you used to tutor?"

"He was my boyfriend." No hesitation, no equivocation, though Damon knew Cain was ready to snap.

Lucy Shaw's mouth was a tight line, her cheeks flushed and eyes burning as the carefully constructed lie she'd tried to make a reality crumbled to dust before her. "I can see you were lying about being ill to avoid the ski trip," she said petulantly, as though this was really the thing she was most upset about.

"Not a lie," Cain said. "I was injured." His eyes were locked on his father, and remained there as he lifted his arm to show the fresh white bandage they'd taped to his arm after showering this morning.

Cain's mother gasped, eyes wide, and her hands reached out as she came forward to inspect his damaged arm. Damon was pleased to see she had a normal, motherly reaction to this, at least.

"Dear God. When the hell did you put all this... this...

trash all over yourself?" she moaned, stepping between Cain and Damon, reaching for Cain's arm.

For the first time since his family had walked in, Cain's eyes met Damon's. His expression was bleak - both sad and unsurprised. The woman was horrified at his *ink*, not his injury. Jesus. Damon shook his head minutely.

The senator stepped forward. "Enough, Lucy. Get out, both of you." He pointed at his wife and daughter. "I'm going to handle this. You two wait downstairs."

"But Daddy!"

"Emmett, he is *my son*! I will have my say."

"You've already had it, Lucy," Emmett said firmly. He didn't raise his voice, nor did he turn to look at her. His eyes seemed to be transfixed by the papers on the desk, and he stared at them as though they might suddenly burst into flames if he focused hard enough. "Go. Now."

Lucy set her jaw, and her fingers tightened on Cain's arm - Damon could see dimples forming beneath each of her red-tipped fingernails. But finally, surprising no one, she relented, pushing Cain's arm away. "There are tattoo removal services," she informed no one in particular. "Come with me, Arcadia. We need to put the groceries away and start dinner. Dinner for *four*," she clarified, in case Damon thought he was invited.

Cady clearly didn't want to budge, but her mother snagged her around the elbow without breaking stride and all but dragged her from the room, shutting the door behind them.

When they were gone, silence reigned again, but this time, it wasn't simply oppressively heavy, but charged with tension. Damon could feel Cain vibrating like a tuning fork, but he resisted the urge to touch him. A demonstration of affection in front of Cain's father would have to come from Cain himself.

The senator heaved a sigh and walked to the leather desk chair where Cain had been sitting, the desk like a tiny mahogany neutral zone separating him from Cain and Damon. Or maybe, strewn with evidence as it was, it was more like a battlefield. Shaw picked up one of the receipts from the desk. He read it, then tossed it back down dismissively.

The leather chair creaked as he sat down, eyes pinging back and forth between them, and Damon instinctively shifted his weight, blocking Cain slightly from view, like that would do anything at all to protect him from what his father might say.

After a minute that lasted a century, the senator turned his gaze out the window. "I've always loved this view," he mused. "When I bought this property years ago, I had the idea this would be our family home, the place where you and Arcadia would bring the grandchildren to visit us, maybe a place where your mother and I would retire. Which was silly of me," he said, giving Cain an off-handed smile, "since your mother would never be happy living in an out-of-the-way place like this. Born to rule society, that one."

He sighed again, drummed his fingers on the desktop in a careless rhythm, and issued his opening salvo. "I debated whether to pretend not to know who you are," he told Damon. "But I won't insult anyone's intelligence."

Damon raised his chin, but otherwise said nothing.

"I would like to know what you're doing with my son, though."

Once again, Damon remained silent. Emmett Shaw could demand an explanation all day long, but Damon wouldn't dignify it with a response. He owed the senator nothing. But behind him, he could hear a subtle change in Cain's breathing. He had no idea what it meant.

The senator shifted his attention to Cain. "You've always been a good son, Cain. A little rebellious, perhaps," he allowed with a smile, "but that's a good thing in a man. Gotta have a spark that lets people know you'll stand up for yourself. I'm proud of you, son."

Jesus.

"Are you?" Cain whispered. His voice was strangled, choked with disgust and sadness and disbelief.

"I am," the senator said heartily. It was as though he couldn't hear any of those notes in Cain's voice. Maybe, like Cain's mother, he only heard what he wanted to hear.

"I will say, though, I'm a little disappointed in what I walked in on here today. Oh, not the kissing," he waved his hand dismissively. "No, I knew it would only be a matter of time before something like this came up. I don't bury my head in the sand about these things the way your mother does, and I knew you couldn't just turn it on and off." He shook his head indulgently, as though his wife amused him. "But I really thought you had better judgment than to get involved with the likes of *him*." He nodded his head at Damon. "Don't you see what's happening here?"

"I think what's happening here," Cain said. "Is that we found all sorts of suspicious invoices in your files."

Shaw gave Cain the same indulgent smile he'd worn when talking about his wife. "*These* invoices? For the house renovation?"

"They weren't for the house renovation," Cain said.

"Oh, Cain. *Prove it.* In case you haven't researched far enough yet, each of these companies is a very real, very well-known local entity. Many of them have clients in local law enforcement."

"Of course they do." Damon ground his teeth together. The bastard was all but admitting the companies were fake, but of course they had all kinds of local politicians and police on their payroll who'd swear up and down to their legitimacy. Hell, they probably all filed taxes. Of course they did.

Shaw shrugged and his smile widened. "I enjoy using local contractors whenever possible. Keeping the community alive."

"You used our family," Cain accused stepping forward. Christ, Cain looked wounded, like even though he'd been kicked a hundred times by the guy, metaphorically speaking, he'd still found a new capacity for hurt in hearing his father all but admit this new sin. "Dragged our family into this bullshit, for what? More money? Power? *God*."

"No, I *protected* you! All of you. The only one using you here is *him*. Mister Damon Fitzpatrick." The senator gave Damon a scathing once-over, and Damon fought to remain calm, not to display how absolutely furious he was in the clench of his fists or tightness in his shoulders. "How's your *brother*, Mr. Fitzpatrick?"

"Cort's fine. So are my sister and her daughter."

Shaw blinked and tilted his head back, studying Damon's face like a chessboard while a small smile played around his lips.

"Jack said you were a miserable bastard. I thought he was exaggerating."

Cain gasped. Damon closed his eyes and shook his head.

"And what did Jack say about *me*, Dad?"

For a second, Shaw hesitated. "He said nothing about you. Why would he?" But it was too late, the moment of hesitation had given him away.

"Did you pay him to sleep with me?"

"Sleep with you? Christ, no. He befriended you, yes. But sleeping with you. No." He looked so genuinely outraged, so close to anger, that Damon almost believed him. "Did he?"

Cain ignored this. "You wanted him to spy on me."

"Not *spy*, Cain, but to keep you safe."

"To make sure I wasn't involved in any relationships that could damage your reputation."

"Or yours! When your father is rich, is powerful, people come out of the woodwork to take advantage—" He glared at Damon again.

"You must have been so sorry to lose him," Cain said bitterly. "Now that you don't have anyone to keep tabs on me."

Once again, the senator hesitated, and Cain recognized it immediately. "Oh, fuck. Who? Who's spying on me now?"

"No one," Shaw lied. "I was concerned for your safety, and Jack was in charge of security for our family. His job was to keep you safe, among other things."

"*Among other things*," Cain repeated in disgust. "Other things like killing Levi and Charlotte Seaver."

Shaw's face paled. He took a deep breath and steepled his hands on his desk. "Levi Seaver was my best friend." He slid open the top middle drawer of his desk and a second later, there was an audible click as he removed a panel from one side. He extracted a package of cigarettes, an ashtray, and a lighter.

"Levi was the one who gave me this desk," he mused. "It's an original Warren, with a hidden compartment. He said it reminded him of me - an antique with hidden secrets. Two years older than he was, and he never let me forget it." He smiled sadly, like he was thinking of his old friend. The lighter cracked and flared as he lit the cigarette, taking a deep drag. "We won't mention this to your mother," he told

Cain, exhaling the words in a plume of smoke. "She thinks I quit years ago."

"God," Cain said in disgust. "How do you live with yourself?"

The senator sucked in a breath through his teeth. "I didn't kill Levi Seaver."

"What happened to not insulting our intelligence?" Damon demanded. "Jack Peabody told us all about what he did… and *why*."

"I didn't kill Levi Seaver," the senator repeated. "Levi killed himself."

"Wow. That's sick," Damon accused. "You — "

"Do you know, when Levi and Jon McMann and I founded Seaver Tech, Levi didn't have a pot to piss in? Mortgaged his house, pawned his guitar, pissed off Charlotte to no end, although she stuck by him, because that's the kind of woman she was. Jon was this newly-minted lawyer, thousands of dollars in debt and saddled with a kid and a wife who'd grown up rich and accustomed to a certain standard of living. I was dating your mother, and determined to show your grandfather that I was good husband material. It was a different time then," he added with a short laugh. Then he sighed. "Such a different time then."

Cain drifted forward to lean against the back of a chair across from the desk. "What does that have to do with — "

"Don't interrupt," the senator told him with a glare. He took another drag of the cigarette, and Damon noticed that his hand wasn't quite steady. "Levi knew his tech would work. Christ, that man was convincing. And confident. I don't know if you remember that, Cain, but he was so confident in everything he did. Sebastian is a bit like that," he mused. "Must come with the genius." He sighed again. "The banks wouldn't lend us money, we were in debt up to our eyes, but we didn't have enough for the demo we needed. We were desperate."

Oh, fuck. Damon sighed as the facts clicked into place in his mind. Just where would three broke not-quite-kids get the money they needed for a start up?

Cain looked back and forth from Damon to his father. "Explain it to me, because I'm not getting it. What did you do?"

Shaw's lip twitched in a parody of a smile. "We went to an unconventional money source. A man by the name of Ilya Stornovich was happy to lend us money… in exchange for a little help from time to time. A little programming job here, design plans there. Side-jobs we called them. Jon hated it - he was squeamish from the beginning, but that's a lawyer for you, eh? Black and white, a firm line between right and wrong. He didn't have a head for business, so eventually we stopped telling him. But Levi, he understood that sometimes you have to nudge the line a little if you want to get ahead."

He flicked his cigarette over the ashtray before taking another drag. "But then, a few years in, Levi started getting cold feet too. *This is the last one*," Shaw said in a sing-song voice, shaking his head. "*No more after this, Emmett. We don't know what they're using this tech for. I want to be a man my sons can be proud of.* Christ. Like *I* didn't? Like I wouldn't have slept easier at night if the Russians didn't know my name, or the names of my kids? But it wasn't about wrong and right at that point. It was about keeping my head above water." He turned to look at Cain. "It was about keeping my family safe."

Damon stepped forward, needing to be closer to Cain. Shaw was starting to make a fucked-up sort of sense, and all of a sudden, up was down and down was up.

"See, the problem was, the Russians liked us just a little

too much. By then, old man Ilya had ceded power to his son, Adam, a bastard in every sense of the word. He wanted to be more than just a moneylender, a leg breaker, a broker for technology like his father had been. He wanted to build himself an empire, get his family a seat at the table in the criminal world.

"We'd repaid our loans a hundred, maybe a thousand, times over, of course. Levi, Jon, and I had become an overnight success story. Jon bought his first hundred-thousand-dollar sports car, which back in those days was saying something. People were writing articles about Levi." He laughed. "He was on the Hot Hundred Most Powerful Millionaires list for this magazine one time. I gave him shit about that *daily*. Hourly, for a while." His smile faded. "But none of it mattered, because the game with the Russians was no longer about what they could do *for* us, but what they could do *to* us. Ruin us in business, for sure, but worse… hurt our families."

He stubbed out his cigarette with violence and promptly lit another.

"Levi had the brilliant idea that he'd start making tech that failed. He'd leave out one crucial line of code, mess up some small mechanism. Maybe then they'd be less eager to use us, right? They'd just forget we'd ever existed." He shook his head. "Remember the time Sebastian Seaver ended up in a car accident, Cain? Rear-ended by that hit and run driver who was never found?"

Cain nodded slowly. "Broke his collarbone."

"Yes, he did. And thank Christ he was driving his dad's Volvo at the time and not riding in that little Boxster Drew McMann drove."

"*Jesus*," Damon breathed, and the senator raised an eyebrow in his direction.

"You can think what you like of me as a father, as a

person, Mr. Fitzpatrick. But if you think I was going to take a chance on having something like that happen to my children, or my wife, then you don't know me at all."

"Things kept on as they had been for a while after that, but then Levi balked again." Shaw took an angry drag and picked at something on his lip. "*We started this company to do things our own way, Emmett. I'm not becoming a slave to the goddamn Russians.*" He stared at the desk, like he was seeing visions of the past in the shining mahogany. His jaw ticked to the side. "And that was about the time Adam Stornovich decided he needed a foothold in American politics." He shrugged.

He looked at Damon and his eyes flared. "Don't you dare feel sorry for me. I wanted power, and I got it. I'm one of the most powerful men in the whole goddamn country!" He looked away again as he continued. "But Levi wanted something different. Fucking *asshole* decided he'd blackmail them back." He was angry, Damon realized, profoundly so. At himself, maybe, and maybe at Levi Seaver, too.

He stabbed out his cigarette, and for a second Damon thought the man might be sick. He looked nauseated, and beads of sweat stood out on his forehead. "You can imagine how *that* went. You can imagine what they demanded of me. And you can imagine what they held over my head."

Cain made a wounded noise deep in his throat.

"And you can imagine what happened when they believed Jack would talk."

Shaw shuddered, and *Christ Almighty*, Damon could almost understand how this man had become what he was. A regular guy - a little too cocky, a little too young – who'd gotten in over his head, and suddenly found he was owned by people who wouldn't take no for an answer, people who threatened his family. And he felt guilty for it.

None of this changed the essential facts, of course.

Emmett Shaw had blood on his hands. He was a manipulator, a con man, an asshole. But as Damon had been reminding Cain for days, it wasn't that simple. Relationships weren't that simple. People weren't that simple.

He found himself feeling reluctant sympathy for this guy. It should have been impossible.

"So, here's where we find ourselves," Shaw said, spreading his hands on the desk. "I am a man with many secrets. If I come forward about them, I die. Or worse, my family does. So, I'm not going to do that. Not for anyone, Mr. Fitzpatrick, and sure as hell not for *you.*" He sat back in his chair and gave Damon a knowing grin. "But that's alright. Because it's not really justice you want, is it?"

Damon frowned. "Yeah, it sure as hell is."

Shaw shook his head, smiling. "No. You just want your life back. You want to be made whole again. You want to reclaim your identity, your job, your family."

Cain turned a questioning glance on Damon, who swallowed hard. Was that what he wanted? It was a part of it, certainly, maybe even most of it. But he wanted justice for Cam and Bas, too. He wanted to know that no one else would be harmed because of the senator.

"You want to keep your loved ones safe," Shaw persisted. "Just like I do. And we're really not so different, you and me. We're too old to believe we can get everything we want, and we're willing to negotiate. We're willing to make the hard choices, to protect the most essential things, even when it means sacrificing others."

The senator reached back into the middle drawer of the desk, like he was accessing that secret compartment Damon and Cain hadn't thought to look for. "What if I were to tell you that I have, right here, a list of account numbers that show Jack Peabody being paid an extortionate amount of money just prior to the Seavers' plane crash? Combined with Jack's cell phone records, which show him having conversations with various known criminals at around the same time, I think you could certainly make a case that you weren't responsible for the crash at all, Mr. Fitzpatrick. Hell, *I'd* believe you."

Damon and Cain exchanged a look. Cain looked excited, like maybe it could all be over just that easily.

Damon knew better. This was the carrot, but there was a stick coming, too.

"And what would I have to do to get those papers?" Damon demanded.

"Hardly anything, and that's the truth. Nobody else is going to die if I can help it," the senator said grimly.

Damon folded his arms over his chest. *Hardly anything* and *nothing* were vastly different, and Damon suspected he was about to find out just how different they were.

"I'm going to give you this documentation, and in exchange, you're going to forget everything you think you know from these files." Shaw nodded at the files on the desk. "I'm telling you - and you can believe it or not, but it's the truth - you won't get anywhere by investigating them, anyway."

Damon looked at the papers in the senator's hand. He had no way of knowing exactly what was on those papers, but then again, the senator had no way of knowing whether he'd keep his promise not to investigate the companies on those invoices. What Shaw was proposing was a standoff that would leave Damon better off than he'd been before. But...

"And my sister? My brother? The Seavers? How do I know we won't all have targets painted on us the second I leave here?"

Shaw pursed his lips. "They'll be in no danger from me or anyone I'm involved with. We have nothing to gain from the Seavers or any of them, apart from ensuring you stick to the agreement. After all, if anything were to happen to any of them, no doubt you'd go to the authorities and spill everything you thought you knew. It would make life very sticky for me, and I'd much rather avoid that."

Damon nodded slowly and stepped forward, hand outstretched for the papers. "Alright. Okay. I can agr— "

"Not so fast," the senator said. He leaned back in his chair, and his gaze danced from Cain to Damon and back again. "One more condition."

Fuck. "What?" he growled.

"This charming little love affair you're having with my son? It's over. Now. Before you have a chance to leak anything to the press."

The shock of it hit him like cold water, and it *shouldn't* have been so surprising, he *should* have expected some bullshit like this, but he hadn't. He'd been lulled into sympathy for this man, and he'd been a fool.

"Fuck you," Damon said clearly. "That's not a thing I'm going to negotiate. *Cain* isn't a bargaining chip."

Shaw smiled, but shook his head slowly. "Bravo, Mr. Fitzpatrick. Bravo. That was an inspiring performance." He turned to look at Cain, and shrugged. "I don't blame you for falling for it, son. He's extremely convincing."

"What the hell are you talking about?" Cain demanded, looking from Damon to his father.

"You two. This… *thing* you've got going on. Let me guess - it started conveniently right around the time Mr. Fitzpatrick realized he'd need leverage over me? So, he gets you to agree that I'm an evil mastermind, so you'll help him on his little witch hunt." He waved a hand around the office, at the papers strewn everywhere. "And if there's nothing to find here, no matter. Of course Mr. Fitzpatrick knows how much of a scandal it would be for me if my son were to be outed in the newspapers. It would only be a matter of time, Cain, before you two were seen in public. Then I'd lose face, lose financial backing, lose my Senate seat, and Mr. Fitzpatrick's revenge plan would be complete. Did I miss anything?" he asked Damon.

"Everything. You missed everything." *My God.* It seemed as if the man really believed what he was saying. What a fucked-up bastard.

"You're wrong," Cain said staunchly. "What's between Damon and me is..."

"Oh, Cain," Shaw shook his head sadly. "There's *nothing* between you and *him.* Nothing except him wanting to get his life back, and you being his best shot at getting what he wants."

"No!" Damon shot back. "Cain and I, our relationship has nothing to do with this." He turned to Cain, who looked stunned and maybe just a little bit worried. "You know that, don't you? Cain?"

Not after the previous night, not after all that had been said and done between them. There could be no doubt anymore, could there?

Cain didn't look convinced, and that was its own form of heartbreak right there.

"Cain, you have to believe that I would never..."

"Oh, you would," Shaw said, supremely confident. "You certainly would. You're using him, and you're not the first." He looked at Cain. "I know you've never forgiven me for the way things ended with that boy back in high school. Puppy love is strong, and you were more than willing to believe I'm the manipulative parent keeping you from your one true love." He sighed. "That's not how it happened, Cain."

"Oh, no? How did it happen then?" Cain demanded. "How did it happen, if it wasn't you threatening to get rid of

Jesse's scholarship, to ruin his life? How is it *currently happening,* if it's not you threatening to take it all away unless I stay in line?"

"I never threatened you. I reminded you about Jesse because your judgment is singularly terrible when it comes to romance. You get stars in your eyes and you miss what's really happening. Jesse knew the score, Cain. He knew you had money, had connections. He was using you. I made him a similar offer to the one I'm making Mr. Fitzpatrick here. I'd give him what he wanted - his tuition paid for, the employment contacts he wanted when he graduated. And in exchange, all he had to do was walk away from you, pretend you'd never happened." Shaw shook his head sadly. "He didn't hesitate. And neither will Mr. Fitzpatrick."

Cain made that same shocked, wounded noise he'd made before, and he stared at Damon, misery clear in his eyes.

"Especially," the senator continued, "if I told you that there was no way I could guarantee Mr. Fitzpatrick's sister's safety, or his brother's, if you don't agree to my terms."

God. He made it sound so reasonable, so obvious. Damon could not believe how handily he'd been manipulated by this man.

"The answer is still no." No way in *hell* would he trust Chelsea or Cort's safety to this monster. No way would he ever allow this man control over any aspect of his life.

Shaw smiled. "And what if I told you Cain would be cut off forever if you refuse?"

At that, Damon hesitated. "Cut off how?"

"Financially, socially. In every way."

At this, Damon hesitated. The senator was not a master manipulator for nothing. Lose Cain, or see Cain hurt by losing his family? No matter how much tension there was between Cain and his parents, how could Damon make a decision that would sever that tie?

He was pretty sure Shaw was bluffing, but he couldn't take that risk. He looked at Cain's ravaged face, and knew that whatever happened, it had to be Cain's choice.

"I'm not going to make the same mistakes you've made," Damon told Shaw. "I'm not going to decide for him." He tugged on Cain's arm. "I'm not Jesse, and I'm not walking away unless you tell me to."

"You have to," Cain whispered, pulling his arm away. "Don't be crazy, you *have* to." *You*, not *we*. Shocking how badly that one word could hurt. And Cain wouldn't meet his eyes.

"No, I don't. We don't." He put his hand on Cain's chin, tilting his head up, and forced himself to continue. "Unless that's your choice. And Cain, I understand, if that's the case. Your family..."

Cain did look at him then, eyes wide with horror. "Not because of *me*. God, no. But your sister! *Molly*."

Damon inhaled, his relief more profound than he could have imagined. "Let me worry about that, Cain. We can worry about that together."

Cain looked away again, focusing on his father. Disgust and anger were plain on his face. "I want to hear about how you'll protect his sister."

Shaw smiled, convinced he'd won. "As I told you," he spread his empty palms. "As long as Mr. Fitzpatrick obeys the terms of the deal, no one has any interest in harming his sister or anyone connected to him."

"So no one will be shooting at him anymore?"

"Shooting at him?" Shaw's eyes narrowed. "No one's been shooting at him."

Cain laughed, pulling up his short sleeve once again to show his bandaged arm. "I beg to differ. Sunday morning, outside a fucking pancake restaurant, your goons shot up the parking lot. Almost killed a little girl."

Shaw blinked. "My goons?"

"Your friends, then. Your business associates? I'm not quite sure what the polite term for the hitmen on your payroll would be," Cain said, cold and calm.

"No one authorized any kind of attack on you, Cain. I didn't even know where you were until..." Shaw turned pale, swallowed, his eyes wide.

"Until when?" Cain's eyes narrowed. "When did you know where we were?"

Shaw licked his lips. "When my associates informed me."

"Have they been watching me?"

"For your safety, I..."

Cain snorted. "For my safety, of course. What have you been doing for my safety?"

"We have your cell phone traced," the senator said. "Whenever it pings a cell tower."

"We?"

"My... associates," he repeated.

"Well, that's fucking awesome," Damon said, heart racing, mind sputtering. "Your associates traced us to that fucking motel in Pennsylvania, and then they came to kill us. They tracked us here. Did they follow us when we dropped off Chelsea?"

Cain looked stricken. "Damon, I am so..."

Damon grabbed Cain by the shoulders and shook him, hard, forcing him to meet his eyes. "I swear to God, Cain, if you apologize for something that had nothing to do with you..."

Cain squeezed his eyes shut.

"Do you hear me, Cain?" Damon shook him again, and Cain nodded, but tears tracked down from his closed eyes.

Damon grabbed him behind the neck, pulling Cain's face into his shoulder.

He looked at Shaw over his son's head. "What have you done?"

Shaw shook his head. "You're wrong. You're lying."

"I'm lying? Your son has a gunshot wound in his arm, for Christ's sake."

"Cain is supposed to be protected." Shaw tossed the papers down and pushed himself back from the desk, all his confidence gone. "Cain is... Cain is to remain safe. That's non-negotiable."

"Well, it seems to me that your associates negotiated without you, Senator Shaw," Damon spat.

Shaw pushed his lips together, and watched Cain trembling in Damon's arms. His jaw firmed.

"Cain. Tell me, yourself, son. Is that what happened?"

Cain lifted his head, his eyes red and shattered. "You want to know what happened? You want to know? You found out Damon was alive at the fundraiser, you went after his sister and terrorized a preschooler." He shook his head. "Damon and I moved Chelsea to a safe house, but you used me... used my phone... to track us. Your associates shot at us. And who the hell knows what's happening to Chelsea and Molly!" He turned to Damon, panic in his gaze. "We need to get in touch with Eli," he whispered. "We need to make sure they're okay!"

Damon gripped his shoulder tightly, trying to reassure him. But in truth, he was more than a little panicked himself. His sister. His niece. *Fuck.*

"You're wrong!" Shaw passed a trembling hand over his face. "You're... you're wrong. I didn't know Damon was alive until the day after the fundraiser when I was informed by security. I didn't know you were with him. I didn't..." He wandered to the window, shaking his head. "I haven't authorized anything involving Mr. Fitzpatrick's sister and niece."

He turned to look at Cain and Damon. "I'm sure you don't believe me. That's fine. But it's the truth. I didn't know."

"You would have used them," Damon said. "You just threatened them right here in front of us."

"Maybe... I don't... Yes," Shaw admitted. "To protect my family, to keep my son safe, yes I would. But I would never have authorized this."

"How much does your authorization mean?" Cain asked softly. He shook his head. "You think you have these monsters on a leash, like attack dogs you can use when you need them. But time and again, they show you that *you* are the one in chains. They manipulate you, they use you, they get you to do unspeakable things. What the *fuck* makes you think they give a *shit* what you authorize? What makes you think they give a shit about breaking your deal?"

Shaw's jaw hardened. "They know I have information on them. Names, dates, videos, records of financial transactions, and all the things Levi provided them. Adam can't take me out."

"But he can sure as fuck threaten you," Damon said in disgust. "They know exactly how to do *that*. How to make sure you stay their obedient little lapdog." He looked the senator in the eye. "I am not taking this deal. I am *not* like you, not even a little. If I have to make hard choices to protect what's essential, then you need to know, *Cain* is essential. I *will* protect him, *and* my sister and niece, *and* my brother."

Damon moved his hands forward, used his thumbs to lift Cain's chin so he could stare into Cain's eyes. So blue, so fucking lost. "I am *not* Jesse," he said again. "I am *not* going to let him manipulate me. Cain, for God's sake, tell me you believe me."

"I *do* believe you." It was that fast, that easy. "But Damon, Chelsea and Molly. You can't just say…"

"Right now, baby, I don't believe for a *second* your father could protect them even if he wanted to. He couldn't even protect *you*." He met the senator's stricken gaze. "Isn't that right?"

The senator's jaw trembled. "Take the papers," he whispered, nodding toward his desk, where he'd tossed them. "Get out of here now. I don't know… I don't know who might be coming later."

"*Jesus Christ.*" Damon hadn't considered they'd be in immediate danger, and he should have. He *should* have, goddammit.

"Take the papers and keep my son safe, Fitzpatrick."

"What about you?" Cain asked. "What about Mom and Cady?"

"We'll be fine. I have my bargaining chips. And you ought to know —" He hesitated, as though he wasn't sure how much to reveal, how much further he wanted to damn himself. "There was a time when they couldn't track you. They wanted me to find out where you were, because your phone had somehow stopped transmitting. I was… I was concerned."

Cain looked at Damon. "When my phone died," he said, shaking his head. "Must have been." He sighed. "Thank you," he told his father, and the senator nodded stiffly.

Damon placed his hand around Cain's waist and propelled him to the door, only pausing to take the papers from the desk. They'd have to grab their things, get to Eli's house by nightfall to check on Chelsea and Molly, contact Drew and the Seavers to make plans…

But Cain leaned into his side and wrapped his arm

around Damon's waist, reminding him that even though things had become exponentially more dangerous, he wasn't alone anymore.

And he knew exactly who he was fighting for.

Cain paused as they reached the doorway, and turned to look at his father. The senator seemed smaller somehow. Just a man, outlined against the indomitable mountain in the distance, a giant stripped of his power.

"I'm not staying silent," Cain told him. "I won't publicize any of the information we found in your files, and I won't say anything about any of the other things you told us, but we're going to clear Damon's name."

Shaw nodded reluctantly. "I know you don't believe me, Cain, but I do care about you. Everything I've done, I've done for you. For our family. I would never have cut you off, not really. You're my son."

Cain seemed to consider this for a second. His hand twitched at Damon's waist, he took a shuddering breath, and shook his head slowly, sadly. "No. That's the lie you tell yourself, but you're wrong. You don't care who you hurt. You don't care who you manipulate. Everything you've done is to protect yourself, to protect your own name and your own power. That's how this all started. And now I... No," he stopped and gave Damon a hard nod. "*We*... are going to finish it."

"CAN'T YOU DRIVE FASTER?" Cain urged as Damon navigated the sharp turns up the mountain to Eli's house. Their frantic calls to Eli's satellite phone had gone unanswered - not surprising, since the man was unlikely to have it turned on unless he was using it.

"Not if we want to survive the trip, babe."

As he had every five minutes for the last hour, Cain turned in his seat, glancing out the back window for any sign they were being followed. As Damon had tried to tell him numerous times already, he'd seen no signs of anyone behind them, and since they'd deliberately left Cain's cell phone behind, he was confident there was no way to trace them either. The senator's information said they'd never been traced to Eli's house, and even if they had, Eli was more than capable of dealing with any unwanted guests.

Still, Damon couldn't fucking wait to get there and see for himself. He pressed his foot just a tiny bit harder on the gas.

"It's going to be okay." He reached out a hand and squeezed Cain's wrist.

"But what if…"

"No more what-ifs," Damon said gently. "From now on, we deal with what *is*. Together."

Cain sat back in his seat, and Damon could feel the weight of his stare, even as he negotiated the last few turns before Eli's house. "Yeah," Cain breathed at length, and the words were like a vow. "Yeah, okay."

Damon glanced at him as they pulled through the closely-packed trees into Eli's front yard. He slid the car into Park, then reached over and cupped the back of Cain's neck. "Okay," he repeated.

The dogs' barking cut off anything else they might have said, and a second later, Eli was greeting them, shotgun cradled in his arms.

"You finished your business already?" he demanded, when Damon eased himself from the driver's seat. Cain, hurried around the car and wrapped a bracing arm around Damon's waist before Eli could offer assistance, and despite everything that had happened that day, Damon had to bite back a smile at the way Cain claimed him.

He wrapped his own arm around Cain's shoulders, claiming him right back.

"Not finished," Damon said, looking down at Cain. "But we've got a good start." He glanced up at Eli. "Everything quiet here?"

"Yep. Quiet as it can be when there's a little brown-eyed chatterbox around, anyway," he said, rolling his eyes, but Damon could tell he wasn't really annoyed at all. "Any reason it shouldn't be?"

"Maybe," Cain said, taking another worried glance around the yard, but then he exhaled and pulled Damon more tightly against him. "Or maybe not."

Damon rubbed a soothing hand over Cain's arm. The initial adrenaline rush was over, but he knew it would be a long time before either of them let their guards down again.

"We'll fill you in when we get inside," Damon said.

Damon could see that Eli's own senses went on alert, feeding off Damon and Cain's tension, but the man shrugged and stepped aside, ushering Damon and Cain ahead of him into the house.

"Best get inside, then, boys. We've got a Thanksgiving dinner to eat!"

Damn. *Thanksgiving*. With all that had happened that afternoon, all the dangers still lurking around them and the work still ahead of them, Damon had forgotten. But with Cain's warm weight against his side, with Chelsea and Molly safe inside the house, Damon was well aware of just how much he had to be thankful for.

CHAPTER TWENTY

Cain woke up when the misty gray dawn over the mountain had just started to turn a glowing pink, and he immediately turned over to stare at the man whose arm he was using as a pillow. He couldn't help but grin.

Damon was lying flat on his back in the middle of their borrowed bed at Eli's house. His left arm was thrown out to the side, but his right leg and arm were tangled around Cain. Cain nuzzled closer, tucking his chilly hands beneath the human space heater beside him. Seemed Eli the Lonely Mountain Hermit didn't believe in heat.

Next door, Molly and Chelsea were tucked into the room they'd been sharing, and Cain let out a soft sigh at the knowledge that they were safe and, even better, *happy* in their new environment. They'd raced here from his parents' cabin the day before, half expecting to find the road littered with gangsters and Eli under siege. Instead, they'd found everyone happily engaged in Thanksgiving preparations, with Molly making hand-print turkeys while Eli and Chelsea debated the merits of butternut squash versus pumpkin, for making pie.

And that wasn't even the weirdest part. Eli had taken one look at Cain and Damon, arms wrapped around each other's waists as they walked up to the door, and grinned. "About fucking time," he'd said, and he'd offered Cain a whiskey.

Molly had adjusted to life at Eli's house quickly, making friends with the ravening beasts, Ripper and Puck, and even wrapping grumpy, sarcastic Eli around her little finger. And she wasn't the only one. If the vibes Cain had gotten from Chelsea last night were accurate, Eli might not be a *lonely* mountain hermit for long.

Ironically, it would not be the strangest pairing to result from the nightmare that his father had created. He reserved that title for himself and the man sleeping next to him. On paper, they should never have worked - too dissimilar in age, interests, family, and finances. But in all the things that couldn't be quantified, Cain had never met anyone more perfect for him, anyone who'd made him feel happier or safer.

His eyes tracked the planes and hollows of Damon's face. Asleep, Damon was a completely different sight to behold than when he was awake. His strong jaw was relaxed, the tiny laugh-lines by his eyes nearly invisible, the constant tension in his frame absent. Cain loved him when he was awake, but he could get used to seeing the formidable man at rest.

Love. He tried the word out again in his mind, waiting for panic to set in. He'd always had the vague idea that if it happened to him, love would feel like an obligation, another conflicting loyalty pulling on his already-shredded conscience, but it wasn't like that at all. There were no competing priorities in his mind as he looked at Damon this morning. Damon had superseded them all.

"I should probably find it creepy that you're watching

me sleep," Damon grumbled without opening his eyes. "But I don't."

What? How had he known?

"Wouldn't you have been embarrassed if I hadn't been? If I'd just been sleeping, or thinking about Richard Armitage from that BBC movie, and how hot he is? Or wondering what Eli is cooking for breakfast downstairs that smells like burnt sugar and coffee?" Cain demanded, but against his will, his fingers tracked over the rough growth of beard on Damon's chin.

"Nope. I'd be asleep," Damon said mildly. He cracked his eyes open and one corner of his mouth quirked up. "You were thinking pretty loud."

Cain rolled his eyes. "And now we add mind reading to your impressive list of skills, Big Daddy!"

The green-gold gaze softened, and Damon asked, "Bet I *do* know what you were thinking."

"Yeah, right. I was thinking about breakfast, and you know because you're hungry, too," Cain lied.

"Nope. Bet me," Damon said.

"You're starting to believe your own press."

Damon grinned widely. "So, *bet me.* I get three guesses to figure out what you're thinking. Winner gets a forfeit."

"What forfeit?" Cain demanded.

"Winner's choice."

"That's dangerous!"

With a shrug, Damon taunted, "Not if you're sure you'll win."

Cain pursed his lips, considering. Winner's choice could mean anything from various sex acts - which he was more than fine with - to a total cease and desist on using Cain's new favorite nickname for Damon - which, curiously, he'd be disappointed to lose.

And then his brain came all the way online and he realized, *duh*, there was no way Damon could win.

"Deal," Cain said smugly.

"Okay. You were thinking about how much you love donuts."

"What? That's stupid. No."

"Really? Because that's what you claimed you were thinking of the first morning we were together, back at Cort's apartment."

Oh. Fuck. So he had. He felt his cheeks burn. "Well, I'm not today." Then he added a trifle smugly, "That's *one*."

Damon's smile grew even wider. "Okay, why don't you think about it again. Concentrate. And I'll see if I can catch it."

Cain shook his head against the pillow and laughed. "You need me to massage your temples while you're at it?"

"Nope. Messes with the energy flow. Just concentrate."

God, the man was silly. They were silly together. This was a side of Damon he wouldn't have believed existed, but he loved it, loved that no matter how fucking complicated and dangerous and *shitty* the world outside was - Russian criminals dogging them, reporters contacting him - everything between them was easy as breathing and made him feel warm from the inside out.

So, yeah, he concentrated. *I love Damon*, he thought. *Love, love, love.*

"Whoa, that's weird," Damon said, eyes widening. "I'm still getting the image of donuts, but now there's also bacon. Do you want donuts and bacon?"

Cain's stomach growled at the reminder of how badly he needed food and coffee, stat.

"That's a good guess," Cain agreed. "But no. And that's *two*. Wow. If you wanted me to fuck you again, you just had to say so, you know."

Damon laughed. "Is that what you'd use your forfeit on? Fucking me again?"

Cain cleared his throat. "I… maybe."

Damon rolled closer to Cain, gripping his waist beneath the blanket, and Cain's heart jumped into a staccato rhythm. "Spoiler," he whispered. "You can fuck me any time you want."

Cain sucked in a sharp breath. "T-that's good to know."

"Thought you might be interested in that," Damon agreed with a wink.

"Anytime, as in *now*?"

"Well, not this very minute. We're in the middle of something here. I have a contest to win first."

Cain sighed. "Damon, I either need bacon and donuts, *or* I need to fuck you. Both, really, but I'll take either."

"One more shot, come on."

"Fine." Cain's sigh could have parted the trees outside. "One more shot."

Damon watched him intently, his smile soft and sure, and once again, Cain felt himself *concentrating*, not because he thought it could help Damon, but because he couldn't help it. *I love you*, you crazy man. *I love you.*

"Got it!" Damon said.

"I can't wait to hear it!" Cain enthused, pushing the covers down so he could be one step closer to either food or fucking. "Does it involve maple syrup? Or lube? Oh! Or maple syrup *as* lube?" He shuddered. "That is maybe the worst thing anyone's ever thought of. But if you're into it…"

"You love me," Damon interrupted.

"W-what?" Cain's mouth dropped open. "Where did you get that?"

"Are you denying it?"

Cain licked his lips, suddenly unsure. Neither of them

had said the words yet, and he didn't want Damon to feel pressured to say them, not when he was still figuring out how he wanted his life to look now that his name was cleared, not when they still had *so fucking much* more work to do in bringing SILA to justice. He tried to read the look in Damon's eyes, but it was the same look he always wore - warm, and loving, and... oh.

Oh.

"No," Cain said more confidently. "I'm not denying it."

Damon's smile was incandescent. "Ask me how I know," he whispered.

Cain bit his lip. "How did you know, *Big Daddy*?" he repeated, loving the way Damon's eyes laughed into his.

"Because I was laying here earlier watching you sleep," he said. He trailed a finger down the tattoo on Cain's arm. "And I was thinking the same thing. I love you, too."

"Yeah?" Cain's chest was a little tight, and he wondered if it was possible to be crushed under the weight of your own happiness.

"Yeah." Damon's index finger found a line of words and traced it. "I was thinking about this quote, too. That as awful as the ends are, they're what make the beginnings possible."

Cain's eyes widened. Poet-philosopher Damon was a new wrinkle, and *fuck*. He would never get tired of learning every facet of this man.

"The things your dad did, whatever his reasons, they were awful. The Seavers are gone, Bas and Cam lost their parents. There's nothing we can do to change that, no way he, or anyone else can ever make it right. But what we do from here, how *we* go on, the beginning we make from it... that's up to us."

He met Cain's eyes. "Both of us have had some pretty shit luck in the past, though I can say for sure my luck has changed since I met you." He brushed the hair from Cain's eyes. "I don't know what is going to happen next. But I know that whatever the future holds, I want you with me. This is forever."

Cain swallowed and nodded, pressing his lips to Damon's with a promise in his kiss.

And later that day, when little Molly pushed Uncle Damon and Cain together to take a picture, no one had to remind him to smile, or to look happy. Cain had almost forgotten how to be anything else.

CHAPTER TWENTY-ONE

One Week Later

"*I'M GAY. It's as simple as that. And while that fact in no way defines me, it's also not something I ever intend to hide again.*"

Cam Seaver looked up from his iPad, where he'd been reading the *Herald* article by Gary North that had gone viral in the hours since its release. Slim and lanky as ever, dark hair mussed and blue eyes serious, he nodded approvingly across the table at Cain, who was currently tucked against Damon's side in Drew's sunny kitchen. "This is fucking awesome, Cain. You're a rebel."

The impromptu breakfast gathering had been Drew's idea - a chance for their unlikely band of friends - friends who'd become something like family - to regroup, discuss all the things they'd learned from the senator, and decide on the next steps they needed to take. But first, Drew had insisted, they needed to have breakfast and reconnect - which seemed to be shorthand for teasing Cain by reading his interview out loud. For once Damon was okay with waiting, at least for a little while.

Cain squirmed in embarrassment at Cam's praise, and Damon smiled as he pulled his man even tighter. "It's not rebellious or awesome. Just… true," Cain demurred.

"Yeah, well. Sometimes admitting the truth is the hardest thing a person can do," Drew said from the other side of the kitchen, where he was making coffee and something that smelled like pumpkin and cinnamon. Damon looked at him curiously. Drew's voice had a hard edge, and his body was imbued with a tension that was totally incongruous with his baggy sweats and perfect brown hair, the bright sunshine floating in through the French doors and the homey smells in the air.

At the head of the table, Bas Seaver pushed his chair back with a loud screech and stood, throwing open the door behind him and letting in the chilly autumn breeze.

"I need some air," he said, stepping outside.

Cam watched his brother worriedly as he walked out the door, but when he moved as if to stand and follow, his boyfriend leaned over and nudged his arm, shaking his head slightly. "Keep reading," Cort urged.

Cam gave one last glance at Sebastian, then returned his attention to the article.

"Cain Shaw's comments are not what one would expect from the twenty-something son of a politician best known for his conservative, and some would say outright discriminatory, views on LGBTQ rights. Until recently, Cain was a highly visible if silent part of Emmett Shaw's campaign fundraising machine, a handsome, intelligent presence that appealed to young women, inspired young men, and gained near-universal parental approval. In other words, Cain Shaw was precisely the type of guy your parents would want you to bring home for dinner."

"Fucker wanted to bring *you* home for dinner," Damon

muttered under his breath. "Wanted to *eat* you for dinner, more like."

"Oh, shush," Cain said, elbowing Damon lightly. "He did not. He's a professional."

"A professional who tried to give you his personal phone number three times even though you were sitting right next to me."

"You mean even though you'd practically *pulled me onto your lap* when we sat down with him?"

Cort laughed out loud and wrapped his arm around Cam, drawing the smaller man close to his side. "I feel you, brother."

Damon rolled his eyes. It hadn't been like that. He wasn't jealous. He was just... invested in making his relationship with Cain clear to all observers.

Okay, so maybe it was the same thing.

"Cain blushes when he hears this," Cam continued, and they all turned to smirk at Cain, who was a deep shade of pink once again at hearing this read. *"He refuses to comment, except to say that he hopes he's far more inspiring to young men in his new role, that of an out-and-proud man who is already fundraising on behalf of social justice groups while he continues his law degree."*

"Badass," Cam said again, shaking his head.

"Not badass. They make it sound like this whole big thing, when I just started organizing *one* Christmas fundraiser for a nonprofit that provides scholarships to LGBTQ youth." Cain shrugged. "It felt right. Important. And organizing is something I'm good at. The law degree part is still up in the air."

Damon squeezed Cain's shoulder. "You have time," he reminded his man. "I'm going to make sure of it."

Cain looked up at him and smiled.

"There is a quiet assurance to Cain, a maturity that sits well on his strong shoulders. He claims he's grown up much in recent weeks,

and attributes that growth to the new man in his life, pilot Damon Fitzpatrick. The mysterious, but undeniably handsome Fitzpatrick, nearly seventeen years Cain's senior, has a rather dramatic past of his own.

"Oh, this is even better," Cort laughed, green eyes dancing as he ran a hand through his dark-blond hair. "The mysterious and undeniably handsome Fitzpatrick. From now on, that's what I'm going to call you. *You know my brother? The mysterious and undeniably handsome Damon Fitzpatrick?*"

"Fuck off," Damon said mildly.

Drew brought a tray of coffee and cups to the table, and Cort immediately poured himself a cup.

"You sure the reporter had a thing for *Cain*?" Drew asked as he returned to the kitchen. "Because I could make a case that he's definitely a *Damon* fan.*"

"Right? He was totally buttering you up for a three-some," Cam said confidently, waggling his eyebrows. "Maybe it can be the follow-up article. I'd read it."

Cort, who had just taken his first sip of coffee, started to choke, and Cam reached over to pound him on the back.

"You okay, babe?"

"Jesus, Cammy," Cort coughed. "Warn your boyfriend before you start going all porn-fantasy on his brother."

"*Cammy!*" Drew crowed from the kitchen, where he was plating muffins or something. "The nickname lives on!"

Damon vaguely recalled that Drew had invented that nickname for Cam… and that Cam loathed it. He stifled a smile.

"No. It doesn't live on," Cam said flatly. "It never lived in the first place."

"The man's got a death wish, taunting you that way, bro," Sebastian said from the doorway. He resumed his seat, carefully not looking at Drew.

"No shit," Cam groused, giving his boyfriend a speaking glance. "I respond to *Cam, Camden, Mr. Seaver, and occasionally Badass.*"

Cort grinned and pulled Cam closer. "Fine, then. *Camden Seaver, my love, badass owner of my heart*, please continue."

Cam rolled his eyes, even as he curled himself into Cort's side, and Damon found himself grinning. He'd been initially pretty skeptical of Cam Seaver, wondering how a relationship between the rich heir of the Seaver Tech fortune, and Damon's foster-brother Cort, could possibly work. Nowadays, though, Damon was all glass-half-full when it came to seemingly impossible relationships.

Cain's hand found his thigh under the table and squeezed. Little wonder what had caused that change.

"Fitzpatrick, as some careful readers may remember, was the pilot at the controls during the tragic plane crash that killed tech genius Levi Seaver, his wife Charlotte, and close family friend Amy McMann over a year ago. Fitzpatrick was presumed dead, as well, and until recently was believed to have caused the crash through negligence. However, the investigation into the crash has been reopened this week in light of new evidence that seems likely to clear Fitzpatrick of any wrongdoing in the incident."

Cam looked up as Drew set a plate of pumpkin muffins on the table and took his seat. "That was thanks to *my* badass boyfriend and his FBI connections. Just wanted to note that since Gary here neglected to mention it." He smirked.

"I appreciate the sentiment, badass," Cort said gravely. "But if you're trying to get me into the three-way with Cain, Damon, and the reporter, that's a *no*."

Cam dissolved into laughter. "Good," he said. He turned his attention back to the article, and his smile softened into something smaller, sadder.

"Mr. Shaw says, 'Damon and I don't want to comment on anything related to the crash, except to say that we are extremely thankful Damon's name will be cleared, and we continue to mourn the loss of the Seavers and Amy McMann, who were and always will be, much loved and missed.'"

Bas ran his hands through his hair, his gaze fixed on the table. Drew's hand hovered in the air, like he wanted to reach out and touch Bas, but he dropped his hand to his lap instead.

Cam cleared his throat and set the tablet down on the table. He ran a hand through his hair, causing the cowlicks to stick up even more prominently and making him look incredibly young. "Thanks, Cain," he whispered. "For remembering them."

"Of course," Cain said softly. "Always."

Bas inhaled deeply, like he was mentally preparing himself for something, and sat up straight. "Okay, so now tell us the un-PG-rated version."

Cain straightened in his chair, as well, and looked at Damon. "Well…"

"Just spit it out," Drew said. "We already started looking into the businesses you sent us. Bas is doing it under the table, low-key, so it can't be traced back to us, so it's taking a while. But I get the feeling you two have a pretty good idea who we're going to find on the other end of this."

"What do you know about SILA?" Damon asked. Sudden silence reigned.

Bas's eyes widened, Drew blinked, Cam looked around in confusion, but Cort flushed red. "The Russian criminal organization?"

"Yeah," Damon said heavily. "That's the one."

He explained everything the senator had told them about his own involvement with SILA, including the fact that Levi Seaver and Jonathan McMann, Drew's father, had been in on it from the beginning.

"I don't believe it. He's lying. He has to be," Cam said, staring around the table like he wanted someone to agree with him.

No one did.

"Bas?" Cam pressed. "You know Dad. He would never."

Bas bent his neck back and stared at the ceiling for a long inhale and exhale. "I don't know about never, Cam." He dropped his gaze to Cam's. "It kind of explains some things I haven't understood for a long time. Where some money came from. Some projects Dad was working on that never seemed to materialize. *Fuck*." He braced his elbow on the table and dropped his forehead to his hand.

"My dad, too," Drew whispered. "He knew all along?"

Damon and Cain exchanged a glance.

"That's what my father said," Cain agreed. "And I don't think he was lying at that point. I don't know why he would. But he did say your father was against it from the start."

"Probably worried it would affect his bottom line," Drew fumed. "Or maybe that his new girlfriend would find out."

Damon recalled Drew's parents had divorced almost immediately after the plane crash, their relationship unable to withstand the trauma of losing their daughter, Amy, so unexpectedly. He hadn't realized there had been problems long before that.

"There's more," Damon added. "Cain talked to his father earlier this week, gave him a heads-up the interview would be running."

"I'm sure Uncle Shaw was thrilled," Bas said wryly.

"We don't call him that anymore," Cam snapped, and

Damon felt a tug of sympathy. The three families had been so close for so long, and the betrayal ran deep.

"He actually didn't have a lot to say about the interview. Probably knew it was too late for that. But he told us he'd talked to his Russian... colleagues," Cain said bitterly. "Apparently the guys shooting at us were part of some faction inside the group, not authorized by the Stornoviches, who are supposed to be in charge. The shooting was part of some crazy internal power-grab. Like who the fuck knew that was a thing?" He shook his head.

"The name of the group means power, babe," Damon said softly, pressing a kiss to Cain's head. "Makes sense that they don't do shit in an orderly, democratic way. They do stupid shit like trying to compromise the senator so they can oust the Stornoviches."

"So what the hell does that mean for us?" Bas demanded. "For your sister and Molly, and everyone else who might be on the radar?"

"It means the heat is off, at least for now," Damon said. "The Stornoviches need the senator in their corner if they want to stay in power, and the senator made it clear we are all under his protection."

He could hear the bitterness in his own voice, and made no apologies for it. He fucking hated that he had to feel beholden to Emmett Shaw for anything, not after all the man had done. But for Cain's sake, for his family's sake, he accepted it.

"Adam Stornovich is trying to consolidate his power inside SILA," Cain expounded. "He's got enough trouble handling things inside his organization, so he accepted that he and my father have arrived at a bit of a stalemate. The senator has information on SILA, and SILA has plenty of information on him."

"Another cold war," Drew said mockingly.

"So, what do we do?" Cam whispered. "We can't just leave things like that. Who knows when they'll get their shit sorted and decide we're lose ends that need tying up? And we need to make them pay for what happened to our parents, to Amy. What do we *do*?"

Cort, who had been locked in silent thought for a moment, tightened his hold on Cam.

"*You* do nothing, babe. You run your company, you live your life."

"No! No. You should know better than to try to push me out when—"

"He's right, Cam," Bas said. He had the shell-shocked look of a man who'd just awoken in an alternate-reality. "We're going to get these bastards and bring them down, but in the meantime, you still have a company to run."

Cam frowned. "I do? I thought *we* did."

"We do, then," Bas agreed. "But this is something I can help with. Financials, finding a needle in a haystack, those are things I'm good at. I have the contacts, I have the tech…"

"Hell no. We should leave this to the professionals," Cort said firmly. "This is dangerous shit you're talking about, Sebastian. If you get caught, you won't be arrested, you'll be killed."

"Like you left it to the professionals when your family was threatened?" Bas retorted, one eyebrow raised.

Cort looked at Damon and sighed. "That was different," he protested, but it was clear even he had trouble believing it.

"This is on me," Bas said. "I overlooked this stuff - the inconsistencies, the discrepancies - for way too long. I need to put a stop to it."

Drew snorted and shook his head. "So you're charging off to the rescue once again. God forbid you sit still for a minute, right? God forbid you actually deal with your *life*. When you need a distraction, any vendetta will do!"

"Bullshit," Bas said, looking anywhere but at Drew. "This isn't a distraction. This is about assuring the safety of our *family*."

"Oh really? Then I'll be happy to help you with your investigation, since compiling evidence is kinda *my* specialty, along with keeping your ass out of jail while you're busy running after bad guys. For the good of our family."

Bas's jaw hardened.

"I think it's a really good idea," Cam said firmly. "Drew's got a level head, and— "

"Drew is fucking clueless," Bas said, glaring at the man Damon thought had always been his best friend.

Drew flushed. "That's the offer, Sebastian. I help you, or I turn over all the information we've learned to the FBI, including the fact that you're attempting to investigate this yourself."

"You wouldn't," Bas whispered, meeting Drew's eyes for the first time.

"Try me."

Tension settled around the table, Cam and Cort, Cain and Damon, all exchanging glances, while Drew and Bas seemed locked in a staring contest.

"She was my sister, Sebastian," Drew said, and Sebastian finally broke.

"Fine," he said, looking away. "Whatever."

"I think my brother means, *Thank you for your generous offer, Drew, and even though you're a little bit of a control freak, I'm glad that Cam will feel reassured knowing you're going to be keeping me safe*," Cam said.

His softly-spoken words broke the tension. Damon

ALSO BY MAY ARCHER

Love in O'Leary Series

Whispering Key Series

The Sunday Brothers Series

The Way Home Series

Licking Thicket Series

(cowritten with Lucy Lennox)

Champion Security Series

(cowritten with Lucy Lennox)

Honeybridge Series

(cowritten with Lucy Lennox)